Edelweiss For Elizabeth

Sylvie's Peace

Edelweiss For Elizabeth

Sylvie's Peace

Andrea Gilbey

Per Bastet

Edelweiss for Elizabeth

Published by Per Bastet Publications LLC, P.O. Box 3023 Corydon, IN 47112

Cover art and design by Andrea Gilbey

ISBN 978-1-942166-72-6

Available in trade paperback and DRM-free ebook formats

Edelweiss For Elizabeth

Sylvie's Peace

Andrea Gilbey

Per Bastet

Edelweiss for Elizabeth

Published by Per Bastet Publications LLC, P.O. Box 3023 Corydon, IN 47112

Cover art and design by Andrea Gilbey

ISBN 978-1-942166-72-6

Edelweiss For Elizabeth
Sylvie's Peace

Dedication

To Ginny Fleming
With thanks for her encouragement and love.

With Grateful Thanks To

Marian Allen
T Lee Harris
Jenny Painter
and
The Southern Indiana Writers

Part One
1946

Chapter One

How The Other Half Lives

I was going to have to speak up; we couldn't sit on the wall in total silence all evening.

I glanced sideways at my best friend, Maureen, crinkling my eyes up against the early evening sun. Maureen was swinging her legs, bashing her heels against the wall — her shoes would be ruined. Her fingers were picking away at the rough cement that the council had used to smooth the top of the wall after they took the railings away for the war effort.

I opened my mouth to speak, but she beat me to it.

"So, what do you think of your first week at the grammar school?" she asked, without looking at me.

"Oh! It's jolly super!" I exclaimed. "The school is enormous, with so many rooms, and the masters and mistresses all wear gowns. We have a lot of prep to do, and some of it's jolly stiff, but my form teacher is Mrs Fleming, you know, the one who took us for the English part of the scholarship exam, and she's wonderful. And a girl called Gwen in my class has lent me her Chalet School book, it's all about girls at a boarding school in Switzerland. It's wizard!"

I slowed to a halt as Maureen was just nodding slowly and staring at me with a weird look on her face.

"How are you getting on with shorthand and typing?" I asked.

"The typing's easy, like playing the piano," she said with a wicked grin. During the holidays, we had both taken piano lessons from Mrs Keele down the road, and Maureen was a natural, while I struggled to read music and my fingers tripped

1

over my thumbs. I'd given up lessons, but Maureen carried on and was about to take her first piano exam. Of course, she would find typing easy.

"The shorthand's hard, though," she continued, still picking away at the cement. "It's like algebra all over again, little squiggles that don't mean a lot. Still, apart from the shorthand I don't have no homework."

"You don't have any homework," I corrected her.

"What?" She looked at me blankly.

"If you don't have no homework you must have some homework." I explained. "It's a double negative, and Mrs Fleming says unless you can write like Shakespeare you shouldn't use a double negative. You should've said 'I don't have any homework,' see?"

Maureen stared at me with that odd look again.

"But you understood what I meant, didn't you?" she asked.

"Well, yes, but. . . ."

She jumped off the low wall with a big leap and brushed down her skirt.

"I'm glad I don't go to the grammar school," she said. "I don't think I could live up to myself. I'll see you tomorrow afternoon, unless you're too posh for the pictures now."

She walked up the path and into her house without looking back, and slammed the door.

I sat still on the wall for a while, thinking. Maureen must be jealous of me because I had got into a good school and was learning to talk nicely and was making new friends.

I slid down from the wall and walked slowly indoors. Mum looked up as I came in and closed the door behind me.

"You two were quiet this evening, considering you haven't seen each other all week," she said, watching me closely.

"Yes. Maureen's acting a bit odd."

I picked up my English exercise book from the sideboard and flicked through the few closely written pages at the start of the clean new book.

I said, "I think she's jealous."

Mum held out a hand to me and pulled me down to sit beside her on the settee.

"Don't forget that Maureen is having a bit of a hard time at the moment with her dad so ill."

I nodded. Maureen's dad had come home from the war quite different. Some days he was perfectly normal, then other days he was silent and sad, and sometimes he would lose his temper and shout about something that wasn't very important. Daddy said it was called shell shock, and a lot of soldiers in the Great War had suffered from it because of the loud noises, the danger they faced, and the horrible things they saw. Mr Fielding never talked about anything that had happened in the war, but we knew that he was one of only sixteen men from his company who had come home. Life in Maureen's house wasn't easy sometimes.

The kitchen door slammed open and my sister Audrey and her friend Brian burst in, battling away with pea sticks as swords, with a lot of "arrr" and "avast". They'd been playing pirates in the garden again.

"Come on, you two; time to put up your swords and cutlasses and live to fight another day," said Mum. "It's about time you were going home, Brian."

They finished their fight with one last swashbuckle and Brian ran off home with a rushed, "Goodnight, Mrs Ford, goodnight, Sylvie, see you tomorrow, Aud!"

"Will you play Scrabble with me, Sylvie?" asked Audrey, comical in her eyepatch.

"I can't, Aud, I've got my prep to do." I replied.

"Homework can wait; you've got all weekend," said Mum. "Give your sister a game." Audrey ran off to get the Scrabble set.

~*~

After Audrey went to bed I sat a little longer with Mum and Daddy, while Daddy smoked his pipe and read the paper and Mum knitted. I gazed unseeingly at the print of Salisbury Cathedral that hung over the fireplace, thinking about school and what Maureen had said.

Mum put her knitting down and the needles clattered together, making me jump.

"Come on Sylvie," she said, "out with it, what's wrong? Are you being teased at school for not having the right uniform?"

Mum and Daddy had been saving money week by week to buy my school uniform, but during the last week of the summer term Audrey had gone down with the measles and had been very ill. We'd had the doctor out for her three times, and she had recovered perfectly, but the bills had eaten into my uniform fund, so I was still wearing my old dark green dress instead of the uniform white blouse and dark green pinafore dress. I wasn't the only one not wearing the right clothes, but I hated feeling different.

"No, Mummy, it's not that, it's just . . . I don't know. . . ." I trailed off vaguely.

"I expect it's just the excitement of the new school and everything being new and different," said Daddy, knocking out his pipe. "You'll feel better after a good night's sleep, and it's Saturday tomorrow, so you can have a lie in and rest. But remember, if there's anything worrying you, it's best to talk about it."

I stood up and went over to kiss him. "I will, Daddy. I'm sure I'll feel fine in the morning, I love my new school, really."

He stood up and wrapped me in a big hug, letting me go with a kiss to the top of my head.

"Goodnight, Ducks, sleep tight, mind the bugs don't bite."

"Goodnight, Mummy," I said, hugging her and enjoying the scent of her lavender perfume from the little sailor boy bottle that Uncle Johnny had brought back from France. Two whole days at home where everything was old and familiar. I smiled to myself as I tiptoed up to bed softly so as not to wake Audrey.

~*~

I rushed home from school on Monday, impatient to share my news. Mum was scraping potatoes in the sink and Audrey was laying the table as I burst through the front door. Daddy appeared from the bathroom wiping his face on a towel.

"Where's the fire?" he asked with a wink, pulling my plaits.

"You've got an invitation!" I said excitedly. "You and Mum. You're invited to a dinner and dance at school on Friday for all the parents of us new third formers. It'll be so glamourous, and you can meet Gwen's parents, and Jasmine's parents, and it's only half a crown for each couple."

I handed the invitation to Daddy while Mum dried her hands and turned to read the invitation over Daddy's shoulder.

"What do you think, Ducks?" Daddy asked her. "Shall we dust off our go-to-wedding-and-funeral outfits and go to this beano?"

"Oh, you must!" I cried, "But it says 'dress — formal'. Gwen says that means black tie and a long dress."

"I'll look a bit funny in a long dress and a black tie," Daddy teased, pulling a face. "We can't afford new evening clothes, Sylvie, you know that. If they don't let us in in our best clobber then they won't get our half-crown and that's the end of it."

~*~

I worried about the dinner dance all week. Gwen described the wonderful dress that her mother had bought to wear, and Jasmine and I looked at each other anxiously. I knew Jasmine's parents didn't have formal evening clothes either.

On Friday evening when I saw Mum and Daddy dressed up I felt so proud of them that I almost forgot they were wearing the wrong things, they looked so glamourous.

"Look after Audrey, Sylvie, and if you need anything you just knock on the wall for Mrs Fielding. She knows we're going out and will pop round to see you before Audrey goes to bed," said Mummy, kissing us both.

"Of course, if they fling us out on our ears we'll be home early and we'll spend that half-crown on fish and chips," said Daddy, picking Audrey up and swinging her round, and then kissing me squeakily, just like grandma did.

~*~

I stayed up to wait for them to come home, as it was Friday. Audrey wanted to stay up, too, but she was asleep on the settee by half past eight, and stumbled upstairs with no argument when Mrs Fielding came round to check on us.

Mummy and Daddy crept in just after ten o'clock.

"Oh, Sylvie! You didn't have to wait up for us, dear," said Mum, closing the door quietly.

"I just wanted to hear how it went," I whispered.

"It was lovely! So nice to meet your friends' parents and some of the teachers! We had a very nice chat with your form teacher; she's so interested in everything and speaks very well of you."

I sighed with relief, suddenly feeling very tired.

"I'm glad you had a good time." I yawned. "In the morning you can tell me what you had for dinner."

I kissed them both and tiptoed upstairs.

~*~

Maureen called for me after dinner on Saturday to ask if I wanted to go to Woolworths with her. She was still being a bit sniffy, and when I told her about the dinner dance and all the people that Mummy and Daddy had been socialising with she just "humphed" as though she wasn't really interested, so I gave up trying to make conversation.

As we walked down the high street I saw a familiar figure coming towards us. Mrs Fleming! I pointed her out to Maureen.

"Oh, I'd better cross the road," she said with a flounce.

"I'm not posh enough to talk to your la-di-da grammar school teacher."

I grabbed her arm.

"Don't be stupid," I hissed. "Say hello and be polite. Good morning, Miss!"

"Hello, Sylvie." My teacher smiled. "I was so pleased to meet your parents last night, and I am so impressed with your mother's sewing skills! She told me that she made her beautiful dress herself!"

I was a bit embarrassed by the subject of Mum's dress.

"I know it's not a proper evening dress. . . ." I started.

"Neither was mine," said Mrs Fleming. "I can't wear long dresses. I'm too short, and as I can't sew for toffee I can't shorten them!" She laughed. "And your father is so knowledgeable about plants! He explained how to prune roses properly. Look, he even drew me a diagram for me." She pulled a paper napkin out of her pocket and showed me one of Daddy's classic sketches of how to prune a plant.

"I'm off to buy myself a new pair of secateurs now!" She beamed.

She turned to Maureen and smiled.

"You must be Sylvie's best friend."

I introduced Maureen and explained that she didn't go to our school, but she was learning to type and take shorthand so she could be a secretary. Maureen gave me a look, but Mrs Fleming was impressed.

"Oh, Maureen, how clever of you! I'll tell you girls a secret: I'm writing a book, and it's taking me absolutely ages because I can't type. I tap away with three fingers! I do admire people who can touch-type."

Maureen gave me another look, but this time she looked more like herself, with a touch of her old smugness.

"Any time you like, Miss, I can come and give you some lessons. It's easy, really."

Mrs Fleming thanked her warmly and said goodbye.

We walked on in silence for a while.

"She's nice," said Maureen. "Not like some of these posh grammar school types who don't have no manners."

"You mean 'don't have any'. . . ." I started, then realised that she was teasing me. I laughed and aimed a smack at her, but she ducked and ran, and we raced giggling down the street.

Chapter Two

Woodcraft

I leaned against the doorframe and sighed as Maureen ran back for "something". She never managed to be on time, even when I told her to be ready five minutes earlier than she needed to be.

The penknife on my belt clunked on the wood as I shifted about impatiently, and I reached down to touch it, smiling to myself. It was my grandad's penknife. It had belonged to Mum's dad, who died before I was born, and the outside casing was silver. I always wore it proudly on my Guide belt, but it could be a bit of a nuisance when we had church parade and it banged on the wooden pew every time I stood up or sat down.

Maureen was ready at last. She called a goodbye to her mum and dad as we closed the door. Mrs Fielding called after us, but Mr Fielding said nothing; he just sat on the settee reading a paper. He must have been having one of his bad days.

"Maureen, wait a minute!"

We turned back. Daddy was standing at our front door waving at us, then he disappeared back into the house. I was starting to feel like we'd never get away. He came running back again with something small in his hand.

"Here, Maureen, take this pruning knife. Sylvie said you haven't got a penknife: this knife is too blunt for proper pruning any more, but it'll do for hacking lumps out of trees, you young vandals!"

"Oh, but we're allowed to! It's for our Woodcraft badge — we have to leave signs on the trees so people following us know where to go. Captain said that's how Robin Hood and his Merry Men did it."

"He knows, Mo," I said, tugging at her arm, "he's just teasing you. Now come on!"

"Thank you, Mr Ford!" Maureen yelled back as I dragged her down the path. "I'll look after it!"

"Do you know all the woodcraft signs, then, Sylvie?" Maureen asked.

"I think so." I frowned. "But anyway, it's Lieutenant taking the test, not Captain, and she won't fail us unless we're really terrible, and if she does. . . ." I looked sideways at Maureen and we finished together.

"Worse things happen at sea!"

Captain was always telling us that: her husband was a captain in the Navy and she knew everything there was to know about the sea and ships.

Maureen kicked a pebble down the gutter.

"Do you reckon they call each other Captain at home?" she asked. "Can you imagine it at the breakfast table? 'I say, Captain, please pass the butter, old thing.' 'Aye aye, Captain.' They'd end up not knowing who was talking to who!" She doubled over with laughter and I joined in, laughing as much at her snorting laugh as at the joke.

"Come on, we need to get a move on. We're supposed to meet Lieutenant and the others at Home Farm at two."

"What time is it now?" asked Maureen.

I shot the cuff of my Guide uniform importantly and looked at my watch. It had been my Christmas present from Grandma last year.

"It's twenty to! We'd better run!"

~*~

We arrived panting at the gate of Home Farm to find the other two girls who were going to take the test waiting for us. They were June and Maggie from the Sparrow patrol. I felt a bit sorry for the Sparrows, they had such a dull badge. Maureen and I were in Kingfisher patrol and had a pretty bright blue bird on our badge.

"Lieutenant's late," said Maggie, no "hello" or anything. She was a bit serious and goody-goody. June said nothing; she never spoke, she just nodded at whatever Maggie said.

Maureen and I hopped up on the bars of the gate and perched on the top rail. The farmyard was quiet with an early afternoon sleepiness. All the animals had been fed and were dozing somewhere. A flash of red caught my eye; a fox was rummaging around in a pile of mouldy-looking turnips, looking for something to eat. It was very skinny and looked scared and jumpy. Probably a vixen who had been feeding her cubs all summer and was worn out and hungry, the poor thing. I nudged Maureen and pointed at the fox, putting my finger to my lips to tell her to be silent, and we watched it digging among the turnips and then standing like a statue to listen for any mice or rats, its head cocked on one side.

A sputtering roar disturbed the fox and it bolted off behind the barn as Lieutenant's Morris Eight came hurtling down the road towards us. Maggie and June joined us on the gate sharpish to avoid being mown down.

"Good afternoon, girls," smiled Lieutenant, climbing out of the car. "I hope you're all set and you've been swotting up on your woodcraft signs?"

We all smiled and nodded.

"Here is what we're going to do," Lieutenant continued. "I have marked two trails through the woods to two points halfway up the hill, one to the left for you, June and Maggie, and Sylvie and Maureen will take the route to the right. I want you to follow the trails until you find a tree which has an envelope pinned to it with your names on it. Sign your names on the envelope, and from the tree onwards I want you to work your way uphill, taking any route you like, to get to the picnic benches at the top, marking a trail so I can find which way you went.

"When you get to the picnic benches, I'll go back to the trees I marked and trace your paths to check your signs. Is everybody clear?"

We nodded again.

"Oh, one more thing," Lieutenant added with a smile. "While you're waiting for me to check your trails, you can collect sticks to build a small fire and a gadget to hold a billy can and brew us all some tea. You'll find water, tea and a billy at the picnic benches. I hope you've all got matches in your pockets?"

We all patted our pockets to make the matchboxes rattle. I noticed that Maggie looked a bit anxious, and her pocket didn't seem to be rattling.

"Right, then. Now remember, this isn't a race, but do try to get to the picnic benches before it gets dark! Off you go!"

~*~

Maureen and I started out on the path that Lieutenant had said was ours, chatting but keeping our eyes peeled for signs. The first one was easy: At the first junction in the path, three long stems of grass had been knotted together and bent to the left, so we went left and followed the path uphill.

"I bet the other two aren't chatting," I said, stopping at the next junction to scan the trees and verges for a sign. "Have you ever heard June speak?"

"Never," said Maureen. "Look, there, two pebbles, one on top of the other, and one to the right. We go right."

"You can't exactly call June Maggie's Yes Woman as she doesn't even say 'yes', she just nods," I mused as we walked on. "It must be odd spending so much time with someone who never speaks."

"Hmm," said Maureen. I suddenly remembered her dad's silent spells and changed the subject.

"I wonder if Lieutenant brought any biscuits along to go with that tea?"

Maureen grinned and fished a small package wrapped in greaseproof paper out of her pocket.

"This is what I went back to get," she said, unwrapping the paper and showing me the contents.

"Oooh! Squashed fly biscuits!"

"Don't let my mum hear you calling them that; she made them," laughed Maureen, "and don't tell her I took them out of the tin, either!"

"There, just ahead, look, something white on that tree."

We ran ahead, and on the ground at the roots of the tree was a circle of stones with one stone right in the centre: the symbol for the end of the trail. Sure enough, a white envelope was pinned to the tree just above our head height with "Maureen and Sylvie" written on it. I reached up and pulled out the pin and we signed the envelope, Maureen bending over to make a "back" for me to lean on to write, and then me doing the same for her. I pinned the envelope back on the tree and we looked around us.

"The picnic benches are right at the top of the hill, and you can see the sunset from there," I thought aloud. "It's now . . . three o'clock, so we need to head uphill towards the sun, and we have to remember to mark the path every time it divides. Got your knife?"

Maureen brandished her knife, like Errol Flynn did with his sword at the pictures, and we marched off uphill. I let Maureen cut all the arrows on the trees and hack off pieces of grass to make knotted signs, as she was so pleased with her knife.

"Should we make a detour for Lieutenant to follow, to make it more interesting?" she asked. I thought for a while.

"Detour, or tea and biscuits?"

She stood and thought for . . . ooooh . . . three seconds.

"What's the symbol for 'straight on' again?" She grinned.

We came out of the wood at the top of the hill, and there was Lieutenant sitting on one of the picnic benches, looking lost in thought.

Maureen put a hand on my arm, and angled her head at Lieutenant. She put her finger to her lips, and made tiptoeing motions in the air with her fingers. I grinned and nodded, and we crept quietly towards the bench, fanning out, and slid onto the seat either side of Lieutenant.

"Aaaargh!" She jumped and put her hand to her heart, laughing. "You frightened the life out of me!" She grabbed us in a rough hug, one under each arm.

"Well done, you two, I'll go and check your trail. You can start building a fire, just a small one, mind, and remember to clear the grass away first. We don't want to burn down the whole of Home Farm!"

She walked off back the way we'd come, whistling softly, and Maureen started gathering twigs while I cleared a circle of earth.

We'd just got the fire crackling when we heard a rustling in the trees behind us. Maureen grabbed up a long stick and winked at me, I knew what she was going to do; she loved the scene in Robin Hood where Little John challenged Robin to a staff fight.

Maggie and June emerged from the trees and Maureen strode forward, wielding her longstaff.

"You may not pass," she challenged. "You must fight me to enter my camp."

Maggie looked her up and down, pushed the stick aside and walked past.

"Don't be so childish," she said. June scuttled past with an embarrassed look.

"Is this all you've done?" asked Maggie sniffily. "Just a fire? What about the gadget to hang the billy can? You've just been messing about, haven't you? June, get some sticks." She plonked herself down on the bench.

June scurried off and came back with a handful of sturdy twigs which, to my surprise, she set about making into a very workmanlike tripod thing to hang the billy can on. Maggie just supervised.

By the time Lieutenant came back with the signed envelopes in her hand, the tea was brewing. Maureen opened her little packet of biscuits and offered them round. I wouldn't have offered one to that stuck up Maggie if they'd been mine, but Maureen's soft sometimes.

"Well, haven't you all done well!" exclaimed Lieutenant. "You all made a very neat job of your trail signs and I'm happy to pass all of you. Congratulations!"

"I did most of the camp work, Lieutenant," Maggie lied smugly, jumping to her feet.

Lieutenant looked from one of us to the next, around the little semi-circle, taking in our grubby appearance compared to Maggie's pristine uniform and clean hands.

"I'm impressed that you managed to keep your hands and knees so clean while doing all the work, Maggie," she said with a twinkle in her eye, and Maggie flushed bright red and sat down again.

We drank our tea and ate our biscuits, looking out over the fields as the sun sank lower in the sky. Maureen had picked up a stick and was whittling away at one end of it with Daddy's old pruning knife.

Lieutenant finished her tea and started dismantling the tripod and kicking out the fire. Maggie got up to help, embarrassed at being caught out lying earlier.

"Would anyone like a lift home?" Lieutenant asked.

I glanced at Maureen and she shook her head just a tiny bit. We'd both had enough of Maggie.

"No, thank you, Lieutenant," I replied. "Maureen and I will walk home."

The other two accepted the lift and the three of them said goodbye and set off down the hill. Maureen and I sat on the bench for a little longer, watching the shadows move across the fields. Somewhere below us the church clock struck five, and a flock of jackdaws flew from the wood, making that strange yapping cry of theirs.

"Look," whispered Maureen, tapping my arm. I turned to where she was pointing and there was a fox — it looked like the same one we'd seen earlier — sitting calmly in a patch of sunshine with its eyes squinted against the light, having a scratch, just like a dog.

"That fox is just like us," said Maureen.

"How do you mean? I asked, puzzled.

"When we saw it down in the farmyard, it was like us during the war, all of us, I mean, the whole country." She frowned and bit her lip, trying to think how to explain.

"We were all a bit hungry and tired, and everything was different and hard, and there were loud frightening noises and scary things happening. Now up here in the sunshine, the fox is like we are now there's peace. We're still a bit scruffy, there are broken buildings, and people can't afford new things, but we're not scared all the time, and we've got time to sit in the sun and relax a bit."

I looked at her with surprised respect. She was absolutely right, and she'd thought it out all by herself. I suddenly realised that Maureen was just as clever as me, but in different ways, and I felt bad that I'd thought she was slow and a bit silly for so long. I reached out and squeezed her hand.

"Come on, let's get home before the sun goes down, and leave the fox to have the woods to itself."

~*~

Mr Fielding was sitting on the front wall smoking a cigarette when we got home; he seemed to have cheered up, and asked us how we'd done.

Maureen chatted away about trail making, laying the fire, making Lieutenant jump, and then showed him what she'd been carving while we were drinking our tea. On the end of a stick about an inch across she'd whittled out a little running fox. Its back legs were still joined to the stick, but its front legs were galloping away, as though it was just running for fun. It was really good carving.

Mr Fielding gently took the stick from her.

"Can I have a go on the other end?" he asked, "I won't damage your fox, I promise. I used to do this sort of thing when I was a kid."

Maureen handed him Daddy's pruning knife and he bent his head over the blank end of the stick, working gently but firmly at the wood as we watched. Under his hands, a tiny rabbit appeared, and it was running, too, chasing the fox! Maureen laughed delightedly and clapped her hands.

"What's happening here?" asked Daddy, appearing beside us. We'd been so involved in watching Mr Fielding that we hadn't noticed him come out of the house.

He looked at the carving on the stick, at Maureen's good but rough fox, and at the beautiful little rabbit on the other end.

"That's really good, Gerry," he said. "Where did you learn to do that?"

"I always used to mess around whittling stuff as a kid," Mr Fielding said. "I wanted to be a carpenter and wood carver, but my dad said I'd do better learning to be a mechanic. He reckoned no-one wants fancy carved stuff these days."

"There's plenty of work around now for a good chippy," Daddy said. "I'll ask around; I know lots of people who need windows and doors repaired. It'd give you something to do, get you out of the house."

Mr Fielding looked down at the carving in his hand.

"Maybe that's a good idea. I've been running away from the fox too long, I should do what this rabbit's doing and chase it away."

Maureen and I looked at each other, confused, but Daddy seemed to understand. He shook Mr Fielding's hand warmly and patted him on the back.

Chapter Three

Birthday

"Happy birthday Sylvie!" Something heavy was bouncing up and down on my feet.

"Hmmm. . . ? Wha. . . ?" I rolled over and kicked out.

"Ow! That's not very friendly when I'm saying happy birthday!"

I opened my eyes and sat up. Audrey was kneeling on the bottom of my bed in her red-and-white striped pyjamas that were passed down from our cousin John, rubbing her elbow and looking cross.

I reached out to the bedside chair for my dressing gown.

"Sorry Aud, but you took me by surprise. I was dreaming I had my feet trapped in a hole; that must have been you sitting on them!"

"Come on, get up! It's your birthday and there are loads of presents on the table; I've been down to look. There's something from me, too, it's mmmmpfff. . . ."

I grabbed her in a hug and clamped my hand over her mouth while she squealed.

"Don't spoil the surprise! Are Mummy and Daddy up yet?"

An amused-sounding voice came from the next room.

"We are, now. Happy birthday, Sylvie!" Mummy appeared in the doorway, tying the belt of her candlewick dressing gown. "You two do realise it's only half past six?"

"Sorry," we said together.

"It's my fault, Mummy," said Audrey, pushing her bobbed hair back from her face. She looked like a Yorkshire terrier in the mornings until she put her hair slide in.

"I went down to the bathroom and saw all the presents on the table and I couldn't wait any longer for Sylvie to wake up."

"Get your dressing gowns on and come downstairs, girls, I'll put the kettle on while Daddy has a wash. As it's Saturday, you can have breakfast in your pyjamas, and Sylvie, you can open your presents once we've eaten."

Audrey was shaking with silent laughter.

"What's so funny?" I asked.

"Having breakfast in our pyjamas."

Mum and I looked at each other, puzzled.

"Why is that funny?"

"Well, we usually have our breakfast in a bowl!" She howled with laughter, curling into a ball, and rocked so hard she fell off the bed and landed with a thud on the floor, still laughing.

Mum and I rolled our eyes and laughed.

"You're going to have a good job writing jokes for Christmas crackers when you grow up, young lady," said Mum.

~*~

The breakfast table looked spectacular! We all huddled at one end to eat our porridge, admiring the pile of parcels at the other end. Audrey scoffed her porridge down without breathing between mouthfuls and bounced in her chair, sitting on her hands, until the rest of us had finished.

"Come on, Sylvie, open mine first!" she cried, as soon as I'd finished my last spoonful, pushing a small soft package into my hands.

I untied the ribbon and unwrapped the package carefully. Inside was a little book, made of pieces of soft felt in different shades of blue, and across the front cover the word NEEDLES was embroidered in chain stitch in a darker blue thread.

Inside the first page of the book were six needles with gold eyes, pinned into the felt in a neat row.

19

"Oh, Aud, did you make this yourself?" I asked, "It's beautiful! You're so clever!"

"Mummy helped me with the embroidery, but I stitched the seam in the middle all by myself, and Mummy let me use her big scissors to cut the felt out," Audrey said proudly.

I hugged her tight. As she grew older, it felt as though the four-and-a-half-year gap between us was getting smaller and smaller. She was really a proper sister-friend, now.

I opened the pile of cards next. They were from all the aunts and uncles, and some had money in them: In all, I had two pounds, ten shillings in birthday money! I felt very rich.

A smaller parcel wrapped in red-and-white striped paper turned out to be a big bar of chocolate. That was from Maureen. She must have saved up all her coupons to get it, which was very impressive, as Maureen loved chocolate. I remembered a long thin package that Jasmine had slipped into my satchel on Friday afternoon at school and ran to fetch it: it was a packet of pencils with rubbers on the ends.

I saved the biggest parcel for last, knowing that it would be from Mummy and Daddy, and everyone gathered round to watch me open it.

I peeled the paper back carefully -- it was a basket! The top of the lid was covered in fabric printed with red strawberries and green leaves on a white background, and it was slightly padded. I opened the hook that fastened it and lifted the lid. It was a sewing basket!

The inside was lined with shiny red satin with little elastic loops stitched round the sides, and held in each loop was something to use for sewing -- a pair of cutting-out scissors, a small pair of embroidery scissors, a tape measure folded up neatly, some white pencils that Mum said were chalk pencils for marking fabric, and some skeins of embroidery thread.

In the bottom of the basket was another wrapped package with a label on it that read "Happy birthday Sylvie, love from

Grandma," and inside this was a beautiful silver thimble, and a pincushion in the shape of a tomato, full of pins with coloured heads, and with a tiny stuffed strawberry hanging from its stalk.

Mum explained that the strawberry was full of emery powder, so if my needles became rusty I could push and pull them through the strawberry and it would polish them up again.

Last of all, in the very bottom of the basket, were some folded squares of fabric: floral prints, spots, stripes, and plain colours, reels of sewing cotton and a bunch of narrow ribbons in colours to match the fabrics, and some paper templates -- a heart shape, a square, a circle, and a diamond.

I gazed at all the wonderful things in the basket, taking out the fabrics one by one and stroking them, completely forgetting about anything except my beautiful sewing basket.

"Look at her face, Tom, I told you she'd love it," said Mum, waking me out of my trance.

"Oh, I do! I do!"

I jumped up and ran around the table to hug and kiss Mum and Daddy.

"Thank you, thank you!"

"I made those paper patterns for you so you can make some lavender bags with the lavender we cut and dried in the summer," said Mum. "I'll show you how, and you can make Christmas presents for Grandma and the aunties."

"I'll start this morning!" I exclaimed, gathering up the porridge bowls to clear the table for my sewing.

~*~

By the time the table was needed for dinner I had made two lavender bags: one for Grandma, which was a heart shape in lilac floral fabric with a purple ribbon loop, and a diamond-shaped one for Auntie Mabel in pale green, her favourite colour, with an "M" embroidered on the front in dark green chain stitch.

Daddy picked up the lavender bags and examined them as I carefully moved my basket into the front room.

"These are very neatly made, Sylvie, well done! You should set up a little production line!"

"Oh! We're having a bazaar at Guides in December," I remembered. "I could make some to sell there! Not from these lovely fabrics, I want to save them for special things, but maybe I could use some of my birthday money to buy some material and tape. May I?"

"What a good idea," said Mum, bringing the casserole to the table. "Why don't you take Audrey with you this afternoon and go down to Ashcroft's? Ask Mrs Ashcroft if she has any remnants of fabric off-ration. Half a yard should be enough to make about ten sachets, and you can measure the ribbon you used on Grandma's one and work out how much tape to buy from that. Good practice for your maths." She winked at me, knowing how much I hated maths.

~*~

The bell over the door of Ashcroft's jangled and Mrs Ashcroft looked up as Audrey and I blew in on a gust of wind.

"Hello, girls." she smiled. "How can I help you?"

"I'm looking for some fabric to make lavender bags for the Guides' Christmas bazaar," I explained. "Mum said to ask if you've got any remnants off-ration, please."

Mrs Ashcroft bustled out from behind the counter and led me over to a wire basket on legs in the corner of the shop.

"Here's the remnant basket," she said. "Anything in here is off-ration, and it's all priced up. There are all sorts of bits of trims in here, too; you might find something you can use for the loops."

I left Audrey gazing at all the beautiful bolts of fabric on the rack and followed the shopkeeper.

"Thank you, Mrs Ashcroft." I bent over to rummage in the basket.

There were some beautiful pieces of fabric: some very small, and some large enough to make a bag or apron.

After a few minutes of picking up completely unsuitable but very exciting pieces, I found half a yard of plain red cotton, marked down from a shilling to sixpence. It had a dirty mark down one selvedge, but that didn't matter; I could cut round that.

Digging through the trimmings, I found a length of green ribbon that had gold stars printed in a line down the middle. It was priced at threepence and was plenty to make enough loops for about five lavender bags. A length of stiff gold braid was marked at ninepence, quite expensive, but it would look lovely on heart-shaped sachets.

I was about to take my materials over to the counter to pay when I had a good idea. Daddy had a small apron-belt that he used for work which was made of dark brown canvas and had pockets all along it to hold his secateurs, string, wire clippers, and all the bits and bobs he needed to hand at work. It was very worn out and Mum had mended it several times. There was a yard of blackout material in the basket which would be perfect to make him a new one. Mum would help me, and she might even let me use her sewing machine.

As I pulled the length of black fabric out, another piece came with it. It was dark blue with white birds on it, and was just enough to make a cooking apron for Mum.

I looked at the price tickets. The blackout material was one and six and the bird material was one and threepence. I had plenty of money. The only problem was how to make Mum's apron in secret, but I decided to buy the material anyway and worry about that later.

I signalled to Audrey to be quiet as we opened the front door and I quickly slipped the bird print fabric out of my bag and stuffed it down inside one of my wellingtons until I could take it upstairs and hide it properly, then nodded to Audrey, and she slammed the door loudly.

"Hello, girls," called Mum. "I've just made a pot of tea; come and have a cup and show me what you've bought."

I showed her the blackout material first, quickly, before Daddy came in for his cup of tea, and she reassured me that making the gardening apron would be easy, and she would show me how to use the sewing machine.

We spread the lavender bag material and trimmings on the table and Mum congratulated me on finding such good bargains.

I drank my tea so quickly that I had already cut out a lavender bag from the red cotton before Daddy had taken more than two sips of his tea, and he watched with interest as I sewed around the heart shape.

"You can't work all day on your birthday, Sylvie," he said, winking at me. "I think we should do something special to celebrate your twelfth birthday. Who'd like to go to the pictures this afternoon? Dumbo is on at the flea pit."

"Oh, yes, please!" Audrey and I cried together.

"This is the best birthday ever," said Audrey, "and it's not even mine!"

Chapter Four

When Johnny Comes Marching Home

"You'll never get that apron finished at this rate," said Mum, finding me craning to peer between the curtains of the front window, a pile of blackout fabric abandoned on the sideboard.

"You've only got a week, and it's the bazaar tomorrow. You've spent so much time at Maureen's this week, I don't know what you two find to talk about."

I smiled to myself without turning round, so she couldn't see my face. I had been spending a lot of time at Maureen's, but all the while we were chatting I had been sewing at the apron I was making for Mum for Christmas. I had to hand sew everything, as Mrs Fielding didn't have a sewing machine, so it was taking ages, but it was nearly finished and all I had left to do was the hem at the bottom.

"I've finished all the lavender bags for the bazaar, and it's the holidays now, so I'll sew all day on Monday after Daddy goes to work," I promised.

"I wonder who's going to move in next door but one," I mused, changing the subject. Mum came to stand beside me and watch as Mr and Mrs Bird went to and fro in the dark, loading their dining chairs into the hired van parked outside.

"Dicky" Bird, whose real name was George, was in my class at school, but his dad had just taken a new job the other side of London, so they were moving out first thing in the morning.

"I'm sure it will be someone nice," said Mum. "Now, let's have a look at that zip pocket you want to put on. Daddy will be pleased with that; he can keep his door key safe in there while he's working. He didn't have a zip pocket in the old apron."

I listened with one ear as Mum showed me how to pin the zip in place, thinking hard all the time. Something was going on. It was nearly Christmas, and Mum and Dad always had secrets at Christmas. I knew there were presents hidden somewhere in the house, but this was different. Lots of letters had been received and sent in the last few weeks, and when I asked who they were from and to I just got silly answers.

"The King," said Mum.

"Mickey Mouse," said Dad.

I sighed as I turned the apron round and started pinning the other side of the zip so I could stitch it before Daddy came home. Adults could be very confusing at times.

~*~

I shrugged into my coat and tugged my knitted hat well down over my ears. It hadn't snowed yet, but the sky had that endless grey-white look that it gets when snow is lurking in the clouds. I pulled on my matching knitted gloves and picked up the basket that held all the things we had made for the handicraft stall at the bazaar. My lavender bags were wrapped in tissue at the bottom, then there were the tea cosies that Mum had knitted from all her left-over oddments of wool, every frilly stripe a different colour.

Daddy had made some teapot stands from odd tiles set into wooden frames, and even Audrey had made some little felt finger puppets with glued-on faces and hair. My Guide hat was sitting on the top of the basket, to put on when I got to the church hall.

"I'll pop along later and see how you're getting on," said Mum, kissing the bobble of my hat. "I hear they've got Father Christmas coming for all the little kids. That'll be fun!"

I was too old for sitting on Father Christmas' knee now, but it would be fun to watch all the little ones.

I heard Maureen's front door open and ran out to meet her. The two of us had been given the handicraft stall to look after together. Maureen was bringing some of her mum's home-made gooseberry jam to add to the table, and her dad had made some little wooden bird whistles.

The church hall was echoing with noise as people unfolded trestle tables and screeched them across the floor. A group of dads were tacking up bunting and tinsel around the walls, and Captain and Lieutenant were pinning wrapping paper over a folding screen to make a grotto for Father Christmas to sit in.

Maureen and I laid our produce out on our table, arranging and re-arranging it to show everything off the best way and encourage people to buy.

Lieutenant left her screen and came over to look at our table.

"Well, you have worked hard, haven't you!" She handed us a small jam jar containing some coins.

"This is your float, a pound in small change, so you have enough change if people only have ten-shilling notes," she explained. "When we cash up at the end of the bazaar, we take a pound off the total, and that's how much money you'll have made."

We nodded solemnly, taking our responsibility very seriously. I had spent the evening before labelling up all the things we had to sell and had worked out that if we sold everything we would make two pounds, one and six. With Mrs Fielding's jam and Mr Fielding's whistles added to the stock, we could earn as much as three pounds, seven and sixpence!

There was a bustle at the door. The Mayor had arrived, and Lieutenant marched off to welcome him. He was wearing his chain, but he only had an ordinary suit on and not his mayoral robes, which was disappointing. Captain clapped her hands for silence and made a short speech welcoming our Very Important Guest and invited him to open the bazaar.

He started to talk about what excellent training it was for girls to be Brownies and Guides, and how much good they did in fundraising, blah blah blah. . . .

Maureen wasn't paying attention; she was picking away at the edge of the green oilcloth that was stuck to the top of our table. I nudged her and she pointed her face in the direction of the Mayor, but I could tell she still wasn't listening. Finally, he ground to a halt.

". . .and so, it gives me great pleasure to declare the bazaar . . . open!"

Everyone clapped and cheered, more from relief that he had stopped talking than anything else. The crowd of people in the hall began to roam around the tables, the Mayor included. He made his way slowly round, making a purchase here, showing interest there, until he came to our table.

"Oh, lavender bags!" he exclaimed, picking up one of the heart-shaped ones with the gold braid loop. "I must buy one of these for my wife, and that jam looks delicious! I'll have a pot of that too, please, girls."

I pulled out one of the ironed paper bags that we had all been saving for weeks and popped in the jar and the lavender bag, twirling the bag over and over to twist the corners, the way the lady in the grocers did. Maureen took the money and smartly counted out change.

We grinned at each other as the Mayor moved on to the next stall. Two sales already!

The hall was filling up and the Brownies had arrived to man the lucky dip barrel in a shift system of pairs. I could see Audrey with her friend Carol, but no sign of Mum or Dad. I thought they would have come with Audrey to see how everything was going.

Our table was one of the busiest in the hall, as we had something for everyone, and our stock soon started to run out. I was busy re-arranging what was left to fill the space when a wide-eyed Audrey appeared by my side.

"Sylv! Look! Mummy and Daddy have just arrived, with Father Christmas! They know Father Christmas!"

"Well, of course they do, or how else would he know where we live?" I asked. I wasn't going to tell her the secret that Mum had told me when I turned ten. She would find out in two years.

I looked across the hall and saw our parents standing beside a tall fat man in the traditional red suit and white beard, talking to Lieutenant. For some reason, they kept looking across at Audrey and me, then Lieutenant nodded and smiled and led Father Christmas into his grotto, where a line of mothers and small children soon formed to see what was in the sack he had brought with him.

Audrey shuffled her feet.

"What is it, Aud?" I asked.

"I've seen a little red car on the toy stall that I want to get for Brian for Christmas," she said, "but I've run out of pocket money. Will you lend me fourpence until tomorrow? Please?"

"All right, here you are." I rummaged in my pocket and handed her the money and she skipped off to the toy stall, forgetting all about Father Christmas. She was getting a bit old for all that, anyway.

~*~

The hall was almost empty by two o'clock. Nearly everything had been sold, and the lucky dip barrel had been emptied out and put away for the summer fete.

We cashed up our takings. We had made three pounds, two shillings and had hardly anything left. Lieutenant tipped the money into her tin cash box and rattled it with great satisfaction.

"Have you two been to see Father Christmas?" she asked as Audrey came over to see why I was taking so long in tidying up.

"No!" I scoffed. "I'm too old for that. Audrey can, if she wants to."

"Hmm, I think you should go and see him. I think he might have something to tell you about what you're getting for Christmas."

I looked over to the grotto. Mum and Dad were standing there chatting to Father Christmas as though they'd known him all their lives. He laughed at something they said and somehow the laugh sounded familiar.

"Come on, Sylvie, let's go and see him." Audrey grabbed my hand and pulled me across the room.

"Ho, ho, ho! Hello, you two," said the jolly fat man in a deep voice. "I think I know what you two are getting for Christmas."

"What, what?" cried Audrey excitedly.

"A new neighbour!" boomed the deep voice.

Huh, I thought, not very exciting, and anyway we knew that.

"Who is the neighbour, do you know?" asked Audrey.

Father Christmas' eyes twinkled and he suddenly whipped off his cotton wool beard.

"Me!" he said in a normal voice.

Uncle Johnny!

Audrey and I squealed and rushed to grab him in a hug. He was so well padded that there was plenty of him to grab.

"You're moving in next door but one?" I asked, as he rocked us to and fro, laughing.

"Yes." He grinned. "The navy have finally had enough of me and I'm home for good."

~*~

We all walked home together, and Uncle Johnny proudly unlocked his new front door and ushered us inside. He didn't have a lot of furniture yet, and some of what he did have I recognised as coming from Grandma's house or ours, but it was going to be wonderful having him living so close.

He filled the kettle and set it on the stove to boil while Mum went back to our house for some cups, and Audrey and I ran about the almost empty house that was so much like ours, but so different. I looked through the front bedroom window and saw Maureen hovering on the pavement: She must have seen that something was going on but she was too shy to knock. As I ran down the stairs, Mum was just coming back in and she brought Maureen in with her.

Uncle Johnny poured the tea and we all looked at him expectantly, our cups raised.

"Speech, speech!" laughed Daddy.

"Well, I don't really know quite what to say except thank you, big brother, for putting in a good word for me with the landlord and helping me get moved in so quickly. Let's have a toast, to family. And that includes you, Maureen!" He winked at her and we all replied to his toast.

"To family!"

Part Two
1947

Chapter Five

Going Up West

I smoothed my new gloves over the arm of the settee and looked at the clock again. Still only a quarter to eleven. I sighed impatiently and tried to distract myself by thinking about something else.

I thought back to Christmas Day. It had been so lovely having Uncle Johnny with us. He came round for breakfast and watched us open our presents. Mum and Daddy were thrilled with their aprons that I had made. Mum was so pleased with hers that she almost forgot to take it off when we left to go to Grandma's.

Audrey and I were still singing, "We wish you a merry Christmas," as we walked back down our road on Christmas evening. It was nearly ten o'clock, and way past both our bedtimes.

"You'll wake all the babies!" said Daddy, scooping up a handful of snow from someone's front wall and throwing it at the back of Uncle Johnny, who was walking ahead of us with Mum's arm tucked through his.

"Ow!" laughed Uncle Johnny. "Come on, everyone, back to my house for a cup of tea. I haven't given these two young ladies their present yet."

Audrey and I ran past the adults and danced backwards in front of Uncle Johnny.

"What is it?" squealed Audrey.

"Wait and see!" he answered, standing back with a flourish to usher us all through his front gate.

When the tea was ready, Uncle Johnny went to a kitchen drawer and took out an envelope.

"You open it, Sylvie, as you're the eldest."

I slid my finger under the flap and opened the envelope. Some small slips of paper fell onto the table, and I picked one up and read it.

"Cinderella! We've got tickets for Cinderella, at the Dominion Theatre! Where is that, Uncle Johnny?"

"It's in the West End. We'll make a day of it and have a meal at the Lyons Corner House before the show. There are five tickets, so you can each choose a friend to come along. The fifth ticket is for me." He smiled as we ran to hug him.

~*~

Maureen was last, as usual. Brian had already arrived and was being shown Audrey's Christmas presents, and Uncle Johnny was chatting to Mum in the kitchen.

"Come on then, kids," he said, picking up his coat. "We'll knock for Maureen on the way. If she doesn't hurry up, we'll miss the trolleybus."

We had never been on a trolleybus before. Brian had, and he had given us a very technical explanation about how they work. I didn't really care, so long as it got us there.

Maureen's front door opened at the same time as ours. She was wearing her new red coat that she'd had for Christmas and looked very smart.

"Off you go, then." Mum waved her tea towel as we set off to walk the mile to Abbeyfield to catch the trolleybus. "Have fun!"

~*~

The trolleybus terminus was busy and a lot of the people there were dressed up as smartly as we were and looked as though they were going into London, too. I watched the queue anxiously. What if there were too many people, and we couldn't get on the trolleybus when it came?

A clang and rumble announced the arrival of our bus, but as we were at the terminus we had to wait while the bus was turned around. Brian explained what was happening as we watched, fascinated.

The driver stopped the bus on the turntable and the conductor jumped down and unhooked a long pole from somewhere on the side of the bus, which he used to disconnect the trolley poles on the roof from the overhead wires. Brian said the pole was insulated so the conductor could touch it to the electric wires without getting a shock from the electricity.

The driver climbed down from his cab and he and the conductor pushed the huge bus all by themselves, so it spun through a hundred and eighty degrees on the turntable to face the right way to go to London.

The driver climbed back into his cab while the conductor hooked the trolley poles back onto the wires and stowed his pole away again. The bus slowly pulled forward to the stop, and we were ready to board.

"Can we go upstairs, Uncle Johnny?" begged Audrey.

"Well, of course!" he replied, straightening her hat, which was tipped over one eye as usual. "This is a special occasion. It's not every day we go Up West; we're going to do this in style!"

I was pleased to see that all the passengers in front of us decided to sit downstairs. They must have all been on a trolleybus before. We raced for the front seats of the top deck. Maureen and I sat on the right, and Audrey and Brian squeezed onto the other front seat either side of Uncle Johnny. Brian wanted to sit by the window so he could watch the conductor, if the trolley came disconnected and needed to be hooked up again.

The conductor rang the bell and we were off.

It was cold on the bus, so cold that I didn't want to unbutton my coat, but I knew what Mum would say,

"If you keep it done up, you won't feel the benefit when you get off."

The window kept steaming up as we breathed, so Maureen wiped it clear with her glove every now and then so we could see where we were going. In the other seat, Audrey and Brian were messing around, fidgeting and laughing so much that their window was completely covered in mist. Audrey saw Maureen wiping our side and decided to write her name in the mist.

"You need to write it backwards, Aud," said Brian. "Then people outside can read it."

"But I don't want everyone knowing what my name is!" she cried indignantly.

"All right, then, if you want them to think you're called Yerdua, that's up to you."

Brian leaned forward and wrote slowly and carefully: NAIRB.

"That's still wrong," said Audrey smugly. "The B, R and N are the wrong way round."

"I don't care, it's better than yours," said Brian crossly.

"If the pair of you don't behave, you'll be in trouble when the conductor comes up for the tickets," said Uncle Johnny, wiping the writing off the window with his hanky just as we heard the conductor come up the stairs.

"One and four halves, return, please," said Uncle Johnny, and the man reeled off the tickets in a long strip.

Brian fidgeted in his seat, waiting for the conductor to go back down the stairs before he burst out, "You can't have four halves! You can have two halves of something, but not four! Four is quarters!"

"Yes, you can," argued Audrey, leaning forward in her seat to glare at Brian. "Four halves makes two whole ones, a half plus a half is one, so four halves equals two, so there."

"If you two professors can stop arguing a minute, I'll explain," said Uncle Johnny, pushing them both back in their seats. "The four of you only pay half fare, because you're children. It has nothing to do with adding up fractions."

Audrey settled back in her seat with her arms folded, sulking.

I took a bag of pear drops from my pocket and offered it round, which helped to calm things down. You can't argue while you're sucking a pear drop, in case it goes down the wrong way.

~*~

It was a long journey. I kept sneaking a look at my watch.

"Will we have time to eat before the pantomime, Uncle Johnny?" I asked anxiously.

"Oh, yes, plenty of time," he replied calmly. "We're nearly at Holborn Circus, where the bus turns round. We've got a bit of a walk from there to Tottenham Court Road, where the Corner House is, but we should be there by one o'clock. The waitresses and cooks there know what time the theatres open, and they'll make sure we get fed in plenty of time to make it to our seats. The theatre is right near the Corner House, so we haven't got too far to stagger after we've stuffed ourselves."

"What do they have to eat there?" asked Maureen.

"Oh, all kinds of things. Bacon and eggs, maybe even real egg, macaroni cheese, anchovy toast . . . all sorts."

"And jelly?" asked Audrey.

"I expect so," said Uncle Johnny. "All good restaurants should serve jelly."

The bus shuddered to a halt and the conductor rang three pings on the bell.

"Terminus!" he shouted, in a severe-sounding voice.

We scrambled down the stairs and onto the pavement. Audrey looked around and frowned.

"Where's the circus?" she asked.

"It's not the kind of circus with acrobats and animals," explained Uncle Johnny. "A circus is just a bit of road that goes around in a circle, like a big roundabout."

"The Romans had circuses," I said informatively. "Terminus is a Roman word, too. A lot of Roman words end with 'us', I learnt that in Latin at school."

Maureen gave me that look she used when she thought I was being a swot.

"Did the Romans have trolleybuses then? Trolleybus ends in 'us'," she asked, but I could tell from her tone of voice that she was just being sarky, so I ignored her.

Uncle Johnny took firm hold of a hand each of Audrey and Brian and shepherded Maureen and me in front of him.

"Stick together, kids, it's busy here."

Everyone seemed to be in a tremendous hurry, people bustling along the pavements and in and out of the office buildings and shops, cars and taxis honking at each other at every junction.

"There's the Corner House." Uncle Johnny pointed with Brian's hand as well as his own, not letting go for a second.

"We cross here, quick quick!"

The Corner House was warm and cosy, and we unwrapped our scarves and coats into a pile on the velour-covered bench in the booth and arranged ourselves around the table.

The Nippy, in her smart black dress, white cap, and apron took our order of lemonade for us girls, ginger beer for Brian, and coffee for Uncle Johnny, and left us with the menu to decide what to eat.

"Oooh, I can't decide," Maureen mused. "What are you having, Sylv?"

"Either anchovies on toast or baked beans on toast. I can't make my mind up."

"I'm having bacon and eggs," said Brian. I looked anxiously at Uncle Johnny. Brian had picked one of the most expensive meals.

"Good for you, Brian." Uncle Jonny closed his menu and beckoned to the waitress. "A proper man's dinner." He winked at Brian.

"Have you made your minds up, girls?"

"Anchovies on toast, please." I folded my menu and piled it on top of Uncle Johnny's.

"The same for me, please, Mr Ford." Maureen was such a copycat!

"Audrey?"

She debated with her head on one side, glancing at Uncle Johnny and Brian.

"Bacon and eggs, please." She closed her menu firmly and glared at Brian, knowing that he was dying to make some comment about her ordering a "man's dinner."

Brian took in the glare and said nothing.

The food was wonderful! And it was so nice to know that we wouldn't have to help with the washing up afterwards. When we had finished our dinners, the waitress came back with another menu for puddings, but we were all so full up we couldn't manage anything.

"I wish I'd known there was pudding," Audrey moaned. "I wouldn't have had such a big dinner!"

"Never mind." Uncle Johnny helped her into her coat. "We can have ice cream at the interval in the theatre."

"Are you going to see Cinderella?" the waitress asked as she collected the money and wiped the table down. "I saw it last week; it's ever so good. The wedding scene is like a dream!" She smiled and waved us off. "Have fun!"

Coming out of the warm restaurant into the cold was quite a shock, and woke us up a bit, as we were all feeing sleepy from so much food.

There was a queue forming outside the theatre already, and I was worried that we had arrived too late and wouldn't be able to get good seats, but Uncle Johnny explained that the seats were already booked and showed us the seat numbers on the tickets. We had five seats in a row, and Uncle Johnny said that we were in the middle of the first row of the Stalls, which he thought were some of the best seats in the house, so we would have a really good view of the whole stage.

As we joined the back of the queue, the big doors of the theatre opened and the line of people started to shuffle forwards. A man in a frock coat and top hat took our tickets and clipped them, with a little bow, and directed us towards an inner door, where a lady looked at the tickets again and showed us which door to use to get to our seats.

The inside of the theatre was breath-taking! Red velvet seats that tipped up, just like at the pictures, only grander, and paintings on the walls, surrounded by gold scroll work, with glittering chandeliers hanging from the ceiling.

We trooped to our seats in silence, taking in the wonderful sights all around, and watching the stream of people spread out and take their places. We were right in front of the stage!

Uncle Johnny had bought a programme from the lady at the door and passed it along the row. The programme had photos of all the actors and actresses, and told what other shows they had been in. We hadn't heard of any of them, but then I was the only one who had been to the theatre before, and then I was only three.

A bell rang, just like the dinner bell at school, and we all looked at Uncle Johnny, who knew everything about the theatre.

"That bell means that the performance is going to start soon. It's to let everyone know that they need to get to their seats. If they're not in the theatre before the curtains open, they won't be allowed in until the interval."

We craned to look around as people hurried to their seats. There were lots of children in the audience; maybe they had been given tickets for Christmas, too.

Behind us, the theatre went back and back, and up and up. There were two more layers of seats above us, and rows and rows sloping up behind us, nearly all full of people, then there were little balconies at the sides of the stage, which Uncle Johnny said were called boxes. You could hire a whole box for yourself, he said, and they would bring your drinks and ice creams into the boxes at the interval so you didn't have to leave your seat, but they were very expensive to hire.

Suddenly music started up, coming from under the stage! The musicians were sitting under the stage in the dark!

The lights in our part of the theatre dimmed and turned off, and the big velvet curtains in front of the stage swished back to show Cinderella sitting in front of a fire, peeling potatoes. She started to sing about how sad and lonely she was, and we settled back to watch.

We knew the story, of course, but the way it was done in this show was quite different. Cinderella's stepsisters were played by men, dressed in really comical ladies' clothes, not like anything a real lady would wear, and they tripped each other up and fell over all the time, showing their bloomers and making jokes. Audrey laughed so hard I thought she would be sick.

At one point, after Cinderella ran away from the ball at midnight, the Ugly Sisters asked for children to come up onto the stage and sing a song with them. Audrey, Maureen, and I cringed back in our seats, but Brian jumped up and ran to the steps at the side of the stage and was up there like a flash! They sang "Run, Rabbit, Run," with actions, and Brian threw himself into it. We all looked at each other in amazement. He was usually so quiet!

After the song, all the children ran back to their seats to wild applause, and the lights came back on for the interval. Ladies with little trays slung on ribbons around their necks walked up and down the aisles selling ice cream, and Uncle Johnny bought us one each. The ice cream came in a cardboard tub, with a little wooden spoon that looked like a miniature shovel.

We just had time to finish our ice creams when the bell rang again and, knowing what it meant, we looked around to see that everyone made it back to their seats in time for the second half.

In the second half, Cinderella was sad again. She had lost her Prince and dropped her shoe. I wanted to call out to her that it would be all right in the end, she looked so unhappy, but eventually Buttons found her, the shoe fitted, and a wedding was arranged!

The waitress was right; the wedding scene was wonderful! Cinderella's dress was beautiful. If they had called children up to the stage during that scene, I would have gone, to see that dress up close. All the characters were on stage for the final scene, waltzing round and round the stage, all the ladies in satin ball gowns and the men in velvet suits.

Suddenly, it was over. The cast came back on to the stage to take their bows, and we clapped and cheered until we were hoarse and the palms of our hands stung.

~*~

We didn't speak as we left the theatre; none of us wanted to break the spell. Audrey danced her way across the red-carpeted floor, humming the tune from the final scene and swishing the skirt of her coat.

Coming out onto the busy road was a big let-down after being in fantasy land for two hours — it was dark now, and cold. We hurried back to the trolleybus terminus, huddled into our coats.

"I wish I could dance like that," said Audrey, still sashaying along. "It must be so lovely to float around in a ball gown."

Brian grunted. "My mum says I've got to start dancing classes when school starts again. My Auntie Lou is starting ballroom dancing lessons at the drill hall and I've got to go. My sisters get away with it; they do piano lessons already."

He kicked at nothing on the pavement and scuffled his feet.

"I'll have to dance with girls."

The expression on his face was so disgusted that I wanted to laugh, but didn't, in case it hurt his feelings.

"Oh, can I come too?" Audrey pirouetted along the pavement in front of us and dropped into a curtsey at Brian's feet, her hands clasped in front of her, just like Cinderella had done when the Fairy Godmother transformed her rags into a beautiful ball gown.

"We can't afford dancing lessons, Aud," I reminded her gently.

"I'll talk to my Auntie Lou," said Brian. "If she really expects me to do lessons, then I want a partner I can get on with. She might let you in for free if I ask her; then I won't have to dance with a girl!"

"Audrey's a girl, Bri, last time I looked." Maureen nudged him, teasing.

"Yes, but she's my friend first and a girl second; that makes a difference." Brian nodded seriously and we all laughed as we clattered up the stairs to the top deck of the trolleybus.

Chapter Six

Dance Hall Daze

Audrey's peal of laughter could have been heard right down the street.

"Oooh, look at you, Valentino," she chirped, opening the door wide so we could see Brian.

"Shut up," he growled. "Morning, Mrs Ford. Hello, Sylvie."

Scamp ran to greet his friend, but Brian pushed him away.

"No, Scamp. These are my best trousers; my mum'll kill me if I get them covered in dog hair."

"Down, Scamp! You look very smart, Brian. Don't take any notice of Audrey; she's always like this when she has to get dressed up." Mum frowned at my sister.

Brian smoothed his brilliantined hair back and hitched the collar of his best coat.

"You ready then, Aud? You're not going to walk down there in your dancing shoes, are you?"

"Of course not," she replied, stuffing her silver shoes into her gym bag and cramming her feet into her battered school shoes.

"Off you go then, you two. Have fun and be good."

I watched them walk down the street, Audrey skipping ahead and Brian trailing behind, scuffling his feet.

A sudden idea popped into my head.

"Mum? I'm just popping next door to call for Maureen. We might go out for a bit."

"All right, but be back for dinner; I'm doing boiled bacon."

~*~

Maureen came to the door with a tea towel in her hand.

"Oh," I said, "are you busy? I wondered if you wanted to come out for a bit."

"Just finishing the washing up. Where did you want to go?"

"Well, Audrey and Brian are having their first dancing lesson today at the Drill Hall, I thought maybe we could go down and watch."

"Will Brian's auntie let us in?" Maureen asked as I followed her through to the kitchen.

"No, but we can look through the window. Morning, Mrs Fielding!"

"You want to spy on your sister and her best friend having a dancing lesson?" Maureen sounded indignant.

"Yes, don't you? It'll be fun! Imagine Brian's face when he has to put his arm around Audrey for a waltz or something. It's too good to miss! They'll never know. We can peep in the side window; they'll be too busy concentrating to see us."

"You are an evil sister!" Maureen laughed. "But come on, then!"

~*~

We crept quietly up to the window and peeped in, crouching so our chins were on the windowsill. A gramophone was playing a waltz tune and about a dozen children were slowly stepping around the room. Most of them were girls, dancing in pairs, but there were two other boys looking unhappy in tight shoes and their best suits, each pushing a girl backwards. One of the boys was tiny but partnered by a girl who was at least a foot taller than him.

"Audrey's actually really good, isn't she? She looks quite graceful." Maureen sounded surprised, and I didn't blame her. We were used to seeing Audrey in scruffy old shorts inherited from a boy cousin, climbing trees and playing football with

Brian. It was hard to recognise that little tomboy in the pretty girl twirling about in her best dress with her hair all smooth and shiny.

"Brian's not bad, either," I said, admiringly. "He hasn't tripped her up yet!"

"He looks miserable, though!"

We watched for a while as Brian's auntie showed the class the basic steps for a quickstep, then she changed the record and set them dancing again. Audrey and Brian were by far the best in the class, and Brian seemed to enjoy the quickstep more; towards the end of the dance, he and Audrey were smiling at each other.

For the last ten minutes of the lesson, Brian's auntie lined the class up and talked through what they had learnt, showing them what they were doing wrong and praising what they did right. We couldn't hear every word, so we got a bit bored and sat down with our backs against the wall, chatting and eating humbugs.

Suddenly we heard a door open and scrambled up. We couldn't let them know we'd been watching! We ran around the back of the hall and cut through an alleyway behind some houses, so if we met Audrey and Brian coming out it would look as though we'd been to the library just down the road.

As we came back out onto the main road, the younger two had just passed the end of the alley, and turned back to us, bubbling over with chatter. I slid Maureen a sideways glance of relief.

"Hello, you two." Maureen acted surprised. "How was your lesson?"

"It was super!" Audrey smiled. "Wasn't it, Brian? Mrs Jackson said I've got good posture, didn't she, Brian? We were the best in the class, weren't we, Brian?"

Brian nodded and grinned.

"So, it wasn't as bad as you thought, then?" I asked him.

"No," he admitted, "it was actually quite good fun once we started dancing properly. Audrey's good; she didn't step on my foot once, and I only stepped on hers a little bit when we tried the reverse step the first time."

"So, you'll be going back next week, then?" Maureen nudged him.

"I haven't got a choice. Auntie Lou is making me go, but I might actually look forward to it next week."

"At least you're not dancing with that really tall girl," said Maureen, forgetting that we weren't supposed to have seen any of the dancing. I widened my eyes at her and she cleverly made a quick recovery from her mistake.

"We saw her leaving, didn't we, Sylv, that really tall girl with the red hair. She must have been in your class; she wouldn't be dressed up like that on a Saturday morning just to go out shopping."

The kids hadn't noticed Maureen's slip; they just took her word for it that we had noticed the girl leaving, although we hadn't even seen her.

"Poor Bill is stuck with her," said Brian. "Her name's Elsie something. She's about three years older than all of us. Auntie Lou knows her mum and got her to come, in hopes that she'll tell her friends and get some older children to join the class. Why don't you two come along? You can have a trial lesson for a shilling, Auntie said, then if you don't like it you don't have to come again. If you sign up for a term's worth of lessons, it's ninepence a week."

I looked at Maureen.

"What do you think, Mo, shall we have a try?"

"Count me out!" she said, backing away. "Don't you remember how bad I was at gym? I've got two left feet!"

"Oh, come on, Sylvie, you come next week. Mrs Jackson said there'll be some older boys coming. Her husband runs the Boys' Brigade and he's going to get some of them to come along," Audrey wheedled.

"I'll think about it," I said.

~*~

The following Saturday, the three of us set off together, dolled up in our Sunday best. Maureen waved us off from her front door.

"I might go out for a walk in a bit," she muttered to me under her breath.

"Don't you dare!" I glared at her and she laughed.

All through the start of the lesson I kept looking nervously at the window, expecting to see Maureen's face peering in. I was partnered by one of the boys from the Boys' Brigade, a spotty, pale boy called Alan. He said he was fourteen, and that was all the conversation we had.

Mrs Jackson called Brian and Audrey out to the front of the class to demonstrate what she wanted us to do, then told all the boys, or girls who were pretending to be boys, to go to their partners, bow, and ask for the pleasure of the next dance.

Some of the girls threw themselves into the part, bowing with a flourish, one even stroked an imaginary moustache, like Ronald Coleman, but the boys all muttered something without looking at the girls' faces and dragged them onto the dance floor.

My partner ambled over, scuffed the floor with his toe and said, "Come on, then."

His hands were soft and clammy. It felt like holding a lump of blancmange in each hand, and he walked through the dance stiffly, looking over my shoulder.

The room was full of muttered "sorry"s and "excuse me"s as the newcomers stumbled around. Some of them quickly picked up the steps and started dancing properly, but Alan was hopeless, and I felt so self-conscious that I couldn't get into a rhythm.

~*~

"So, will you be back next week?" Audrey asked as we changed our shoes.

"No, I don't think so, Aud. I'll leave it to you. You're much better than I am."

Mrs Jackson heard me and came over.

"It's not for everyone, Sylvie, I quite understand. Your sister, here, is very good, and although I shouldn't say it, with him being my nephew, so is Brian. I can see these two entering competitions and winning medals in the near future."

"I know what, Sylvie!" said Audrey. "If I'm going to be a proper ballroom dancer, I'll need lots of dresses. I can design them, and you can make them for me. I'll have my own personal dressmaker!"

Mrs Jackson laughed.

"This one has got it all organised. She'll go far!"

"Next stop, the Tower Ballroom, Blackpool!" laughed Audrey, twirling away down the room.

Chapter Seven

The Green-Eyed Monster

Jasmine was waiting for me at the end of the road. I waved goodbye to Maureen as she turned off to her school and slipped my arm through Jasmine's.

"Mum said you can come 'round after school tomorrow so we can do our history homework together," said Jasmine, offering me a mint imperial.

"Oh, super! I'll ask my mum tonight, but I'm sure she'll say yes," I mumbled through my sweet. "It'll be much easier doing it together. We can test each other on all those wives to make sure we've got them in the right order. What was it Mr Dawes said: divorced, beheaded, died, divorced, beheaded, survived?"

"Yes, that was it," Jasmine frowned, "but it's remembering which queen did which. It would be so much easier if they weren't nearly all called Anne or Catherine!"

We laughed and skipped down the road, chanting, "Divorced, beheaded, died, divorced, beheaded, survived!"

I was looking forward to seeing Jasmine's house. She lived in one of the newer houses, down past the church, that had nice big gardens, and I knew she had a swing in the back garden. Her dad had collected scrap metal for the war effort after he was invalided home, and when the war finished, he had built the swing from various bits and pieces. I was glad Audrey wasn't invited. If she was there, I'd have to pretend that I was a bit old for playing on swings, but I didn't think I was at all.

Maureen was waiting at the top of the road on the way home. She nodded to Jasmine, but never had a lot to say to her.

"See you tomorrow, Sylvie. Don't forget to ask your mum," said Jasmine, waving as she crossed the road.

"Ask your mum what?" Maureen questioned me.

"Jasmine's invited me round to her house after school tomorrow, so we can do our history homework together after tea."

"Oh." Maureen looked down at her feet, balling her hands in her coat pockets. "I was going to ask you to come round for tea tomorrow. Mum's been sorting out the linen cupboard and she's got some old dresses she said we could have to cut down and make something for ourselves. I thought we could have a sewing session, you're so good at making things over."

I bit my lip. "Sorry, Mo, Jasmine got in first. Maybe we can do it at the weekend?"

"I can't." She shook her head. "I've got a piano exam on Saturday morning, then Dad's taking us over to see Auntie Jean — you know, the one who's just come back from America — then on Sunday it's church parade, and after that I've got to help Mum tidy up the under stairs cupboard so we can put some of my old toys away. You know what she's like with tidying; she finds old photos and things and has to sit down and look through them and the whole job takes forever."

"Oh, well, maybe next week then?"

She shrugged offhandedly. "If you like."

She didn't seem that bothered. I felt bad about turning her down, but Jasmine had asked first.

~*~

It felt weird walking past my road and not going home. We left school at the usual time, but Maureen wasn't waiting at the corner as usual. I could see her marching off down the road towards home. I called after her, but she didn't hear me, she just kept on walking. She had no reason to wait, really, I wouldn't have been walking down the road with her, but I thought she might have stopped just to say hello.

"How long have you and Maureen been friends?" asked Jasmine, breaking my train of thought.

"Oh, forever, since we were babies. We've always lived next door to each other."

"It must feel weird for her, now you're not at the same school."

"It feels weird for me, too," I said, slightly annoyed that Jasmine was feeling sorry for Maureen, when Maureen was being so grumpy and jealous.

"I know," Jasmine frowned, "but you're at a new school, new teachers, new friends, new everything, while nothing's changed for Maureen except that her best friend doesn't sit beside her anymore."

I hadn't thought of it like that.

~*~

Jasmine's house was so tidy compared to ours, but she didn't have a little sister running in and out and leaving toys everywhere, or a dog bringing in chickens and letting them run around the house, like Scamp did now and then, and her mum didn't work, so she had plenty of time to dust and tidy.

"Come in, Sylvie, lovely to meet you; Jasmine's told me all about you." Jasmine's mum opened the door wide and smiled as we walked in.

Jasmine caught my arm as I was about to go into the front room and glanced down at my feet. She had taken her own shoes off and was padding about in her socks. I quickly heeled my shoes off and grinned at her.

"Hello, Mrs Willis. Thank you for letting me come 'round."

"You're very welcome, dear. Tea's almost ready. Would you like a glass of lemonade?"

"Oh, yes, please."

Mrs Willis led us through to the kitchen. The table was laid with a white cloth embroidered with little bunches of flowers in the corners, and the teapot had a knitted cosy that looked like a little thatched cottage.

A big plate was piled with bread and butter, and there were pots of home-made jam, each with a pretty cotton cover tied with coloured thread. Our places were set with china plates and cups, and bone-handled knives to spread our jam. And napkins!

I glanced across at Jasmine as we sat down. She didn't seem to be acting "company", so maybe they always had their tea like this. I knew Jasmine was a scholarship girl like me, and I'd imagined they didn't have a lot of money, but everything in the house seemed new and posh. Of course, Jasmine's dad ran his own business, so that would make a difference.

"Does your dad work late?" I asked. "My dad goes out early, so he's usually back for tea."

"Dad works until he's finished," said Jasmine through a mouthful of bread and jam. "People turn up at the scrap yard at all kinds of times, so he has to stay and help them. But he's his own boss, so if he wants a day off, he can just do it."

"Salvage centre, dear, not scrap yard," Mrs Willis corrected as she poured tea into our cups, "and don't talk with your mouth full."

Jasmine winked at me and carried on eating.

We helped clear the table and wash up, then settled down to our history homework. Mrs Willis replaced the pretty white tablecloth with a green check oilcloth one, so we didn't spill ink on the table or make grooves in the wood with our pens.

We had to write a two-thousand-word essay about one of Henry VIII's wives, writing as though we were the queen, talking about why she married him and what being his queen was like.

"Which queen are you going to be?" Jasmine asked, chewing the end of her pen.

"I'm going to do Anne of Cleves. She's the most sensible one, and she wasn't married to him very long, so there's not too much to write about."

"I think I'll be Anne Boleyn. She's the most interesting and dramatic one." Jasmine opened a clean page in her exercise book and wrote "Anne Boleyn's Story" at the top, underlined it neatly, and started to write.

Mrs Willis fussed in and out of the kitchen, asking if we wanted any more tea or lemonade, as though she didn't know what to do with herself.

I had just written the last line of my essay when the kitchen door opened, and Jasmine's dad arrived.

"Hello, you must be Sylvie." He grinned. "I won't shake hands; I'm all dirty."

He bent and kissed Jasmine on the top of her head as Mrs Willis bustled in, tying on her apron. Mr Willis kissed his wife carefully, poking his head forward so he didn't make her dirty.

"Go and get changed, Dennis. I'll get your dinner started. The girls have finished at the table now."

I quickly packed up my pencil case, leaving my exercise book open to the last possible minute to let the ink dry, but Jasmine carried on writing, in no hurry.

Mrs Willis collected cutlery from the drawer, slid the cruet onto the corner of the table and fidgeted impatiently while Jasmine's pen scratched across her book.

"And then the sword came down and I died," Jasmine read as she blotted the page and shut her book with a flap.

"You can't write 'and then I died'!" I exclaimed. "How can you tell a story if you're dead?"

"It's History, not English." Jasmine stuffed her book and pencil case in her satchel.

"Anyway, it's done. It's either right or wrong. Let's go out into the garden and forget about school until tomorrow."

We grabbed our coats and ran down to the bottom of the garden where the swing stood under a big apple tree that had no leaves on it yet. It was an unusual swing, because the seat was wide enough for two people to sit on it at once.

It was dark already, but good to be out in the cold fresh air after slaving over our books.

"Dad built this as a swing seat that he and Mum could sit on in the evenings, but Mum didn't like it," Jasmine said as we sat down and pushed ourselves to and fro. "She wanted a proper swing seat with a back rest and a canopy and everything, but Dad didn't have time to build it like that, so it's ended up being my swing."

Jasmine was quiet for a while.

"Your mum works, doesn't she?" she asked.

"Yes. Not as much as she did during the war, but she still works at the nursery a few days a week."

"I wish my mum had a job." She sighed. "I think she's bored. All she has to do all day is embroider or clean the house. I can't leave anything anywhere without her picking it up and tidying it away."

"Your house is lovely, and your mum's a great housekeeper," I said. "Our house is always a bit of a mess. I bet your mum makes lovely cakes and things. My mum never has time except at weekends."

"Well, Mum's actually not a very good cook. She can follow a recipe, but nothing ever tastes very interesting! Oh, that reminds me, we've got Home Economics tomorrow, baking day! Have you got your half of the ingredients ready?"

"Oh, yes, we've got to make fairy cakes, haven't we? I've got the flour, sugar and icing sugar; you're bringing the marge and eggs, is that right?" Having seen Jasmine's house, I didn't feel so bad that she was bringing the most expensive things, although the sugar for the cakes had used up half of our coupons for the week, but Daddy said he didn't mind, if it meant he got extra cake.

~*~

Maureen was playing ball up the wall in the front garden when I got home.

"Did you have a good time at Jasmine's house?" she asked without taking her eyes off the tennis ball.

"Yes; she's got a lovely house, everything's so neat and tidy, and she's got a double swing in the garden. I'll ask if you can come, too, next time."

Maureen stopped bouncing the ball and looked at me.

"Don't bother," she said flatly. "There's only room for two on that swing; I'd just be in the way. You don't need me, now you've got Jasmine."

She walked into her house and shut the door without saying goodnight.

~*~

Next morning, Maureen didn't bother to wait for me. For once, she was early. I heard her front door slam as I was still putting my shoes on, and by the time I left the house she was halfway up the road.

Jasmine was waiting in her usual place.

"I just saw Maureen. Have you two fallen out? She seemed in a really bad mood and just walked straight past me."

"I think she's upset because I came 'round your house yesterday. She thinks I don't want her as a friend anymore."

"That's just silly," said Jasmine. "You can be friends with more than one person and like them all the same amount, just differently. I'd have invited Maureen, too, only she doesn't have homework like we do, so she'd have been bored waiting for us to finish. Just leave her in peace for a while; she'll get over it. You'll see her at the weekend anyway, and it will soon be light enough to play out after school."

"She's busy this weekend, so I won't see her except at church parade," I said gloomily. "I don't want this . . . whatever it is to go on too long. Maureen's my best friend. We can't fall out after all this time."

~*~

It was one of those days that started badly and just got worse and worse. In my hurry to pack up at Jasmine's house, I'd left my pencil sharpener behind, so I had to keep asking to use the teachers' desk sharpeners in every lesson, then I fell over in hockey practice and grazed my knee, and the Home Economics lesson was the last straw.

I had weighed out my ingredients and carefully labelled the jars "flour", "sugar" and "icing sugar". We made up our cake mixture, spooned it into the tin and set it in the oven. Halfway through the second part of the lesson, while everyone's cakes were browning in the ovens and we were washing up our utensils and bowls, there was a horrible sticky, sweet, burnt smell, which seemed to be coming from the oven that Jasmine and I shared. I opened the door to see what looked like a boiling volcano pouring out onto the floor. Our cakes looked like molten lava!

Miss Goodchild hurried over, switched off the oven and snatched the tin of runny goo out, throwing it into the sink.

"What have you two done? Look at the mess all over the oven! This will all have to be cleaned up. I'm marking you both as nought out of ten for this lesson. You'll have to stay behind at lunch break tomorrow and do it all over again, if you don't want to go to the bottom of the class for this term."

Jasmine and I looked at each other in dismay. Neither of us was very good at cookery, and we dreaded Miss Goodchild's lessons, as she was so strict and particular.

"I don't understand, Miss," I said, risking another telling off. "We mixed everything up exactly as the recipe."

Miss Goodchild looked at the sticky mess in the sink, then picked up the jar marked "icing sugar" from our table. She dipped a clean teaspoon into the jar and tasted a little of the white powder.

"This is flour," she said, slamming the jar down again. "You put the icing sugar in the cakes; that's why the mixture turned to toffee."

The rest of the class was giggling quietly, partly because of the silly mistake and partly because they were relieved it wasn't them being told off.

I looked at Jasmine. It was all my fault, and now we both had detention, and all the ingredients were wasted.

Jasmine looked back at me and the corners of her mouth started to twitch. A large blob of runny mess slid out of the tin that had been flung into the sink and broke the hush with a big "plop" as it hit the tiled floor. It was too much for Jasmine. She started to laugh and laugh and couldn't stop. She laughed so much that the whole class joined in, despite Miss Goodchild getting more and more angry and trying to control the class.

"BE QUIET!" the teacher yelled, slamming a wooden rolling pin onto a table. There was an immediate shocked silence.

"Sylvia and Jasmine, go and stand in the corridor for the rest of the lesson, one at each end, and no talking. The rest of you, get on with what you were doing, in silence."

We scuttled out of the class and did as we were told — well, almost. Jasmine mouthed words and made signs at me, telling me not to worry, but I had never been in real trouble at school before, and dreaded going home and telling the story. All over a few cakes!

~*~

I was still gloomy on the way home, despite Jasmine's attempts to cheer me up.

I don't think Maureen deliberately waited for us, she just happened to arrive at the top of the road at the same time.

"What's wrong with you two? You look like you've lost half a crown and found sixpence."

I glanced at Jasmine.

"I'll tell you when we get home. See you tomorrow, Jasmine."

Maureen popped next door to leave her satchel and tell her mum she was home, then ran through the back hedge and in at our lean-to door. Mum had made a pot of tea and pushed a cup across the table to Maureen.

"Come on, Sylvie, tell us what's happened. It can't be that bad, surely."

I poured out the story of the mixed up sugar and flour, described the horrible sticky mess, and told how we had lost control and laughed until we cried, finishing off with the part about being made to stand in the corridor and having to lose our lunch time to make the cakes all over again.

"And it means I need all those ingredients again," I finished miserably.

Mum's mouth was twitching just as Jasmine's had, and I could tell that Maureen was jiggling her leg under the table like she used to do at school when she wanted to laugh but couldn't. I suddenly saw the funny side and let out a giggle, which set the other two off and we laughed until our sides ached. Daddy walked in in the middle of all the laughter and it was a good few minutes before anyone could stop laughing enough to explain to him.

"I've got an idea," Maureen said. "I'm just popping home for a minute to ask Mum something."

While she was gone, I told the story again, while Mum started making the tea.

"I'm sorry, Daddy. It's all my fault for labelling the jars wrong, and now all the ingredients are wasted, and you didn't get any cake."

"Never mind," he said, hugging me. "These things happen, and it's not the end of the world. Neither of you is planning to be a master baker to the King or anything, so failing a cookery lesson is hardly going to stop you getting a job. You'll just both have to marry husbands who can cook." He winked at me and stuck his tongue out at Mum as she turned around from the stove, laughing. Daddy was a really good cook, and when they first married, he had taught Mum how to make all his favourite dinners.

Maureen burst back in through the door.

"Problem solved," she announced triumphantly. "I talked to Mum. She's on a diet, so she hasn't used up any of her sugar coupons, and Dad doesn't take sugar, so you can have our ration."

"Oh, Maureen, you don't need to do that," Mum cried. "We can manage."

"And here's the other idea," Maureen went on. "Mum suggested that Sylvie and Jasmine come to our house after tea and practice. We'll help. I'm really good at making fairy cakes. Then when they have to do it again tomorrow, they won't make any mistakes."

"You are a good girl, Maureen," said Mum. "I'll come back with you and say thank you to your mum. Sylvie, run to Jasmine's and tell her. Tom, you keep an eye on the tea and Audrey; she's upstairs learning her spellings. I'll be back in a minute."

~*~

We trooped into Mrs Fielding's kitchen, which was just as spotless as Jasmine's, but without all the shiny new things that Jasmine's mum had.

Maureen handed us each an apron and took my recipe sheet out of my hands.

"We don't need that," she said, dusting her hands in an efficient manner.

"Right, Sylvie, you weigh an egg, and whatever it weighs, you need to weigh out the same amount each of marge and sugar."

I weighed the ingredients into the mixing bowl.

"Now, Jasmine, you beat the sugar and marge together until they're really fluffy, then beat in the egg. Sylvie, weigh out the same amount of flour and put in a teaspoon of baking powder — not that much! A flat teaspoon!"

Jasmine glanced at me and smiled, amused at Maureen's bossiness.

"Now, fold the flour and baking powder in. No! Don't stir it, fold it, like this. You've got to keep the air in the mixture, or it won't rise."

Jasmine took the bowl back and meekly did as she was told. We spooned the mixture into the tin and slid it gently into the oven.

"We'll look in after a quarter of an hour and check them. No peeping!"

Mrs Fielding opened a bottle of ginger beer, and we sat at the kitchen table to wait for the cakes to be done.

"Anyone home? It's quiet in here." Mr Fielding put his head around the kitchen door.

"What are you girls doing, having a séance?" He kissed Maureen and her mum, ruffled my hair and nodded and smiled at Jasmine when Maureen introduced her.

"We're baking," Maureen explained. "These two are hopeless and got into trouble in cookery at school, so I'm giving them some extra tuition. Sylv, tell Dad about the icing sugar."

I told the tale again, to much laughter from Maureen's parents, and by the time we'd all calmed down again, it was time to look in the oven.

Maureen pulled the tray of cakes forward on the oven shelf. They looked nice and brown and had risen well.

"Now, gently press the top of one of the cakes with your finger."

We both leaned in and pressed.

"Feel it bounce back? That means they're done. If they don't bounce back like that, they need a few more minutes cooking."

Jasmine carefully lifted the tray out of the oven and slid the cakes out onto a cooling rack.

"Well done!" Maureen praised us. "They look lovely. Can't wait to try them! All you have to do tomorrow is exactly what you've just done, and you won't have any trouble."

"Thank you, Maureen. You've been so helpful." Jasmine hugged her. "Sylvie's lucky to have you as her best friend."

Maureen hugged back.

"I suppose people have all sorts of friends for all sorts of reasons, and they're all 'best' friends in different ways," she mused. "If you're not doing anything next weekend, why don't we all go to the pictures together, then we can get fish and chips afterwards?"

"What's on?" I asked.

"The Three Musketeers is on at the Empire," Mr Fielding chimed in.

We looked at each other and grinned.

"One for all!" said Maureen, holding her wooden spoon in the air.

"And all for one!" Jasmine and I chorused.

Chapter Eight

First Impressions

Audrey sat on the back step, throwing a tennis ball down the garden for Scamp. I stood in the kitchen doorway watching her for a while; she wasn't really playing with him, just throwing the ball, taking it off him when he brought it back, throwing it again, all the time gazing into space, deep in thought.

The little dog must have noticed her mood. He dropped the ball at her feet and as she reached down to pick it up, he pushed his muzzle into her hand, asking for a cuddle. She put her arm around his neck and pulled him close, tickling his ears, but in an absent-minded way. He gave a little "wuff" as if to say, "You're not paying proper attention!"

I sat down on the step beside her and stroked Scamp's back, his tail lashing against my knees.

"So, how was the first day at the Big Girls'? It's all a bit different, isn't it, after being one of the oldest at infants' school? You'll get used to it." I leaned closer and bumped my shoulder against hers affectionately.

"Oh, it's all right," she said, shrugging. "The work's not hard, and most of the girls in my class are nice. It's just odd, not having Brian and the other boys around, and some of the girls are so . . . prissy!"

I laughed.

"I know what you mean. I remember listening to the older girls talking about film stars and hair styles and thinking how boring it was, just like you, when you hear me and Maureen talking about fashion magazines," I teased her.

"It's not just the older girls," she said, frowning and rubbing Scamp's ears between her fingers. "Some of the girls in my class said I was boyish, just because I wanted to kick a ball around at lunch break and not play skipping or ball up the wall. Why can't girls play football, if they want to?"

"Well, they can, I suppose." I frowned. "It's just that most probably don't want to. I've never really thought about it."

"We were talking about our friends from our old schools, and a couple of the girls weren't very nice when I said my best friend was a boy. They asked if he was my boyfriend." Her cheeks turned pink. "I told them that was just silly. We're only eight years old. He's just a friend who happens to be a boy."

She looked so confused and miserable that I put my arm around her and gave her a hug.

"Don't take any notice of those girls. They're just silly. There's nothing wrong with Brian being your best friend; don't let them spoil it for you. Aren't there any nice girls in your class who you can be friends with?"

She brightened up when I asked that.

"Yes, there's one girl called Nancy. She's really nice and she said the same as you, just to ignore those girls. Nancy's good at maths and drawing too; we came joint top in the mental arithmetic test this morning. We're going to ask if we can sit next to each other tomorrow. Nancy's dad is a carpenter and he's teaching her how to make furniture for her dolls' house. She said I can go 'round after school one day and he'll teach me, too, but we're not going to let the Awful Girls know about it. They'll say it's boyish."

She grinned.

"How many Awful Girls are there?" I asked. She made them sound like a pack of wild animals.

"Three, really. Kathy is the worst; she makes everything you say into a joke against you, and Barbara and Peggy just giggle and agree with her."

"Well, three out of a whole class isn't that many, and the other girls will soon realise they're not very nice, so they'll find themselves without many friends, won't they?"

She nodded. "Thanks Sylvie, I feel better now."

I hugged her again.

"Why don't you go and call for Brian and see how his first day went? You'll have loads to talk about."

She stood up and dusted down her skirt.

"I will. I'll take Scamp. We can give him a walk while we talk." She hesitated and looked at me seriously.

"And I won't tell Brian what Kathy said about him being my boyfriend."

"No, just forget about that." I held out my hand so she could pull me up. She was nearly as tall as me, now.

"Off you go, but don't be late back."

"Yes, Mum," she cheeked me, and ran off.

Mum looked up as I came indoors.

"You two had a long chat out there. Is Audrey all right? She was very quiet when she got home from school, but she said she'd had a good day."

I sat down and picked up my sewing. I was hand-rolling the hem of Audrey's new dance dress. One of the Whitefield girls at Grange Park had given Auntie Maude one of her old evening dresses that she didn't want any more, and Auntie Maude had given it to me to make into a dance dress for Audrey to wear when she and Brian took their bronze ballroom exam at the end of term.

"There are a couple of girls in her class who aren't being very nice to her, calling her a tomboy and things like that. I told her to ignore them. It sounds as though she's found a new friend, though, a girl called Nancy, another one who's good at maths. Wait till the three of them get together — Aud, Brian and Nancy! I'll give them my maths homework to do!"

I shook out the dress to see how much more hemming there was to do.

"You've made a lovely job of that, Sylvie." Mum smiled. "I bet Princess Elizabeth's wedding dress won't look half so nice."

Dad came in from the shed and I held the dress up for him to see.

"You're a good little seamstress, Ducks," he said, kissing the top of my head. "Audrey will dazzle the judges so much that they'll end up giving her gold, not bronze!"

"Sylvie said one of the girls in Audrey's class is picking on her, calling her a tomboy," said Mum. "She should see her in that dress with her hair up. That would make her think twice!"

I looked up at Mum and smiled. An idea had just come into my head.

~*~

I finished the hem before bedtime and took Audrey upstairs to try it on again in front of Mum's long mirror to make sure the hem was level.

"Is Miss Sandys still at your school?" I asked as I trimmed off a loose thread. "Does she still organise a concert at the end of the Autumn term?"

"She's still there," Audrey said over her shoulder, twisting about to check the dress from all angles, "but I don't know about a concert. I've only been there one day," she reminded me. "Why?"

"I was just thinking: If there's a concert, you should do a demonstration dance." I turned her to face the mirror, holding her by her slim waist above the layers of chiffon and net that made up the skirt of the dress, and held her hair up off her neck, as though it was pinned up in a dance style. "I mean, look at you. You're so . . . boyish!" I winked at her through the mirror and she grinned back.

~*~

The whole family turned out for Audrey and Brian's bronze exam. Uncle Johnny said he was going to sit in the front row and cheer and whistle every time they danced past.

Brian looked horrified until Audrey explained that he was only joking.

The two of them had improved so much since their first term that neither of them was the slightest bit nervous about the exam, running ahead, kicking stones, and teasing each other, while I had terrible butterflies in my tummy as we walked to the Drill Hall.

I was chatting to Brian's mum as we walked, and hadn't noticed Audrey go quiet until I realised she was walking beside me and had slipped her hand into mine. I glanced sideways at her questioningly.

"Kathy," she whispered, without turning her head.

Three girls were walking towards us, looking at Audrey and Brian and nudging each other. They gave a smothered giggle as they came closer and I could feel Audrey tense up. It was obvious which one was Kathy. She had long dark hair which she flicked about like a horse tossing its mane, showing off to the other girls, who presumably were Barbara and Peggy.

"Ignore her," I muttered out of the corner of my mouth. "Smile and ignore her."

Audrey set her face in a smile and lifted her head, turning to me and laughing as though I had just said the funniest thing ever.

Kathy and her sidekicks walked past, giggling, and either Peggy or Barbara stuck out a foot and tripped Brian, who stumbled, but recovered.

Audrey whirled around, her eyes flashing, and made to grab at the girl, but I was too quick for her and spun her back towards me, slipping my arm through hers in a tight grip.

"Ignore them," I hissed in her ear. "They want you to react, so don't."

~*~

The Drill Hall was buzzing with excitement as the pupils primped and preened or nervously ran through their steps.

Parents chatted, and younger siblings ran up and down, sliding on the polished floor.

Mrs Jackson played a flourish on the piano to get everyone's attention and walked slowly and gracefully to the middle of the floor.

The audience sat quietly as she explained the order of the dancing and introduced the three judges who would be awarding the medals. I slowly craned round to look towards the back of the hall where the dancers were lined up, waiting to perform. I could see Audrey warming up; stretching up on her toes and down again to limber up her feet, her face set and determined.

It wasn't a competition — each couple was performing against a set of rules and steps to win a medal for their own next level of dancing, so all the children smiled and clapped as each couple took to the floor, encouraging each other to do well.

Audrey and Brian, as beginners, were among the first to dance in the ten years and under class, performing an old-fashioned waltz. I could see that Brian was a bit nervous, but Audrey was really strung up and excited after her encounter with the Awful Girls, her head high and proud.

As the music started, Audrey seemed to relax and somehow grow at the same time, so she was taller and more graceful than normal. She and Brian swooped and dipped with the tune, faces set in their "performing" smiles, feet gliding across the floor, perfectly in time with the music and each other.

The dance swirled to an end, and they paused, frozen in a deep curtsey and bow. For a second, I thought no-one was going to clap, then the hall erupted in noise: clapping, cheering, stamping feet.

Audrey and Brian came up out of their bows and grinned at each other.

Once the dancers had performed, they were allowed to sit with their family and friends. Audrey, between Mum and me, kept up a whispered running commentary on how all the other dancers performed, while on my other side I could hear Brian and Uncle Johnny muttering about football.

After the very last couple had danced, Mrs Jackson changed the record on the gramophone and invited everyone to take to the floor and dance for fun, while the judges added up their scores and decided who deserved a medal.

Some of the parents shyly got up and started dancing, while the younger children jumped about excitedly, relieved to be able to move after hours of sitting still.

Daddy and Uncle Johnny went outside to smoke and talk in peace, and Brian slipped out after them, but Audrey stayed in her seat, watching everything and smiling to herself.

"Do you think you passed?" I asked her.

She looked at me as though I had asked her what day of the week it was.

"Of course!" She wasn't smug about it, she just knew they'd done well. It was as though her body was separate from her and she had trained it to do the dance correctly, then let it get on with the job. I looked at her with a new respect, but at the same time didn't want to encourage her to be cocky.

"Well, we'll see soon, won't we?"

She looked sideways at me, curving one side of her mouth up in a smile.

"You sound like Mum."

Mrs Jackson called the hall to order and began to announce the awards. Some of the dancers looked nervous; fidgeting with hair or ties, while others slumped in their seats, knowing they'd made a mistake and would have to take the exam again.

Audrey sat relaxed and still, confident that she and Brian would have won their medal. Brian looked as though he didn't care much either way.

"Bronze medal in the age ten and under category, and also the judges' highly commended award, goes to Audrey Ford and Brian Jackson."

Audrey dragged Brian out of his seat to go and collect their medals. I noticed one of the judges having a quiet word with Audrey, and hoped she wasn't praising her too much. We'd never get her head through the front door.

Audrey bounced back to her seat and passed her medal and certificate along the row so everyone could look at it closely, before letting Mum pin the medal to her dress.

"The lady judge in the red dress wants to talk to you and Daddy when everyone goes," she told Mum. "She says she wants to take me for a Latin dance class. I didn't tell her I don't learn Latin yet; do you think I should have?"

Audrey looked worried, but Mum laughed.

"Latin is a type of dancing, nothing to do with the language Sylvie's learning. Do you remember that little doll you had that Uncle Johnny gave you? The one that came from Spain, that had the big frilly skirt? She was a flamenco dancer. That's Latin dancing."

"Ooh! I'd like to wear a dress like that! Sylv, do you think you could make me a dress like that?"

I looked at Mum over Audrey's head and we both grinned.

"We'd better speak to the lady judge first, Audrey, but I'm sure it can be managed."

Mrs Jackson brought the lady in the red dress over to us when everyone else had gone.

"This is Mrs Winchester. She would like Audrey to sign up for Latin dance lessons."

Brian was slowly backing away towards the door, but his auntie saw him and laughed.

"It's all right, Brian, you won't have to dress up as a matador. Mrs Winchester is only looking for girls to join a flamenco troupe."

I'm sure I heard Brian mutter "Olé" as he slid out the door.

~*~

After a few weeks, we were all regretting Audrey learning flamenco. Every time she walked on a hard surface, she practised her steps. She flamencoed on the kitchen lino doing the washing up, she flamencoed on the little wooden bridge across the pond in the park when we fed the ducks, and, most embarrassingly, she flamencoed out in the street.

While my sister stamped and flounced around the house, I got on with her dress. Mum had an old pair of curtains with deep orange flame-coloured satin lining, so we took the lining out and cut it up to make a dance dress. I was glad that Mum had taught me to use her sewing machine, as it would have taken forever to hem all the yards and yards of frills in the skirt, but when it was finished and Audrey tried it on she looked lovely in it. We let her swish around in it for half an hour, then made her change so she didn't ruin it.

~*~

On the last Saturday before the end of the Winter term, it rained and rained. I spent the morning learning my lines for the end of term play while Audrey dashed through the rain, wrapped in Mum's raincoat, to her flamenco lesson. She hadn't mentioned anything about the end of term concert at her school, and we had both been so busy making Christmas presents, practising for concerts, and going to parties that I hadn't had a chance to talk to her about the Awful Girls and how school was.

She usually arrived back from her class at ten past eleven, so at eleven o'clock I put my play script away and went downstairs to make a cup of tea.

Daddy was out — he'd gone with Uncle Johnny to get a Christmas tree from Park Grange — and Mum was in the front room listening to a radio play and finishing the gloves she was knitting Daddy for Christmas, so when Audrey came home I whisked her into the kitchen and sat her down for a chat.

"How are things with the Awful Girls?" I asked directly.

She sipped her tea and looked at me over the cup, her eyes twinkling.

"They're still Awful, but I don't care."

She put her cup down and leaned forward over the table, words tumbling out.

"I remembered what you said about not reacting, so I'm doing exactly what they think I'll do; being even more tomboyish than I really am. It's like acting, only I'm just being me. Miss Sandys gave out the parts for the concert but didn't give me anything because we've already arranged that I'm going to do my flamenco dance as a surprise at the end, but the Awful Girls are smug because I've been left out."

"Did you tell Miss Sandys that they were being horrid to you?"

"I didn't have to. She saw I was upset and spoke to me about it and I told her what you'd said about not reacting to them, and that's when I told her your idea of me doing a dance. She rehearsed me doing it on the school stage at lunch break, so I know what to do, and she's going to play the guitar for me to dance to. I haven't told Mummy and Daddy; I want to surprise them, too, so I'll need you to help me get my dress to school on Monday."

"I have to take my costume to school on Monday, so we'll put your dress in the bag with mine, leave a bit earlier, and I'll drop you off. You can put your dance shoes in your gym shoes bag."

She grinned, and we made our secret signal; linking our little fingers together and shaking up and down three times.

~*~

The school hall was packed with parents, grandparents, uncles, aunts, and brothers and sisters, all squashed onto long wooden forms or perched on little chairs. The windows were steamed up from all the people breathing, so it looked as though it was foggy outside.

Miss Young walked on to the stage and clapped her hands. She made a speech about how hard all the pupils had worked preparing for the concert, then introduced a singing group from Class 1.

Three girls shuffled and giggled their way onto the stage. It was Kathy, with her sidekicks, Barbara and Peggy. They were all in floral dresses and had their hair done up in Victory rolls on top of their heads, and they were wearing lipstick.

Kathy looked across at Miss Young, who started up the gramophone. A swing band started to play, and the three girls sang the first lines of Chattanooga Choo Choo in harmony.

They were doing all right, then either Barbara or Peggy forgot the words and stopped singing. Either Peggy or Barbara was confused and stopped as well, leaving Kathy singing on her own. Red faced, she carried on with the song while her friends stood still.

Miss Young applauded loudly when the song finished, to encourage the audience, but there was no need; everyone felt sorry for Kathy and admired her for carrying on. The three girls took a quick bow, then ran off stage. I think Kathy was crying.

Mum nudged me. "Where is Audrey? I thought she was in the concert?"

I shrugged, "Maybe she got scared and decided not to sing."

Some of the second-year girls were on next, with a comedy sketch including impressions of the teachers, and then five girls from the third year read a long poem that they'd written together, each girl taking one verse.

The last performance was an orchestra made up of twelve fourth-year girls who played a very slow and serious piece of classical music on violins, flutes, and a clarinet, then followed it up with Jingle Bells, which even the smallest children in the audience could sing along to.

As the orchestra filed off the stage to loud applause, and the curtains were closed, Miss Young came back and held her hands up for quiet. All the children who had performed slipped into the hall and sat with their families.

"There is one more act tonight, a very special finale. Please welcome on stage, the mysterious Senorita Conchita!"

The curtains swung back to show a small girl in a flame-coloured dress standing alone on the stage, her back to the audience, one arm held high in the air. I could hear Mum, Daddy, and Uncle Johnny gasp, and smiled to myself.

Mum nudged me again. "Did you know about this?"

I grinned at her and nodded.

Miss Sandys, sitting at the side of the stage, a guitar on her knee, slowly started playing a tune.

Audrey's feet began to tap, slowly, then faster and faster, stepping on the spot; then, as the music got faster, she whirled round to face the audience, stamping her feet, swishing her skirt, and clicking the castanets that she held in her raised hand.

Kathy and her friends, a little red around the eyes, were sitting in the front row with their parents, so I couldn't see their faces, but I could imagine their gaping mouths as their "boyish" classmate swished her frilly skirt.

Audrey swished and tapped towards the front of the stage, and I saw Kathy shrink down in her seat as her victim made eye contact with her, eyes flashing, feet stamping harder and harder. Just as it seemed that Audrey would stamp her way off the stage into the laps of the front row, the music stopped; and with a final stamp, Audrey held her pose, head high, skirt swishing around her feet, her cheeks flushed and her eyes sparkling.

The whole hall erupted, standing up, clapping, cheering and whistling.

Audrey made a deep curtsey, grinning all over her face, then bunched up her skirt, sat down on the edge of the stage, and slid to the floor, running through the audience to get to us.

Daddy swept her up in a big hug and set her back down gently. Mum smoothed her hair and kissed her, and Uncle Johnny knelt at her feet and took an imaginary rose from between his teeth, presenting it to her with a flourish.

The crowd started to thin out as people made their way home, but I could tell that Kathy was hovering. I tapped Audrey on the shoulder and pointed to Kathy.

"I think someone wants to speak to you."

The two girls approached each other slowly, then both started to speak at the same time. They broke off and laughed.

"You first," said Audrey.

"I just wanted to say, your dance was wonderful! I had no idea you could do that; how did you keep it such a secret?"

"It was a lot of fun." Audrey grinned. "And your singing was lovely; you were so brave, standing out there singing on your own. I couldn't do that."

The girls smiled at each other.

"Maybe next Christmas, we can perform together," Kathy suggested, shyly.

"That's a wonderful idea." Audrey took Kathy's arm and linked it through hers.

"We've got a whole year to get to know each other and plan something."

Part Three
1948

Chapter Nine

An Island Holiday

"It's not fair!"

Audrey flopped down on the settee and folded her arms.

"Why can't I go, too?"

"Come on, Audrey, you heard what Auntie Mabel said," Mum soothed her. "You know she hasn't been well. She needs a nice holiday where she doesn't have to worry about anything. Sylvie's thirteen now; she's old enough to be responsible and help your auntie on the journey, and if Auntie Mabel doesn't feel well enough to go out, then Sylvie can go bus riding or walking on her own."

"But Sylvie could look after me!" Audrey argued. "I wouldn't be any trouble, I promise. Please let me go. What am I going to do on my own all the Easter holiday?"

"It's not all the holiday, it's just a week, and you've got Brian to play with. Auntie Mabel said she'll pay for Sylvie's holiday as a treat, so we can't ask her to pay for you, too, and we can't afford it. I'm sorry, dear. There will be other times when you can have a special treat."

"Come on, Audrey." I sat on the arm of the chair and pulled her towards me in a hug, but it was like hugging a rock. "I'll send you postcards, and bring you back something nice. And you can help me choose what to pack; you're good at deciding which outfits go well together."

Scamp nuzzled at Audrey's knee and she unfolded her arms to tickle him.

"And if we were both away, what would Scamp do? He needs you to play with him and take him for walks."

She bent her head over Scamp and kissed him so we couldn't see her tears.

"Just think," I went on, "in three years' time, I'll have to get a job, and then you'll still have all the school holidays while I'm at work. Then I'll be the one saying 'it's not fair!'"

She looked up and sniffed.

"Save me all your train tickets? Please? And the ferry ticket?"

I grinned and hugged her.

"Of course."

~*~

Uncle Johnny drove Auntie Mabel and me to the station in his van, with me sitting in the back on the suitcases, so we didn't have to lug them down the hill through town.

We'd packed as light as possible, but I was still a bit worried about how we were going to manage the two cases, as Auntie Mabel wasn't strong enough to carry hers very far.

As we climbed out of the van, Uncle Johnny handed me a small purse.

"Here are some shillings. When you get to London, find a porter and ask him to help you with the cases. You can do that every time you need to change trains, but make sure you tip the man a shilling for his trouble each time."

"Thank you, Uncle Johnny." I kissed him and helped him lift the cases out while Auntie Mabel went to buy our tickets.

"And remember, you've got the telephone number for my office, and you know how to use a phone box, so if you have any problems you can ring me up. Not tomorrow, though —It's Sunday!"

"Ready?" Auntie Mabel tucked our tickets into her pocket and took her case and handbag from Uncle Johnny, kissing his cheek.

"Off we go then, Sylvie. See you in a week, Johnny. Thanks for the lift."

~*~

I had been on the train to London a couple of times before, so that part was fine, but I was a bit worried about having to find where to go once we arrived in London. I knew we had to use the underground to get to our next station, then another over-ground train for the long journey to Portsmouth, and then another train for a short ride to the ferry port in Southsea.

I hadn't even started to think about the ferry and how we got from there to where we were staying on the Isle of Wight.

"Don't worry, Sylvie." Auntie Mabel smiled at me. "We'll be fine. If we don't know where to go or what to do, we'll just ask someone. Just sit back and enjoy the journey."

Changing to the underground was quite scary. Everyone moved so quickly, and they all seemed to know where they were going. A nice man stopped to help us find the right platform and explained where we had to change to get to the main line station. The tube train was crowded with people, but we managed to find a seat for Auntie, so I piled the cases one on top of the other and stood, holding on to a leather strap in the ceiling, which I could only just reach.

"I hope the train to Portsmouth isn't this crowded." I leaned down to talk to Auntie so she could hear me above the clatter of the train.

"Don't worry; I've booked our seats, so even if it is crowded, we get to sit down."

The main line station was enormous. Great high ceilings with glass panels, long platforms stretching into the distance, and people in all directions. I found a porter and asked him to help us find the right train and carry our bags, and he swiftly lifted the cases onto a little wheeled trolley. He asked to see our tickets and led us straight to our carriage in the Portsmouth train, even lifting the cases on to the rack above the seats for us.

"You're going to the end of the line, so you'll have plenty of time to sort yourselves out when you get there; no rush to get off," he said, with a smile.

I thanked him and handed him one of Uncle Johnny's shillings, feeling very grown up at tipping someone.

The man touched the peak of his hat and grinned.

"Thank you, Miss. Have a nice holiday!"

No-one had ever called me "Miss" before!

Auntie Mabel looked tired. I wished I'd thought to buy some boiled sweets at the station, but we had been so busy trying to find our train that we'd walked right past the kiosk.

A whistle screamed and made me jump.

"Mind the doors, please!"

The train jolted a little, then slowly started to pull away. We were off!

We were still in the suburbs of London when the ticket inspector came through with his little clippers. He looked at our tickets and smiled.

"Going on holiday, ladies? It's quite a long way to Portsmouth, so, if you get hungry, the dining car is just in the next carriage. They'll be serving soup and sandwiches with tea and coffee in about half an hour."

Auntie Mabel thanked him, and I sat back with a sigh of relief. I hadn't even thought about where we were going to eat lunch!

The upholstery of the seats was very clean and smart, and looked brand new. I remembered Daddy talking about how the railway lines all over Britain were now part of British Railways, instead of all being run separately. They must have re-covered the seats of the trains to make them all the same.

The scenery passing by the window was more countryfied now; houses scattered few and far between among green fields. We sat watching the world go by, not talking for a while, just recovering from all the busyness of London.

As the train settled down into a rhythm, our holiday started to become real. We were going to be travelling on a boat to an island, to stay for a whole week.

I glanced across at Auntie Mabel and saw that she was smiling to herself. She met my eyes and grinned.

"We're on holiday!"

She pulled a piece of paper from her handbag and handed it to me. It was a page from a brochure, telling about the bed and breakfast where we were going to be staying. It was in a place called Ventnor, and the information said that it was close to the sea, and that there was a pier, an esplanade, a park, and winter gardens.

"The island is quite small, but there's plenty to do," Auntie told me. "There are trains that run between the towns, and a good bus service. I think we can buy bus and train tickets for the whole week, so we can go anywhere we like. Ventnor is supposed to be the best place to go if you've been ill. It's high up, so it catches all the healthy sea air."

Actually, Auntie Mabel was already looking better, just from the excitement of being on holiday.

"Are you hungry?" I asked her.

"Ravenous!" She grinned.

~*~

After our lunch of cheese sandwiches and tomato soup, we settled back in our seats. Auntie closed her eyes and had a nap, and I took out my book. We were studying Tess of the d'Urbervilles by Thomas Hardy at school, and I enjoyed the story so much that it didn't feel like homework.

I was so lost in my book that it came as a surprise when the train pulled into Portsmouth.

Auntie woke up with a start and we pulled the cases down from the rack.

"Southsea and ferry port. All passengers for Southsea and the ferry port this way."

We grinned at each other. This was going to be easier than London.

~*~

The sea, which Auntie said was called the Solent just there, was calm, so we sat out on deck and watched the mainland disappear behind us as the little island grew nearer. We just had to catch one more train, from Ryde, where the ferry would land, straight to Ventnor and our hotel.

~*~

"Here we are," panted Auntie Mabel. "Sea View."

"I should think they're all called Sea View." I laughed, pointing down the hill behind us. The town was set on the side of a hill, with the houses ranged in tiers, like seats in a theatre, so every house had a view of the sea.

Auntie rang the bell and the landlady of the hotel came to the desk to greet us.

"Breakfast is between half past eight and ten, guests must be out of the bedrooms between eleven and four, and you may use the lounge at any time up to half past ten in the evening. Room sixteen; up the stairs, second on the right."

As we clattered our suitcases through the doors to the stairs, Auntie Mabel muttered "Yes, Sergeant," making us both giggle.

Our room faced out towards the sea and was decorated in blue and yellow, with a pretty dressing table with a frilled cover standing between our beds. We argued for a while about who should have which bed, but Auntie Mabel was firm that I should have the window side, as I'd never been on holiday before.

We unpacked quickly and washed our hands and faces, then set off for a walk around town and to find somewhere to have our tea.

We found a little shop that sold postcards, and as it was also a post office, we wrote a card home and posted it, telling Mum and Dad that we'd arrived safely.

I spent a long time looking at the postcards and deciding which to buy. Auntie came to see why I was taking so long, so I explained my plan to her.

"I'm looking at these to choose things we can do, and places we can go. If I buy a card from each of the places we plan to visit, I can send one to Audrey each day, telling her what we've been doing; then she won't feel so left out."

Auntie agreed that it was a splendid plan, and we carefully chose six postcards of places we wanted to visit, then bought enough stamps to send one a day.

> Sunday —
> Ventnor Esplanade and Winter Gardens.
> Dear Aud,
> We're here! We arrived yesterday in time for tea and went out for fish and chips. We're staying here, in Ventnor, so today we decided to explore locally. We went for a walk on the esplanade this morning, then a show in the Winter Gardens pavilion this afternoon, and tea in the café above the theatre, looking out at the sea. I put an X on the picture where the café is.
> It's very steep here, so we'll be fit by the time we come home!
> More tomorrow.
> Love, Sylvie. XXX
>
> Monday —
> Carisbrooke Castle.
> Aud! We've been to a royal house! Princess Beatrice lived here until a few years ago. She was Queen Victoria's daughter. Now it's a museum about the castle. Charles I was in prison here, the king who had his head cut off.
> You and Brian would love it here. I can imagine you playing knights on the battlements! When I'm older and earning money, I'll bring you for a holiday.

More tomorrow. Auntie sends her love,
Sylvie. XXX

Tuesday —
Freshwater Bay
Dear Aud,
We came here by train today. We bought train tickets for the whole week, only 7'6 for a whole week to go anywhere! (I'll save you the ticket.)

It's lovely here. We're having a day of just resting, and I've done some sketches. Tennyson lived near here. Remember that poem you had to learn at school, the Charge of the Light Brigade? That was him. Fish and chips for tea again today. Auntie says I'll turn into a cod!

More tomorrow, love to everyone,
Sylvie. XXX

Wednesday —
Osborne House
Aud, we're mixing with royalty again! This is where Queen Victoria lived and where she died. Apparently, Edward VII gave it to the nation, so I suppose we own a little bit of it!

It's very grand inside, but I think I like the gardens best. Auntie bought a tea towel for Grandma with a picture of Queen Victoria on it. She'll like that.

More trains today. Tell Brian I'm writing down all the engine numbers for him, but I don't know if it's cheating that he didn't see them himself.

More tomorrow,
Love, Sylvie. XXX

Thursday —
Godshill
Dear Aud,

Auntie's having a rest today, sitting on the esplanade reading and knitting, so I've come here by myself on the bus. It's very pretty here; you can see the thatched cottages in the picture. I've done lots of sketches, so it'll be just like you've seen it yourself. The holiday's going so fast. Just one more day here!

I'll see you very soon. Wish you were here.
Love to all, including Scamp,
Sylvie. XXX

Friday —
Newport
Dear Aud,

Our last day! We're in Newport, which is the biggest town on the island, but as it's Good Friday, everything's closed, so we're just exploring the town. We're going to have a slap-up dinner in a proper restaurant this evening, to finish the holiday in style. Auntie's feeling so much better, and we've both got a bit of a suntan!

See you tomorrow.
Love, Sylvie. XXX

The sight of Uncle Johnny leaning against his van and smiling at us as we came out of the station was the best thing that two weary travellers have ever seen.

He loaded our cases into the van and hugged us.

"You two look so fit and well! I think I might try a seaside holiday, myself."

We piled into the van and headed for home, Auntie Mabel giving Uncle Johnny the full story of our holiday, with me reminding her of anything she left out.

As we pulled into our road, Uncle Johnny suddenly stopped the van a few houses before ours.

"What's the matter?" asked Auntie Mabel.

"There." He pointed down the road. "The postman. He'll be bringing Sylvie's last postcard for Audrey. I want her to have a chance to read it before Sylvie gets home. She's been so excited about those postcards."

We sat in the van for a good ten minutes. I couldn't wait any longer.

"She's a fast reader; she must have read it by now! Let's go in."

I ran up the path, but didn't get a chance to even knock, as the door flew open and there was Audrey, with my Friday postcard in her hand.

"Sylvie!" She flew at me and hugged me. "You're so brown!"

"Only bits of me." I laughed, rolling up my sleeve to show her my white arm.

She dragged me into the house where Mum and Dad were waiting, big smiles on their faces.

"Welcome home, Sylvie!" Mum hugged me. "Mabel, will you stay for a cup of tea?"

"No, Amy, thanks all the same. I'd better get back to Mother. Thank you for letting me borrow Sylvie for the week; she's been a great help and a lot of fun to be with."

"Thank you for giving her such a lovely holiday," said Daddy, kissing his sister. "We've all enjoyed the postcards."

"Maybe when Audrey's a bit older, we can have another girls' holiday," said Auntie, winking at Audrey.

"Come on then, Johnny, let's go and see how much Mother's missed me."

~*~

I opened my case and pulled out the presents I'd bought for everyone. There was a cigarette box for Daddy, with a picture of the Needles lighthouse on it, and another for Uncle Johnny;

a tea towel for Mum with pictures of flowers from Osborne House gardens; a set of soldiers from Carrisbrooke Castle for Brian; a keyring with Queen Victoria on it for Maureen; and for Audrey, a tall glass tube with a domed top and heavy base, full of layers of different coloured sand.

"I've got a present for you, too, Sylvie," said Audrey. "I made it myself."

She handed me a big piece of cardboard. On it was a map of the Isle of Wight, which she'd drawn in coloured pencils. She had drawn in all the railway lines and roads, and marked all the towns and villages, as well as all the places we'd visited. At each of the places we'd visited she had written "Sylvie went here" in red letters, and stuck on a small piece of paper where she'd copied what I'd told her about each place.

"It's lovely, Aud. Thank you. And maybe next time we'll all go on holiday together."

Scamp jumped up and barked.

"Yes, you can come too, Scamp!"

Chapter Ten

Car Trouble

"Damn and blast it!"

"Lieutenant! Watch your language in front of the girls!"

"Sorry, Captain, but the b . . . dratted fan belt's snapped."

Maureen and I giggled as Lieutenant opened the bonnet of her car and rummaged around inside.

"Can I help?" asked a familiar voice.

Maureen giggled again and nudged me while I rolled my eyes and turned slightly away.

Uncle Johnny kept turning up to walk us home from Guides, even though it was early summer, and still light at half past eight, not to mention us being thirteen and quite old enough to walk home on our own, which we'd been doing for years anyway.

He said he'd heard stories of young girls being pestered in the evenings, but Dad reckoned he just liked looking at Lieutenant.

"Are you wearing stockings, Miss?" he asked, to more giggles from Maureen.

"Mr Ford!" Lieutenant sounded shocked, but she was smiling, so I knew she wasn't really. "That's a bit of a cheeky question, and in front of the girls."

"He's quite right," Captain's voice was brisk and no nonsense.

"Go behind that wall and take your stockings off, then this young man can make them into a fan belt that'll last long enough to get you home. When I was in the ATS, they taught us to do that."

"Exactly my plan, Ma'am," grinned Uncle Johnny, snapping into his smartest Navy salute.

Lieutenant emerged from behind the wall with her nylons in her hand.

"Go to it, then." she said, handing the stockings to my uncle. "Let's get this heap of junk moving again."

Uncle Johnny bent over the car and dug his hands into its works, untangling the old fan belt and fashioning the stockings into a new one, watched approvingly by Captain.

"You seem to be in safe hands with this capable young man, so I'll say goodnight. Must be off to get the Captain his supper."

Uncle Johnny saluted again, leaving a streak of oil across his forehead.

"Whew! What a battleaxe!" He laughed.

Lieutenant leaned close and whispered in his ear.

"Oh, sorry, no offence intended. Anyway, I seem to have won her over with a bit of naval respect. There, that should hold long enough to get you home. Do you know of a reliable garage? If not, I recommend this chap. Tell him I sent you and he might knock a few bob off the bill. . . ."

He pulled a cigarette paper and a stub of pencil from his pocket and wrote down a name.

"Gosh, thanks. Now, can I offer you all a lift home? I know you're only a few streets away, but it's the least I can do. We'll be fine, provided you all jump out while the engine's still running."

~*~

Uncle Johnny came in for a cup of tea and a chat with Dad over a cigarette in the garden, while I told Mum and Audrey the story.

"I thought Captain was going to tell him off when he mentioned Lieutenant's stockings, but she backed him up, and of course once he saluted her and she saw he was Navy, and her being married to a Captain, he couldn't do a thing wrong."

The men came in just in time to hear my last sentence.

"Well, that should stand you in good stead," grinned Dad.

"Don't be silly!" Audrey laughed. "It's Lieutenant he fancies, not Captain."

Uncle Johnny looked a bit pink around the neck, but kissed us all goodnight, and Dad walked him to the gate where I could hear them laughing some more.

~*~

On Saturday afternoon, Maureen and I were leaning over the front fence just chatting, when a car r roared down the street and stopped outside Uncle Johnny's house. My uncle came running out and jumped into the passenger seat and the car sped past, with a toot and a wave.

"Well!" Maureen folded her arms and grinned, looking just like her mum. "Your Uncle Johnny walking out with Lieutenant! Now we know why he was so keen on seeing us home from Guides."

"They're not exactly walking out," I said, annoyed with Maureen's smug grin. "Maybe there's something wrong with his van and he needed a lift somewhere."

"And maybe Gene Kelly's working at the local chippy."

~*~

Uncle Johnny and Lieutenant had been out together a few times before he brought her to our house for Sunday tea. I felt awkward about it, with her being my superior officer and everything, but she was very friendly and chatted away to Audrey about her dancing.

I noticed Mum looked a bit put out when Lieutenant brought out a packet of cigarettes and offered them round, and she quickly cleared the table and made another pot of tea.

I had Latin homework to do, so I went and sat at the kitchen table, partly so I could concentrate, and partly because it felt weird having Lieutenant in the house as a guest.

Mum was clattering about with the tea things; tutting at the lipstick marks on Lieutenant's cup as she washed them out for

94

another round of tea. Audrey had turned the radio on and was practising her dancing in the lean-to, and the three in the front room were chatting and laughing, so I couldn't concentrate.

I gathered up my books and a cushion, and took myself off into the garden, closing the lean-to door harder than I meant to, as I had my arms full.

I curled up on the new garden bench that Dad had built and tried to work out why the sentence I was composing didn't look right. The wind blew the pages of my Latin dictionary to the wrong place, and I dropped my pencil as I tried to flap them back.

"Damn and blast it!" I muttered, then started guiltily when someone laughed close by.

Lieutenant was walking down the path with a cup of tea in each hand and a cushion under her arm.

She put the cups on the ground at each side of the bench, settled her cushion beside mine, and curled up with her feet tucked under her.

"I won't tell anyone, especially Captain!" She winked. "Latin, is it? Let's have a look."

I handed her my exercise book and explained what I was trying to say.

"Well, the sense of it is fine, but you've got the wrong tense here, and the word order should go like this. . . ." She picked up the pencil I'd dropped and quickly wrote a sentence under mine.

"You see. . . ." She flipped open the dictionary and explained where I'd gone wrong. It was simple, really!

"Oh, thank you, Lieutenant. I understand now. Mum and Dad didn't do Latin at school, so I've got no-one to help me. Some of the other girls' parents went to grammar school, so they can help with homework, but Jasmine and I struggle a bit."

"Any time you need help, you can always ask me." She smiled. "And I think while we're out of uniform you can call me Gill. Lieutenant is a bit formal, and I'm only nine years older than you."

"Thank you, Gill," I replied, feeling a bit shy at using her name. I wasn't sure Mum would approve of me calling a grown up by her first name, but I couldn't call her "Auntie Gill," especially as she was seeing my uncle; it would be like saying she ought to marry him, and maybe they weren't that serious.

We worked through the rest of my Latin essay together, and, with Gill explaining the grammar, it suddenly seemed much easier to understand.

"There, finished! Thank you ever so much. I might start getting better marks, now I understand it."

She smiled and passed me my tea.

"Come on, drink up before it's stone cold, then we'll go and help your mum clear away the tea things."

She swung her legs down from the bench and there was an ominous tearing noise. We looked at each other and then down at her skirt. She had caught the heel of her shoe in the hem and ripped the stitches out.

"D and B it?" I asked, with a grin.

"I couldn't have put it better myself." She twisted round to look at the damage.

"It's all right, nothing's torn, it's just that the stitches have come away. I can fix that in no time. You can wear one of Mum's skirts while I mend it."

We trooped into the house, laden with books, cups, and cushions, and showed Mum the damage.

"Can Gill borrow one of your skirts for a bit while I sew up the hem? It won't take long."

Mum sniffed a bit — I wasn't sure whether it was at me saying "Gill" or the idea of loaning out her skirt — but she took our guest upstairs and found something for her to wear while I fetched my sewing box.

Gill sat beside me and watched as I pulled out the torn threads, pinned the hem into place, and quickly slip stitched it back where it should be.

"I'm impressed, Sylvie." She took the skirt and showed Uncle Johnny my repair. "Look how neat the stitches are. You can't see a thing on the outside. I wish I could sew, but my mother always had me outside doing active things when I was a kid, so I never learned."

"I'll teach you!" I offered. "In return for help with my Latin." I turned to the others, "Gill's really clever at Latin. She explained it much better than my teacher."

"Oh, she's a very clever young lady; don't let the lipstick and cigarettes fool you." Uncle Johnny winked at his girlfriend, then looked directly at Mum. "She's no flighty piece; she got Matriculation Exemption, you know; she could have gone to university at sixteen."

Gill blushed and tried to change the subject, but I was watching Mum's face, and suddenly she looked at Gill differently.

"That would be lovely, Gill, you helping Sylvie with her Latin, and her teaching you to sew. We can't afford extra tuition, and I know she's been struggling with her Latin. It'll be nice for her to have an older friend, too, someone sensible to set her a good example."

Out of the corner of my eye I could see Uncle Johnny's mouth twitching, and when Mum took Gill upstairs to change back into her own skirt, he laughed out loud, and winked at me, saluting at the same time.

Chapter Eleven

Queen For A Day

"You do realise you get beheaded, Mo?"

That stopped her in her tracks. She stopped swishing down the street, waving her Guide hat graciously and bowing to invisible crowds, and turned to face me.

"What do you mean?" She frowned.

"Well, I know you're pleased at being Anne Boleyn because she was glamourous and exciting, but you know Henry had her beheaded, don't you?"

"That's not going to be part of the pageant, though, is it?" she asked.

"Well, no. . . ."

"Are you upset at being Anne of Cleves because Shirley said she was ugly? She didn't mean you're ugly; you know Shirley, she's just tactless."

Maureen was right, and anyway, Shirley was in her class at school, so she ought to know what she was like.

In the few months since she moved to the area, Shirley had upset just about everyone at Guides, one by one. She wanted to make friends, but she was a bit too pushy, and something of a liar. She was always making up stories about things that had happened to her, and every time she found a new friend, she said something tactless and upset them.

"I do think it's a bit off that she got Jane Seymour, though. She's new; she should have got Catherine Howard or Catherine Parr, one of the later wives."

"But didn't you say Catherine Howard was pretty and had loads of boyfriends?" Maureen asked. "Trust Miss 'I'm so popular' Maggie to get that one. And Catherine Parr was sensible and nice? Shirley's neither of those things. She's pale and insipid and annoys people."

"You're right. She's perfect for Jane Seymour."

I laughed. "I can't wait to see Captain all dolled up as Catherine of Aragon. She'll look like a Spanish galleon in full sail!"

"And Lieutenant bringing up the rear as Catherine Parr, the one who got stuck with Henry to the end," Maureen added.

"Well, there's probably a reason for that." I pointed up the road to where Uncle Johnny was hanging over his front gate giving Gill a goodnight kiss. She must have sped away from our meeting and popped in on her way home. "Uncle Johnny's playing Henry VIII. Lieutenant and I are making his costume. It's hilarious. We're putting pockets inside it to put pillows in to make him fat."

"Do you think they'll get married?" Maureen asked. "Then you'll have to call her Auntie Lieutenant." She giggled and nudged me.

"Don't be daft, she's got a name; she's called Gillian. I call her Gill when we're not in uniform; she asked me to. And I hope they do get married; she's really nice."

Gill pulled away from Uncle Johnny and spotted us coming down the road.

"Hello, girls, are you excited about the pageant? We've still got a lot of sewing to do, Sylvie. There's Henry's costume to finish, then my dress, and all the headdresses, and we've only got three weeks. I'll be here on Saturday morning, so pop round as soon as you can and we'll get cracking on finishing John's outfit. Can you sew, Maureen? We could do with some extra hands."

Maureen pointed to the Needlewoman badge on her sleeve and grinned.

"Sylvie taught me all I know."

"Me, too!" Gill laughed. "See you on Saturday, then. Bye, John, see you tomorrow."

She climbed into her car, blew my uncle a kiss through the window, and roared off at her usual speed.

~*~

"Ow! That was my neck!"

"Ftamd ftill, den," mumbled Gill, through a mouthful of pins.

"Are you going to be much longer?" asked Uncle Johnny, "Only there's some shopping I need to do, and the shops close in an hour."

Gill popped the last pin into his collar and stood back to study her handiwork.

"There, all done. Let's get you out of this, then you can go and play football or go to the pub, or whatever it is you want to do. Shopping! When do you ever go shopping?"

She helped him out of the padded suit and picked loose threads off his shirt.

"I go shopping when I need to buy something, and I need to buy something today." He grinned and kissed her. "Still want to go to the pictures tonight?"

"Yes, provided you haven't spent all your money on your shopping! Come on then, girls. Sylvie, you help me cut this dress out while Maureen gets started on sewing the headdresses."

~*~

You couldn't exactly call it a dress rehearsal, as there wasn't anything to rehearse; all we had to do was stand on the float, three of us on each side of Henry on his throne, but we all got dressed up to make sure everything fitted properly, and so we could sort out how to wear our hair under the headdresses.

Lieutenant brought out a cardboard box and emptied it onto one of the trestle tables.

"Jewels!" she cried. "Not real, I hasten to add!"

We oohed and aahed over the paste jewels, gilt chains, and pearl beads, sorting out what looked best with each of our outfits and swapping things back and forth until everyone was happy.

I nearly laughed when I looked at Shirley; she was decked out like a Christmas tree in everything that no-one else wanted to wear. There wasn't one piece of jewellery left over.

"I thought Jane Seymour was a prim and proper person," I muttered to Maureen.

Lieutenant heard me and frowned.

"Don't forget to leave some things for the King, girls," she reminded us. "We can't have Henry wearing fewer jewels than his wives. Shirley, don't you think you've got too many chains there?"

Shirley sheepishly removed a few chains and rings and put them back in the box, but she kept looking at them, like a magpie, for the rest of the evening, as we practised walking in our dresses without tripping, and climbed the steps of the church pulpit to make sure we could tackle the ladder that we'd need to use to get onto the float.

"Guides!" Captain clapped her hands and called us to attention.

"The parade forms up at 0-nine-hundred hours on Saturday morning. I want you all there, dressed and ready, half an hour before. Is everyone clear on that?"

"Yes, Captain," we chorused.

"Very good. We won't have Taps tonight as this is an informal meeting, so I'll wish you all goodnight, and see you on Saturday."

She saluted smartly, and we returned the salute, although it looked a bit odd, six Tudor ladies giving the Guide salute.

~*~

The dairy yard was full of people, all dressed in different historical costumes. Stone age men with fibreglass clubs mixed with Regency bucks with tin foil buckles on their dress shoes, and Victorian ladies in black bombazine looked enviously at our silk and brocade dresses, which did look impressive, even though they were made from old curtains.

Uncle Johnny was sweating in his padded costume, false beard, and velvet hat, and he seemed really twitchy.

"I wish you and Gill had put pockets in this costume," he complained. "I've got nowhere to put anything."

"What do you want to put?" Gill appeared behind him and tried to link her hands around his padded waist. "You don't need money, or car keys, and I hope you're not going to light up a fag. Henry VIII smoking cigarettes would be too anachronistic for words."

"Nothing particular," he replied, pulling away. "It's just . . . if I wanted to put anything somewhere, I can't."

"You could use your. . . ." She winked and nodded downward at a particularly personal part of his costume, then swished away to round up the rest of the queens, leaving Uncle Johnny red-faced.

~*~

The lorries pulled in to the dairy yard one by one, and each historical group clambered up and settled itself.

We scaled our stepladder without mishap, and clustered around Uncle Johnny on his golden throne.

Captain and Lieutenant, as the tallest, had the positions nearest to the throne, so they had something to hold on to, but the rest of us had to balance as best we could, hanging on to each other as the float went around the corner and onto the main road.

The plan was for all the floats to pull up around the green by the library, where everyone would dismount, and the Mayor would make a speech about the town's history, and how grateful we were to be living in peace once again, blah blah blah, then the procession would mount up again and head towards the park, where refreshments would be available, and a band would play music from all the centuries represented.

I was looking forward to hearing some stone age music; that would be a challenge to the town brass band.

We could hear the Medieval minstrels on the float in front squealing as they crested the hill and zoomed down the other side, so we all held hands. Shirley was next to me, and I squeezed her hand so tight she squeaked.

"Ow, Sylvie, that hurt," she whined, rubbing her hand. There were rings on three fingers of each hand. She must have snuck back to the box of jewellery again. If she hadn't been wearing so many rings, it wouldn't have hurt. I had no sympathy.

~*~

The sun beat down as all the pageant cast, plus friends, relatives, and most of the town, gathered around the Mayor's podium to hear his speech. Uncle Johnny was standing between me and Lieutenant, and sweating furiously. He kept fidgeting with a certain part of his costume.

"John, stop fiddling with your codpiece!" hissed his girlfriend.

"I'm missing something, Gill!" he whispered back.

I saw the back of the Victorian lady in front of him stiffen, and watched her force herself not to look round.

"What have you lost?" Lieutenant muttered.

"I can't tell you," he replied, sounding anguished.

"Then stop fiddling; it's embarrassing!"

"Shhhh!"

The lady in front turned around and hushed them, carefully keeping her eyes above waist level.

~*~

We climbed back onto our float for the journey to the park; downhill again. Uncle Johnny was the first up the ladder, searching the floor of the trailer in a panic.

"Where is it? Where is it?" he muttered.

"Parade . . . forward!" The pageant master was enjoying himself.

We were off again, round the green and down the hill to the park. The four of us who didn't have a throne to hang onto gripped hands again, and once again Shirley made a fuss, wringing her hands and complaining that I'd crushed her fingers. I looked at her hands. She now had four rings on her left hand.

"Where did you get that ring?" I asked her.

"What ring? From the jewellery box, of course."

"No, you didn't, not that gold one with the diamond. It looks too real."

She flushed.

"Someone gave it to me."

"Who?"

She shrugged.

"A boy. At the dairy yard. He said I was the best looking of all the queens and gave me the ring."

"Don't talk rubbish! Why would anyone just give you a ring? And what boy carries expensive rings about?"

Our argument was loud enough for Uncle Johnny to hear. He craned around Captain to look at us, still waving graciously to the crowd.

"What's this about a ring? Sylvie, what's going on?"

"It's Shirley. She said some boy gave her a ring at the dairy yard, but she didn't have it at the start of the parade."

He looked hard at Shirley, really stern, just like he really was a king.

"Shirley, when we get to the park, you will see me immediately, in private. Sylvie, you come with her to make sure she does."

Shirley blushed and bowed her head. I could see her fidgeting, trying to get the ring off, so I grabbed her hand again and squeezed it hard.

I dragged her down that ladder and we followed Uncle Johnny behind the pavilion.

"Now then, Shirley, let me see that ring."

She slipped it off her finger and held it out to him.

"I didn't steal it, honest. I found it. Someone dropped it. I thought it was just a ring that one of the other Guides had lost."

"And the box?" Uncle Johnny stood with his arms folded and his feet planted wide apart, frowning, his mouth pursed up.

"Wh . . . what box?"

"A little dark blue box, lined with dark blue velvet, with "Hall's Jewellers" written inside the lid in silver."

I looked at Uncle Johnny questioningly. How did he know about the box? He grinned sheepishly, then switched back to his stern "off with her head" attitude.

Shirley opened the pomander hanging from the girdle of her dress and pulled out a small box.

"I did find it, honest. I was going to tell someone, but I thought the ring would be safer on my finger. . . ."

"Go. Just go."

He looked so kingly that Shirley forgot he was only her friend's uncle and curtseyed to him, then ran away, sobbing.

I looked at Uncle Johnny.

"Good thing she didn't know where you were keeping it."

We both roared with laughter.

Uncle Johnny draped his arm around my shoulder as we walked back to the others, still laughing.

He let go when he saw Gill, and turned to me, grabbing both my hands.

"There's something I need to do, Sylvie. Keep watch and make sure no-one comes near, please? And wish me luck!"

"Luck? Why. . . ?" He was running across the grass towards Gill, his padding bouncing as he ran.

"Good luck!" I called after him.

Gill turned as he reached her, panting from his short run, and laughed at him in his sweaty fat suit. Until he went down on one knee, and held out a small, dark blue box.

Her hands went to her mouth, then she took the box and opened it.

Uncle Johnny swept off his velvet hat and looked up at her.

I saw her nod and give a beaming smile, then he stood and slipped the ring onto her finger.

They held hands for a moment, just smiling, then grabbed each other in a hug that ended in a long kiss.

~*~

The official engagement party was held at our house. Grandma and Auntie Mabel came down on the bus, Grandma refusing to ride in the back of Uncle Johnny's van, or allow Auntie Mabel to do so.

Maureen and her parents were invited, too, as they were practically family, and we all squashed into the front room, waiting for Gill and her parents to arrive.

Uncle Johnny was at the door almost before Gill had knocked, ushering his in-laws-to-be into the house.

"Good afternoon, Sir, do come in."

Gill's dad was tall and grey, very upright, very much a military man. Uncle Johnny had said he was in the Navy, too.

Gill ushered her mum into the room and my mouth dropped open.

"Captain!"

Maureen automatically saluted, even though she wasn't in uniform.

Captain walked across the room and kissed me.

"I think, under the circumstances, you might call me Auntie Agnes. Only out of uniform, of course."

Part Four
1949

Chapter Twelve

Breadwinner

Audrey opened the paper bag and peered inside.

"Oooh! Chelsea buns!"

Mum scooped up the bag and lifted it out of her reach.

"Sticky fingers off! When your dad's finished in the bathroom you need to go and wash your hands. Sylvie, can you clear your sewing things off the table, please?"

I gathered up the school blouse I was mending, wondering why Dad had bought the buns. We usually only had cake for Saturday tea if it was someone's birthday.

"What are we celebrating?" I asked, laying out the tea plates as Dad came back through from the bathroom.

"Oh, wait till I come back!" Audrey called, running past Dad to wash her hands.

"Let's sit down and pour the tea, then I'll tell you."

Dad made space on the table for the pot stand and opened the paper bag, placing a bun on each plate.

Audrey bounced into her seat and started unrolling her Chelsea bun, picking out the pieces of dried lemon peel and dropping them on my plate.

"What is it, Daddy?" she asked through a mouth full of peel-less bun.

Dad stirred his tea and grinned across the table at me.

"How do you fancy a little job for the summer holidays, Sylvie?"

"A job? What kind of job?" I asked, with my cup suspended halfway to my mouth.

"Dales the bakers need someone to help out in the shop for a couple of weeks while their daughter's away on holiday. Do you fancy it? It would only be four days a week for two weeks; Monday, Tuesday, Wednesday, and Saturday, and they close at twelve on Saturdays."

I sipped my tea and thought for a while. It would be good to earn some money, and to have something useful to do. Maureen might be upset though, if she had no-one to go around with for a couple of weeks.

"It'll be ten shillings a day, even the half-day Saturday. It's a lot of money, but they need someone in a hurry, so they're willing to pay well."

I grinned, working out the sun on my head. I would earn four pounds in two weeks! "I'll take it!"

~*~

After tea, I tapped out the signal for "I need to talk to you" on the wall between our house and Maureen's, and strolled into the garden with another cup of tea, Scamp following behind, just in case I felt like letting him drink some cold tea from my saucer.

Maureen appeared through the gap in the hedge with a bag of humbugs in her hand and sat down beside me on the bench. Scamp positioned himself between our feet, looking hopeful.

"What's up?" Maureen asked around her humbug, bending down to tickle Scamp's ears.

"Dad's found me a job for a couple of weeks at Dales' this holiday, so I won't be around much the first two weeks."

"Lucky thing!" Maureen looked grumpy. "You can eat cakes all day. I've got to go and work with Dad at the wood yard. Taking orders from customers, answering the telephone, and making tea."

"But you'll get paid?" I helped myself to another humbug.

"Yes, but I won't have much free time."

I nodded.

"That's what happens. Growing up is good, we're allowed to do more things on our own, but soon we'll be working full time — no more long holidays."

"Do you think you'll go to university?" Maureen asked. "You're clever enough."

I picked at some flaking paint on the arm of the bench.

"No, Mum and Dad could never afford it. I'll have to find a job as soon as I leave school."

"But not at the baker's?"

"No. I'd like to be a dressmaker, but I'll probably end up working in an office. Anyway, if I worked at a baker's full time, I'd be the size of a house!"

Maureen laughed.

"Oh, well, we'll still have Saturday afternoons and Sundays, plus some money to spend!"

~*~

The "closed" sign was still on the door when I arrived for my first day at work. I tapped nervously on the glass and waited, then tapped again.

"We're not open yet!" came a voice from inside.

I bent down and called through the letter box, "It's Sylvie Ford. I'm here to work."

A shape in a white overall appeared and bolts and locks rattled.

"Come in, then, but tomorrow you go to the back door."

I slid through the partly open door and it was slammed and bolted behind me. The manageress, Miss Norton, looked me up and down. She was not a favourite of anyone from my school, as she hated kids going in the shop at lunchtime. She said we made too much noise and took too long choosing what we wanted, so she had made a rule that no more than two school children were allowed in the shop at once.

"You look clean, anyway." She frowned. "But you'll need to put your hair up in a cap; you can't have that long plait hanging down. Come with me."

She led me through a door at the back of the shop and showed me where the toilet was.

"Hang your cardigan up here, then go and wash your hands while I find you an overall and cap."

The overall was a bit too big, and I struggled to get my hair tucked up into the paper cap, but eventually Miss Norton was satisfied and took me back into the shop.

She had already stocked the shelves, and led me round the shop, asking me to tell her what each kind of bread or cake was called. I must have got them all right, as she just grunted and took me over to the till to explain how to work it.

"I'm not going to let you use the bread slicer until I've seen that you're sensible and don't make mistakes, so if anyone wants their bread sliced, you call me. I'll be in the back getting the next batch of rolls ready. Have you got that?"

"Yes, Miss Norton."

"Now, do you wear a watch?"

"Yes, Miss Norton."

"Good. At nine o'clock, and not a moment before, you can unlock the door and turn the sign to 'open.'"

"Yes, Miss Norton."

~*~

My first customer was our milkman, stopping off from his round to buy a bun for his breakfast, while his horse fidgeted and whinnied outside.

I held my breath as I rang up the price of the bun and pressed the key to open the till.

"That's one and eight change, Mr Metcalfe, thank you."

"Thank you, Sylvie. You look very smart in your overall." He smiled, waving goodbye as he closed the shop door behind him.

As the morning went on, I started to relax and enjoy the job. I had to call Miss Norton out twice to use the slicer, but apart from that I managed to serve all the customers without making any mistakes.

Miss Norton came into the shop at twelve to help with the lunchtime rush, and I could tell she was watching me closely, so I tried to be as efficient as possible, even when friends and neighbours came in, calling them "Sir" or "Madam" when I would usually call them "Auntie" or "Uncle".

Miss Norton treated all the customers the same way — polite but brisk. She rarely smiled at them, just giving them a stiff nod and a "good morning" or "good afternoon", until a tall, friendly looking lady walked in.

"Oh, good morning, Mrs Dale, how lovely to see you. How is Mr Dale?"

Miss Norton was suddenly all smiles.

"We're both very well, thank you, Miss Norton. And this must be the young lady who's covering for our Patricia."

Mrs Dale smiled at me.

"Yes, this is Sylvie. She's doing all right so far, but of course I haven't let her use the bread slicer yet, and I will personally cash up at the end of the day."

I tried not to show how offended I was, but I could feel my cheeks glowing warm. Of course, Miss Norton didn't know anything about me, but she made me feel as though I couldn't be trusted.

Mrs Dale smiled at me again.

"I'm sure Sylvie will be very helpful and efficient. Now, I'd like two Viennese whirls, please, Sylvie."

I carefully placed the cakes in a bag and twisted the top, wondering whether I should charge the owner's wife, but Mrs Dale was already opening her purse to give me the exact money. I rang up the sale smartly and handed her the bag.

"Thank you, Sylvie. I'm very glad you're here. Enjoy the rest of your two weeks."

~*~

The afternoon flew by, with plenty of customers and a delivery of dried fruit, which Miss Norton let me deal with, as she was just taking a batch of Eccles cakes from the oven.

I counted the bags of fruit and signed the delivery boy's docket. Miss Norton bustled over to double check and sniffed. I had the feeling that she was waiting for me to make a mistake and was disappointed when I didn't.

~*~

At a quarter to five, Miss Norton told me to push all the left-over cream cakes into the front of the window, as any not sold would have to go in the pig bin. The bread and buns would need to be put away in airtight tins overnight.

A few last customers came in on their way home from work, but there wasn't much to do.

"Shall I start sweeping the floor, Miss Norton?" I asked.

"No, you will not! This shop closes at five sharp, not a moment earlier. We sweep after we shut for the day."

At a few minutes to five, a scruffy-looking man, hopping on crutches, with one trouser leg pinned up below the knee, and a patch over one eye, fumbled the door open.

"Any leftovers, please, Miss?"

I looked at Miss Norton, unsure what to do.

"I've told you before, we are not a charity." Miss Norton sounded angry, and the man struggled back through the door, letting it slam behind him.

"There are too many of these people begging for handouts," she grumbled, starting to collect up the day-old cream cakes and pile them in the pig bucket.

"Some of them think they can stick a bandage on, claim to have been injured in the war, and get something for nothing. That's what the new welfare state is for; it's not down to hard-working people to hand out charity."

"But surely that man really is missing a leg," I protested. "He looks as though he hasn't eaten properly in months, and all those cakes are just going in the pig bin."

"That's as may be, but if we start giving food away free, word will get around and we'll have all the beggars and layabouts in town on our doorstep. Now, you get that floor mopped, then you can go. I'll see you tomorrow, five to nine; don't be late."

~*~

Over tea, I told Mum and Dad about the man with the missing leg, and what Miss Norton had said.

"I know there's still rationing, and the pig bin food isn't wasted, but surely the men who fought and helped us win the war should be looked after first?" I asked.

Dad sighed.

"I agree, Sylvie. It's wrong that people who gave so much are lacking food and proper housing. Mr Attlee promised lots of things under this new welfare state, and it was a good idea, don't get me wrong, but the government hasn't got the money to look after everyone. There are too many people like your Miss Norton who think, 'I'm all right, Jack,' and don't care about anyone else."

"And Miss Norton doesn't own the shop," put in Mum. "She's just the manageress, so she probably wouldn't be allowed to give away food, if she wanted to."

"She doesn't want to," I said, scraping up the last of my shepherd's pie. "And she acts like she's just waiting for me to steal a load of bread or run off with the money in the till."

"Be patient," Mum advised. "It's only your first day. When she sees that you're sensible and can be trusted, she'll ease up on you."

~*~

The man with the missing leg turned up again at closing time the next day, and again Miss Norton turned him away.

I tried to look as sympathetic as possible, to show that if I had my way, he would get a cake to take home.

~*~

On Wednesday afternoon, I called Miss Norton into the shop.

"We're running out of change, Miss Norton." I showed her the cash drawer.

She sniffed and tutted. "I suppose you've been taking ten shilling notes and using up all the change. Really, Sylvie, you must ask people for the right money. Now I'll have to go to the bank quickly before they close."

"I'm sorry, I didn't know," I apologised. "I've never worked in a shop before."

"That's quite obvious," Miss Norton sniffed. "Now, if I'm not back before five, you can start tidying up, fill the pig bin, close up and start cleaning, but don't leave the shop until I come back."

"Yes, Miss Norton."

At five to five, I fetched the pig bin and started sorting what would be good for another day from what needed to be thrown out.

Just then, the bell jangled and the man with the missing leg appeared.

"Any leftovers, please, Miss?"

I stood stock still, a cream split in my hand. Quickly, I poked my head out through the open door. There was no sign of Miss Norton.

I grabbed a paper bag, dropped the cream split into it, added another, and shoved it into his hands.

"There, take them and enjoy them, but please don't tell Miss Norton."

The man gave me a sketchy salute and limped away.

I turned the sign to "closed" and carried on tidying the shop.

Miss Norton bustled in through the back door just after ten past five.

"All right, Sylvie, you can go. I'll check everything and lock up. I'll see you on Saturday."

~*~

I was glad to have two days off. The work wasn't hard, but having Miss Norton watching me suspiciously all day was tiring.

Thursday was early closing day, so she would manage on her own, and on Fridays, Mrs Dale worked in the shop and banked the week's takings, so I wasn't needed until Saturday morning.

~*~

I made sure I arrived early on Saturday, to try to make up for my mistake with running out of change.

Miss Norton was sitting at the little desk in the kitchen where Mrs Dale did the books and looked at me sternly.

"Don't bother changing into your overall, Sylvie," she said, folding her arms.

"Why, what's happened?" I asked.

"You know very well, young lady. When I went to cash up at lunchtime on Thursday, I checked the pig bin. The money in the till was short by two cakes. I didn't find those cakes in the pig bin. You gave them to that tramp, didn't you?"

Her snooty attitude made me angry. I tried to stay calm, balling my fists until my fingernails dug in, but I could feel my temper rising.

"Yes, I did, and I'd do it again. It's not fair that we have perfectly good food and it's being fed to pigs, to feed people who can already afford to eat."

"That's enough, young lady. You can go. I will be speaking to Mrs Dale tomorrow; you'd better come here at five o'clock to apologise to her."

I could feel my face burning, and there were tears in my eyes, but I held my head up and stalked out of the shop. I resisted slamming the door behind me.

I went to the park to have a sit down and a think. Mum and Dad were at work. So was Maureen, and Audrey was at Brian's house. I didn't want to go home and sit there on my own, but I couldn't decide what to do.

I drifted off into a daydream, still fuming, and going over and over what had happened in my mind. When I looked at my watch, it was eleven o'clock. Dad had a lunch break at twelve, so if I started walking now, I could be there to meet him when he stopped work. It was a long walk, but gave me some thinking time.

Dad's friend Ernie was outside the bothy when I arrived.

"Hello, young Sylvie, is everything all right?"

"Yes and no, Uncle Ernie. Is my dad around?"

Just then Dad appeared, pushing a wheelbarrow. He looked anxious when he saw me, and I hurried over to him.

"It's all right, Daddy, everyone's fine . . . it's just. . . ." I gulped. I didn't want to cry, but seeing Dad made me want to be a little girl again and have Daddy put everything right, despite the fact that I was old enough to work.

Dad took my hands.

"Just what?" he asked gently.

"I've been saaaaacked!" I wailed, and burst into tears.

~*~

When Dad and I got home and told the others the story, they agreed that Miss Norton had been unfair.

Dad offered to come with me to see Mrs Dale, but we talked it over and decided it would be better, and more grown up, if I went on my own.

"Just be polite, explain, but don't argue," he advised.

~*~

I didn't sleep much on Thursday night, and luckily Mum had the day off on Friday, so we spent the day tidying up the cupboard under the stairs, which took my mind off the upcoming interview.

At two minutes to five, I grabbed the doorknob at Dales' bakery, took a deep breath, and walked in. I decided I'd better use the shop door, as I didn't work there any more.

Mrs Dale was cashing up, with Miss Norton standing beside her, looking uncomfortable.

Mrs Dale looked up and smiled, which was a surprise.

"Sylvie, thank you for coming in. Let's go through to the office so we can talk."

We trooped through the shop and Miss Norton and I were told to sit at the table, while Mrs Dale leant against the counter where the staff made tea and coffee.

"Firstly, Sylvie, Miss Norton has my full support in dismissing you, as you failed to follow her instructions."

I bowed my head.

"I'm very sorry, Mrs Dale, and I'm sorry I lost my temper, Miss Norton."

My ex-manager nodded graciously, silently accepting my apology.

"However," Mrs Dale continued, "I do think you have made a valid point, and from now on, we will keep the shop open for an extra ten minutes at the end of the day, and all the food that is not going to last another day will be given away to anyone in need. And we will not question the level of anyone's need."

She looked sternly at Miss Norton as she finished.

"Your job is reinstated, Sylvie, and here are your wages for this week. Now, off you go, both of you. I'll lock up this evening."

~*~

Dad was waiting for me when I closed the shop door behind me. He tipped his hat to Miss Norton, and she gave him a chilly smile.

"Everything all right, Sylvie?"

"Yes." I puffed out a breath of pure relief. "Mrs Dale is going to start giving leftovers to wounded servicemen at the end of each day, and I've got my job back!"

I opened my pay packet.

"Oh! Two pounds! But I didn't work Wednesday; Miss Norton sent me home. Do you think Mrs Dale made a mistake?"

"No, I think she knows a good worker when she sees one."

"Let's get fish and chips on the way home, to celebrate. I'm paying!"

~*~

Audrey came running home from Brian's on Monday afternoon, waving a copy of the local paper.

"Sylvie, you're famous!"

She threw the paper on the table, open at an article headed, "Local bakery helps wounded ex-servicemen."

Mum handed the paper back to her and laid out the place mats.

"You read it to us, Audrey, while I get the tea."

Audrey cleared her throat importantly and read:

> "Dale's the baker's has come up with an idea to help local wounded ex-servicemen and their families. Each day, at the close of business, the shop will stay open for an extra ten minutes, when the staff will be giving away any food that cannot be kept over night to those in need.
>
> "Bakery owner Mrs Dale said, 'The idea came from our newest and youngest member of staff, Sylvie Ford, who is working with us during the school holidays. She pointed out a way that we could help local people who gave so much to help us win the war.'
>
> "The scheme started today."

"Well, Miss Norton won't be too pleased about that, but I've only got to work with her for four more days. Fancy going to the pictures tomorrow afternoon, Aud? My treat."

Chapter Thirteen

Saturday Afternoon

"Dum diddle-um diddle-um diddle-um diddle-um-pum-pum-pum pum pum pum pum. . . ."

Audrey and Brian raced ahead down the cinema steps and along the street, singing the theme tune to "Dick Barton — Special Agent", firing imaginary pistols at each other, and hiding behind trees.

Maureen and I ignored them as we talked about the film, gossiped about school, and discussed what we planned to wear for Jasmine's birthday party.

As we passed the end of Gordon's passage, as we called the alley beside the newsagent in the high street, Brian suddenly stepped out in front of us, feet spread wide, hands in pockets, shirt collar turned up, and tipped an imaginary hat to us. Maureen jumped about a foot in the air and screamed; she wasn't as used to having Audrey and Brian around as I was.

"Briii-yaaan!" Maureen exclaimed.

Brian grinned and ran off to hunt down Audrey's escaping Russian spy.

"Aud!" I called after them. "We're going down to the pool for an ice cream. Tell Mum I'll be home for tea in a bit."

She flapped a hand over her shoulder in acknowledgement as she ran, then ducked behind a rubbish bin to pull the pin from an imaginary grenade with her teeth.

"Those two make me feel tired." Maureen sighed, in an unconscious imitation of her mum, as she slipped her arm through mine.

I jiggled my feet to get in step, so we weren't bumping hips as we walked, and we strolled down past the station and across the railway line to the swimming pool.

It was warm for early September, and the place was full of kids, running, shouting, and splashing, despite the pool manager's resigned call of, "No running! No jumping!"

"Oh, good, the Hokey Pokey man's here!"

Maureen pulled her purse from her pocket and shook some coins out.

"Tuppeny cone?"

She didn't bother to wait for my answer but marched straight over to join the short queue at Mr Amorelli's cart.

"'Ello young Maoreena, what can I do you for?"

Mr Amorelli was one of my most favourite people. He had been a prisoner of war, working in the nurseries alongside Dad, so he was almost family; when he'd arrived, he'd hardly spoken any English at all, so he had learned most of his everyday phrases from the wireless, by listening to comedy programmes like I.T.M.A. and Much Binding In The Marsh, which made his conversation unusual, to say the least. His ice cream, however, was the best in the area.

A loud splash and yell from behind made me turn around so that the vanilla cone Maureen handed to me almost went in my ear.

"Don'ta forget the diver!" laughed Mr Amorelli.

A small, skinny boy surfaced spluttering from the pool and scrambled up the ladder, showering everyone nearby with water. He was fully dressed, so obviously hadn't come intending to swim.

He ran full pelt towards a taller boy with dark hair and dark brown eyes who was laughing hysterically. In fact, he was laughing so much that he didn't see trouble coming until the smaller boy swung a highly accurate fist at him and knocked him flat on the ground.

"Oooh! Poor Bobby!" Maureen was open-mouthed, her ice cream about to drip all down the front of her dress.

"Bobby? The little one?" I mumbled, licking up the last of my ice cream and crunching through the small wafer cone.

"No, Bobby Hemmings, the tall, good-looking boy. Maybe we should go and help him. He could be hurt."

Some of the other boys had pulled Bobby's attacker away from him, and were calming the smaller lad down and drying him off.

Maureen scuttled over to the injured party, who was holding a handkerchief to his eye.

"Oh, Bobby!" she cooed. "Are you all right?"

He peeled the handkerchief away from his eye. It wasn't bad; just a small scratch on his eyebrow and a red patch that would probably be a nasty bruise in a few hours; but it was too much for Maureen. Her knees wobbled, she flumped down onto one of the wooden benches, and her untouched ice cream took a nose dive straight onto the ground.

"Oh, for goodness' sake, Maureen!"

I pulled my clean hanky from my pocket and handed it to her.

"Make yourself useful. Go and ask Mr Amorelli for some ice from his cart and wrap it in this to make an ice pack."

I pushed the tall boy down onto the bench and dabbed the blood away from the cut with his pristine hanky, which he handed over reluctantly, as his friends grouped around us to look at the damage. Maureen came rushing back with the ice and handed it to me, hanging back.

"Here, hold this against the eye for a bit. It'll stop it bruising too badly."

"Thanks." He smiled, looking up at me out of one eye.

"You're Sylvia, aren't you? You're in Jasmine's class?"

"Yes, but most people call me Sylvie. Are you a friend of Jasmine's?"

"Sort of; we went to the same junior school. Are you going to her birthday party next weekend?"

"Yes, we are, aren't we, Mo?" I turned to Maureen who was standing with her arms folded.

"I might. I might not." She turned away and pretended to be fascinated by two little girls who were playing catch with a beach ball almost the same size as them. I took the hint.

"Anyway, if you're all right now we'll be off. We've got to get home for tea."

"See you next week."

~*~

We walked almost all the way home in an awkward silence, until Maureen finally broke it as we turned into our road.

"'Most people call me Sylvie,'" she mocked, in a fake-sweet girly voice, swishing her skirt and looking up under her lashes with a simpering expression.

"Oh, knock it off, Maureen; if you weren't so squeamish, he'd have talked to you. It was only because of the ice pack."

"And who fetched the ice?"

"You did, but only because I told you to!"

"Who wants a boyfriend, anyway? Boys are smelly."

"He's not my boyfr. . . ."

She slammed her front door before I even had time to finish the word.

~*~

Maureen avoided me all week, except on the Wednesday morning when we both left our houses at the same time, and she couldn't really pretend I wasn't there.

"Morning," she grunted, as I closed the door behind me.

"Morning, Mo. Are you still going to Jasmine's party on Saturday?" I tried to be normal and friendly.

"I'll see what I feel like. Actually, a boy has asked me to go with him, but I haven't decided yet."

I rolled my eyes. She was probably making it up.

"Which boy?"

"His name's Ted; he was at the pool the other day. Got to run, bye!"

~*~

I was quite surprised when Maureen knocked for me on Saturday afternoon.

She acted as though nothing had happened; as though there hadn't been a frosty silence between us all week, and I assumed that the mysterious Ted had either let her down or didn't exist in the first place.

As we turned towards the church at the top of the road, I heard someone call my name.

I looked round, and two boys were running towards us, dressed in their best suits, with their hair slicked down — Bobby, and the smaller boy who had punched him at the pool.

"Well, that's a turn up for the books," I muttered to Maureen, but she wasn't listening. She was simpering, just like she had when she mocked me, and batting her eyelashes at the smaller boy.

"Hello, Ted. You look awfully smart."

"Hello, Maureen, hello, Sylvie." Ted grinned, and his blue eyes sparkled. He looked friendly enough; I hoped he wasn't planning to start punching people again.

As the path was quite narrow, we split into two pairs — Bobby and me behind the other two. Ted was making jokes, but I could tell that Maureen wasn't getting them. He was trying too hard to impress her.

"So, are you two friends again?" I asked Bobby.

"Oh, yes, it was jus . . . one of those things, you know? Ted's a good chap. Of course, his family haven't got two pennies to rub together. That's his dad's old suit he's wearing."

I laughed, "Same here. This dress was my mum's; I cut it down and altered it to fit me."

"Oh." He looked taken aback. "Well . . . that's very clever of you, Sylvia."

125

"I wish you'd call me Sylvie; I feel like I'm in trouble at school when you say Sylvia."

"I don't like shortened names," he replied, seriously. "I wish everyone would stop calling me Bobby. I'm fifteen; Bobby's a kid's name. I'd much rather be called Robert."

"Oh, all right, then, I'll call you Robert, if you'd prefer."

He smiled, and ushered me ahead of him as Jasmine's mum opened the front door for us.

I was quite surprised that Jasmine's mum had let her invite so many people, knowing how house proud and fussy she was, but we were quickly bustled through the house into the garden, where pasting tables were laid out, laden with sandwiches, sausage rolls, and jugs of squash.

The French doors to the sitting room were open, and Jasmine's dad stood by the piano sorting through a pile of records and arranging them in order, so he could keep the gramophone going all afternoon.

We found Jasmine among a group of girls and gave her our presents, while the boys wandered over to the tables to find something to eat.

Bobby — Robert — came back with two full plates and handed me one, but Ted just helped himself and strolled back to us, munching on a sausage roll, with a piece of cake in the other hand.

"I don't know what you like, Maureen, so I'll leave you to choose for yourself."

I almost wished Robert had done the same, as he'd brought me a huge spam sandwich with so much mustard that it nearly blew my head off.

After everyone had eaten, Jasmine's dad came out and placed some big cushions around the garden, then announced that we were going to play Musical Cushions. Robert decided to sit it out — he thought it was childish and didn't want to spoil his suit — but the rest of us pranced around wildly and threw ourselves down onto cushions every time the music stopped, laughing until we couldn't breathe.

There were just three people and two cushions left when there was a nasty scraping noise from the gramophone.

"Blast, the needle's broken," cried Jasmine's dad.

A mass groan went up.

"Anyone here play the piano?" he asked.

Ted winked at us and stepped forward.

"I do!"

He bounded in through the French doors, sat at the piano stool and flexed his fingers dramatically, then began to fumble his way through a few bars of Twinkle Twinkle Little Star.

Everyone laughed and jeered, but Ted just grinned, then launched into a fast, lively boogie-woogie tune, both hands flying and his feet tapping the pedals.

Everyone cheered and started dancing. Jitterbugging, jiving, or just jumping around.

I glanced over at Robert, to beckon him to join in, but he was examining the turn-ups of his trousers and didn't see me looking. Perhaps he couldn't dance and was too shy to try.

After three or four tunes, Jasmine's mum appeared in the kitchen door with her tea towel in her hand, looking anxiously at all the dirty plates and cups. I nudged Maureen.

"Time to go home, I think."

She nodded, danced her way to within Ted's eyeline, and made a slashing motion across her throat with her hand. He nodded, and brought the tune to an end with a flourish, closing the piano lid as he stood up and the partygoers cheered.

Jasmine's dad clapped him on the back.

"I think we'll be hiring you for all our parties from now on, young man."

Ted grinned and sauntered across to join Maureen and me in thanking Jasmine for the party.

"Where's Robert?" I asked, looking around.

"Oh, he left ages ago," said Ted, "He's not really a joiner-inner."

"Oh, he must be shy, poor boy."

Ted gave me an old-fashioned look that I couldn't work out.

"Something like that," he said.

"So," he continued, "how do you girls fancy coming to the Boys' Brigade outing next weekend? It's at Home Farm. Everyone's welcome from 2 o'clock. Bring your own picnic, but tea, lemonade, and ginger beer will be free."

"Is Robert in the Boys' Brigade?" I asked.

He laughed.

"No, he thinks it's childish." He shrugged. "His loss."

I looked at Maureen and she nodded.

"We'd love to come! We'll see you there."

He sketched an American-style salute at us and strolled away, hands in his pockets, whistling.

~*~

"Do you think Bobby will mind you going to the picnic?" Maureen asked as we ambled home.

"No, why should he? Just because he doesn't want to, it doesn't mean I can't."

She nodded and we walked on in friendly silence.

We stopped at our front gates and she turned to me with a serious expression.

"Ted's a funny one," she mused. "He said something really odd to me while we were playing Musical Cushions; he said,'Be alert, Maureen, Britain needs lerts.' I don't know what he meant by that."

"Haha! That's really good!" I laughed.

"What is?"

"Be alert. Be. A. Lert. Be a-lert. ALERT! It's a joke; a pun."

She looked at me blankly.

"But 'lert' isn't even a thing. How can I be one when I don't know what it is?"

I had no answer to that.

Chapter Fourteen

Pride and Prejudice

"Aaargh! Why is it doing that?"

The needle bobbled up and down through the loose fabric and the thread spooled wildly. Audrey held her hands up in panic, losing control completely.

"You need to put the foot down," I sighed, for the twentieth time. Teaching Audrey to sew was like teaching a puppy to do a jigsaw puzzle.

"I thought you meant put my foot down! As in go faster!"

I unravelled the loose stitching and handed the cushion cover back to her.

"Try again. One last seam, then it's finished."

She concentrated, tongue out, levered the sewing machine foot down with a deliberate flourish, and stitched a perfect seam.

"See? You can do it, when you concentrate."

She turned the cover through to the right side and stroked it admiringly.

"Isn't it the most beautiful cushion cover ever?"

Dad came in from the kitchen with a cup of tea and kissed the top of her head.

"Beautiful, Chicky. Now, weren't you supposed to be over at Brian's for three o'clock? I thought you were meant to be listening to the football results together?"

The two of them had a game that they had cut from a newspaper where they had to choose a certain number of football teams to follow; every week, they had to mark on a chart their teams' points; at the end of the season, they could send the charts in to the paper and try to win a prize.

"Oh! Yes! I must run; and Sylvie has to get ready for her double date."

She poked her tongue out at me and winked, and was off, out of the house before I had a chance to grab her.

I could feel my cheeks growing hot. It wasn't a double date, just me and Maureen having a lemonade and a cake with Robert and Ted at the café.

"I'll go and brush my hair," I mumbled, and ran upstairs.

I quickly changed my shoes and nipped into Mum and Dad's room to use the mirror over their dressing table, as mine was too small to see all of me at once.

As I brushed, I could hear faint voices, which seemed to be coming up the chimney from the sitting room.

I didn't mean to listen, but when you hear your name spoken, it's hard not to.

"I hope Sylvie's not going to be hurt by this Robert boy," Mum said. "He hasn't exactly rushed round to see her since the party."

"I know his father," Dad replied. "He's a bit of a cold fish. He's an accountant; did some sort of audit up at the nursery. He didn't seem to want to lower himself to mix with us grubby sons of the soil; he only spoke to the bosses. Maybe he's brought the boy up to be a bit of a snob. Sylvie's got a good head on her shoulders, though, and she's only fifteen. It's nothing serious."

I brushed my hair slowly, looking at my red cheeks in the reflection, and remembering how Robert had commented on Ted's second-hand suit, and how he hadn't wanted to play any of the party games, or go to the picnic. Maybe he was just really shy. And if he was used to having a lot of money and new things, he was probably a bit embarrassed about being around people who couldn't afford them.

I took my hairbrush back to my room, picked up my bag and ran down the stairs.

"I'm off. See you later; I'll be back in time for tea."

My parents' replies were muffled by the closed front door.

~*~

I knocked for Maureen, who was in good spirits, and cheered me up with her chatter.

"Do you think Ted will bring Dennis?"

Dennis was Ted's best friend, who we had met at the Boys' Brigade picnic. He and Maureen had got on like a house on fire, much to Ted's amusement.

"You can't have five people on a double date," I told her, forgetting that I had not long ago told myself that it wasn't a double date. "And what does Ted think about you and Dennis being so pally?"

"Oh, he doesn't mind. Ted's nice; we're good friends and that, but he's not really my type. I don't follow half of what he says when he starts making all those dreadful puns. Dennis doesn't, either, but he says Ted's like the brother he never had. He's really kind, and good fun to have around."

~*~

Robert and Ted were already at the café when we arrived, and had taken a table.

Robert stood up and held my chair for me while I sat down, but Ted just grinned hello and handed out menus.

While we chose our cakes and drinks, Maureen rattled on, talking about the picnic, and managing to mention Dennis' name every few seconds.

"...and then when Dennis fell in the horse trough, I thought I'd die laughing!"

"Have you noticed, Sylvie," asked Ted, winking at me, "how many times since the picnic Maureen has mentioned Dennis?"

I laughed.

"Oh, yes, Ted, I believe you're right. I hadn't noticed!"

Robert didn't look amused.

"Have you noticed, SylviA, that since the picnic, all you've talked about is the picnic?"

I was taken aback.

"You could have gone. Everyone was invited."

The waitress arrived with our cakes and drinks, so we stopped talking for a minute and each swayed to one side as she put down the plates and glasses.

"If I'm invited somewhere, I don't expect to be told to take my own food." Robert said, huffily.

Maureen let out a snort of laughter.

"But it was a picnic, Bobby. That's what they're like. You take your own food. Haven't you ever been on a picnic?"

"Of course." Robert looked superior. "But we take the car, and have a fold-up table and chairs so we can eat properly with knives and forks. And besides. . . ." He stopped and looked uncertain.

"Besides what?" Maureen pushed him on.

"My parents are very particular about who I mix with, and, well . . . no offence to you or your family, Sylvia, I'm sure they're very nice people with good manners, but. . . ."

"What? Out with it." Maureen was getting angry.

"Well, the area you live in . . . my mum calls it the slum end of town. It's all council housing."

I could feel my face burning. I stood up and loomed over the table towards him.

He tried to bob up, like the little gentleman he pretended to be, but I pushed him down.

"No. You sit. You sit, and you listen to me. 'No offence'? You've just managed to offend me, my family, my best friend, and all my friends and neighbours. 'Slum end of town'? How dare you! You're so stuck up you don't know how to enjoy yourself. If you spend your whole life looking down at people, you'll end up with no friends, and then what? You think you can live on your precious manners and your money? Well. . . ." My voice was rising, and people at the other tables were starting to look round.

"Well . . ." I continued, shaking with anger, "you can take your money, and your shiny new suit, and your posh manners, and you can . . . you can . . ." I tried to think of the rudest thing I dared to say in public, "you can shove them where the monkey put his nuts!"

I turned to leave and Maureen got up to follow.

"Just leave me alone, please, Mo. I'll see you later."

I closed the café door behind me and started to run up the hill towards home, tears pouring down my face, then slowed as I realised that I wasn't ready to go home and explain what had happened.

I turned towards the park and wandered down to the duck pond. There were a few young children playing on the other side of the pond, but no-one else around, so I sat down under the big chestnut tree in the shade to have a good cry and a think.

Dad had been right. Robert was a snob, and a crashing bore, too. He wasn't shy, just arrogant. To call our lovely house a slum!

I felt humiliated. It had been so nice arriving at Jasmine's party with such a good-looking boy who had such lovely manners, but now I could see the truth; he hadn't wanted to mix with the people at the party because he thought we were all common. I half laughed and half sobbed when I remembered that, although Jasmine had a nice house and new things, her dad had made his money from scrap dealing. If Robert had known that, he wouldn't have set foot in the house.

I picked up a pebble and tossed it into the pond. The ducks scattered to the far side in alarm, running across the water comically.

I chose another pebble and threw harder; not aiming at the ducks, just wanting to throw something to vent my anger.

Pebble after pebble followed as I muttered all kinds of dire insults under my breath.

"Snob. Middle-class, stuck-up bore. Thinks himself too good for everyone 'round here. . . ."

A larger splash interrupted my musings and a voice spoke from behind me.

"That wasn't a very big rock, but it's probably a little bit bigger than Bob's brain."

Ted sat down beside me and handed me another large pebble. I hurled it into the water with some enjoyment and we sat in silence for a while.

"Are you all right, Sylvie?" Ted asked. "That was pretty bad of Bob to say those things to you in public, or at all, come to that."

"Yes, I'm all right." I turned to face him. Oddly, I didn't mind him seeing my blotchy, tear-streaked face. "I'm sorry I shouted at your friend, though."

He shrugged.

"We're not really close friends. He tolerates me because I'm the only one who'll put up with his nonsense, even though I'm common as muck." He grinned at me. "You have to have a pretty thick skin to be friends with Bob, but in a way I feel sorry for him; he pushes people away all the time."

"He's so tactless. Like that time you hit him for laughing at you when you fell in the pool. I felt really sorry for him then, but he probably deserved it."

"Fell in?" He laughed. "Dear Robert pushed me in! And he knows I can't swim. He was just showing off in front of you and Maureen."

I laughed, but inside I felt guilty for thinking that Ted was a troublemaker who had picked a fight over nothing.

"Did Maureen stay at the café after I left?" I asked, changing the subject.

"No, Dennis was passing on his bike just as you ran out, and he came in to see what was going on. Maureen told him, in detail, so loudly that she got herself thrown out; so she went off with Dennis to get an ice cream elsewhere. I gave Bob another piece of my mind about how he'd treated you, then I left, so he had to pay the bill."

"He's so much richer than us slum dwellers, so he can afford it." We laughed.

"I'm glad you can see the funny side, Sylvie." Ted patted my hand. "Just forget him, he'll find out the hard way that being a snob doesn't do him any good."

I glanced at his watch.

"Oh! Look at the time! I must get home for tea."

"I'll walk with you." He smiled, pulling me to my feet.

"Do I look . . . blotchy?" I asked him.

"No, you look fine, really. Come on."

We strolled through the park, talking about all kinds of things, anything except Robert, and carried on talking, standing at the gate.

Dad came whistling along the road and smiled at Ted as I opened the gate for him.

"Dad, this is Ted. He's the one who invited us to the picnic."

"Hello, Mr Ford. Nice to meet you."

Dad shook his hand.

"Oh, you're the musical lad. Sylvie told us about your virtuoso turn on the piano. Why don't you come in for tea with us?"

"Oh, I'd like to, Mr Ford, but I've got band practice in half an hour. Speaking of which, here comes our newest member of the percussion section."

We turned to follow where he was looking; Audrey and Brian were crossing the road towards us, still talking football results.

"Hello, Ted!" Brian greeted him.

"Are you coming to band practice, Brian?"

"Yes, I'm on my way there, now."

Audrey was nudging him, fidgeting from one foot to the other, desperate to say something.

"Ted? I thought Sylvie was going out with . . . mmmfff. . . ."

I didn't want to hear that name, so I clapped my hand over her mouth and dragged her towards the house.

"Excuse my sister, she talks nonsense when she's hungry. Come on Audrey, inside for tea. See you soon, Ted."

Ted grinned and strolled away, with Brian talking at him about football and drumming.

Over tea, I told the family what had happened.

"Good for you, Sylvie, for standing up for yourself," said Dad. "That Ted seems like a nice, sensible boy. You must invite him for tea sometime soon."

~*~

The next morning, Maureen and I had a good chat over the front garden wall and agreed that Robert was definitely out of our circle of friends.

Mum came to the door, sleeves rolled up, flour all over her apron, and a rolling pin in her hand.

"Sylvie, your dad's up at the allotments helping Bert. Can you run up and tell him dinner will be half an hour? You know what those two are like when they get nattering; they're worse than a pair of women. I'm not sure which is Bert's allotment, but just follow the pipe smoke."

I turned to open the gate, and froze. Swaggering up the road, accompanied by a younger boy who was listening admiringly to his talk, was Robert.

"Uh, oh, here comes trouble," muttered Maureen.

I backed slowly up the path towards the door, but Maureen grabbed my hand.

"Oh, no, you don't; you're not going to run away from him in your own street. Stand your ground and ignore him."

Robert saw us, hesitated for a split second, and carried on walking, his voice a little louder.

"Yes, this road is a total dump, isn't it? And that's where she lives. That's her; that's the haybag, standing at the gate."

I grabbed the gate to open it and fly out into the street, but Mum beat me to it. She flung the gate open and advanced on him, brandishing the rolling pin.

"And I, young man, am the 'haybag's' mother. I suggest you remove your superior self from this 'slum' before you catch something nasty, like a dose of good manners. And don't rush back."

He looked startled, stepped backwards, tripped and fell. His lip started to tremble and his eyes filled with tears.

I felt awful afterwards, but Maureen and I started laughing and couldn't stop.

"Haybag?" wheezed Maureen, "Is that the best you can do? Doesn't Mummy let you know any other bad words?"

Robert picked himself up off the road and ran for his life, leaving the three of us doubled up, with tears streaming down our faces.

Part Five
1950

Chapter Fifteen

All Work and No Play

"'Jack's garden is on a hill, with a gradient of one in ten. The bottom of the garden is six feet lower than the top. If Jack wants to put fence posts every six feet along one side of his garden, how many posts will he need?'" Audrey chewed her pencil and gazed into space.

"Sooo . . . a six foot drop at one in ten means the garden is sixty feet long in a straight line, but then use Pythagoras . . . six times six is thirty six, sixty times sixty is . . . nought times nought is nought, six times nought is nought, six times six is thirty six . . . add the two numbers and find the square root . . . ummm. . . ."

I stuffed my fingers in my ears and tried to concentrate on Feste's speech from Twelfth Night, but Audrey kept tapping her pencil on the kitchen table while she calculated out loud, and Mum and Dad were talking over the wireless in the front room.

"Aud, can't you go over to Brian's to do your maths homework, or at least think silently?"

"No; it's not homework, it's a practice paper. We're not allowed to work together; we have to do it by ourselves, then hand it in tomorrow for marking."

"Well, then, can you at least think in your head and not out loud? I'm trying to learn this speech and I can't concentrate. You won't be allowed to talk to yourself in the actual Eleven Plus exam, anyway; can you imagine a room full of a hundred children, all doing different maths problems out loud?"

"Can't you learn your speech upstairs?"

"No. I need to write notes, and I don't want to get ink all over the bedcovers. You work upstairs; you're still at juniors, you still write in pencil! This is really important, Aud, it's for my School Certificate. Whatever job I end up doing might depend on what marks I get in this exam."

"Mine is just as important! If I don't win a scholarship to the grammar school, I can't go; you know that. Just because you got in doesn't mean I will if I don't get good marks. They're not going to say, 'Oh, Audrey Ford, she's not that clever, but we'll let her in because her sister's such a blooming genius.'"

Her voice had risen enough for Dad to hear.

"Audrey!"

"I only said 'blooming'. It's not a proper swear word."

Dad walked into the kitchen and Audrey quietened down.

"Audrey, let your sister work in peace. She's right, you know, you won't be allowed to talk out loud during the real exam."

Audrey slammed her books together and stood up, stuffing her work in her satchel.

"Sylvie's right. She's always right; it doesn't matter about me getting into the grammar school because Sylvie's already done it. It's not that special, because Sylvie's already done it! Well, I'm going upstairs to practice my dancing. I've got a gold medal exam coming up, and that's special, because she hasn't already done it!"

She grabbed the gramophone from the sitting room and lugged it upstairs, and after a few minutes I could hear waltz music playing and steps overhead. Surely the steps were much heavier than usual for a light, floaty waltz?

I sighed and gathered up my work.

"I'm going round to Uncle Johnny's to try to learn this speech," I told my parents, as I put my coat on. "There's only one of him in his house, and, as far as I know, he doesn't think out loud all the time. I'll be back by nine."

I checked up and down the road, hoping not to see Gill's car. Much as I liked her, if she was visiting Uncle Johnny I couldn't very well go barging in asking for peace and quiet to study.

There were no cars in sigh except for Uncle Johnny's van, so I walked quickly up his front path. Just as I raised my hand to knock, the door opened, and there stood Uncle Johnny in his coat, keys in hand.

"Sylvie! Is everything all right?"

"Oh, yes, I was just coming round to ask if I could study at your house this evening. Audrey's having a temper tantrum over her maths homework for the Eleven Plus and her dancing exam, and Mum and Dad are listening to the wireless. I can't concentrate."

"Well, I'm just off to the pub, but you're welcome to come in and use the silence. I'll give you the spare key; if you finish before I get back, just lock the door behind you and pop the key through the letter box."

"Thanks, Uncle Johnny, you're a life saver."

It was weird being alone in someone else's house, and it took me a while to get used to the silence, but after a few minutes, the rhythm of the verses calmed me, and before I knew it, the clock was striking nine.

I cleared the table, checked that I had collected everything, scribbled a thank-you note for Uncle Johnny, and turned out the light, closing the door and posting the keys back through the letter box.

Back at home, all was quiet. Mum was washing up the supper things, and Dad was listening to the nine o'clock news. Audrey was nowhere in sight; I hoped she was already in bed and sleeping.

"Hello, dear, did you get everything done?" Mum asked as I hung my satchel on the back of the kitchen chair.

"Yes. Uncle Johnny went out to the pub just as I got there, so I had the place to myself. How's Audrey? Has she calmed down?"

"She wore herself out with her dancing practice and went to bed. Go easy on her, Sylvie. I know you sailed through the Eleven Plus; and for you, with the war and everything, there were other distractions, but for Audrey, this is her first big challenge. It's just as important as your exams."

I hugged her.

"I know; she's more wound up about things than she pretends. I just wish she wasn't so noisy! Was I that noisy at that age? I don't remember if I was."

Mum laughed.

"Don't forget you were an older sister with a tiny baby in the house. You had to be quiet. Maybe it's being born at the start of the war that made her so noisy; she had to compete with the bombs to be heard! She'll grow out of it, I hope. Now, off to bed with you."

I crept up the stairs as quietly as possible, avoiding the creaky bits, tried not to rustle too much while changing into my pyjamas, and slid into bed. Audrey's back was turned towards me, hunched under the covers, but I could tell from her breathing that she wasn't asleep.

"Aud? Are you all right?" I whispered.

"Shh. . . ," she mumbled. "Be quiet, you're disturbing me with your noise." She pulled the covers tighter around her shoulders and wriggled closer to the wall.

In my own bed, I turned my back to hers, pulled the covers over my head, and settled down to a sleepless night.

~*~

After tea the next evening, instead of stacking plates and running water, Mum and Dad put their coats on. Audrey and I looked at them in surprise.

"Right then, girls, you can do the washing up and putting away, then one of you can work in the kitchen and the other can use the card table in the front room. You can close the kitchen door, then you won't disturb each other. We're going out."

"Out?" I asked, feeling guilty. "You don't have to go out; we can work quietly."

"We're going to the pictures," said Mum, checking her handbag. "We haven't had a proper grown-up night out that wasn't a school function since Sylvie was born, and it's about time we started catching up. You're nearly sixteen, Sylvie, and quite old enough to be responsible for an evening or two a week. Uncle Johnny's only next door but one if you need him. We'll be back before eleven. Lock the door when you go to bed, but don't shoot the catch, or we'll be locked out all night! We'll see you in the morning."

They kissed us both and left, arm in arm.

Audrey looked at me, her mouth open.

"Well I never!" she gasped. "I never thought about parents going out to the pictures or anything like that, but I suppose they must have done before they had us."

"I wonder how they met?" I mused. "I've never asked them."

Audrey put down the pile of plates she was carrying to the sink and looked thoughtful.

"Of course they must have met at some point, but I'd never really thought about it. They've always been together since I've known them, so I can't imagine them not knowing each other, although I know there must have been a time when they didn't. Weird, isn't it!"

"Very," I agreed with her. "Now, let's get this washing up done and put away, then we can decide who's going to work where. Shall we toss for it?"

"Here's an idea," she said, waving the wet dishcloth in the air. "Whoever gets the kitchen has to make a pot of tea at seven o'clock, and whoever gets the sitting room has to answer the door to anyone who knocks. Agreed?"

I could tell that this meant she didn't want to have to answer the door.

"Agreed," I replied, flapping her on the bottom with the tea towel. "Milk, no sugar, please. And a Bourbon biscuit if there are any left."

~*~

I finished my Latin essay and closed my book with a sigh, wriggling my fingers to unstiffen them. Five to seven. I stood up to go and remind Audrey about the pot of tea. All was quiet in the kitchen, apart from a muffled snuffling noise; probably Scamp asleep in his basket by the stove.

I opened the door quietly, in case Audrey was in the middle of something.

Her head was down on the table, resting on her arms, and she was sobbing softly. Scamp had abandoned his cosy bed and was sitting beside her, his front paws resting on her knee as he tried to comfort her.

I pulled up another chair beside her and wrapped my arm around her shoulders.

"Aud! Whatever's the matter? Don't you feel well?"

She lifted her head, pushed her hair out of her eyes, and sniffed.

"I'm not ill, it's just. . . . everything!" she wailed.

"All right, just calm down a bit and tell me what's worrying you. Is it the exam?"

She nodded, fumbling in her sleeve for her hanky.

"The exam at school, and the dance exam, and Mummy and Daddy not being here. I know they've only gone out for the evening, but it feels odd. And us having a row, and Scamp's getting old, and we're getting old, and what if I fail everything? I'm not as clever as you."

She started sobbing again.

"Listen to me," I said gently, rocking her like Mum used to do when we were little and crying about something. "One thing at a time. You are just as clever as me, in a lot of different ways.

146

You're good at maths and science, you draw well, you can dance, you're good at games, and you have plenty of friends. You'll pass the Eleven Plus, and the dance exam, and if you don't, it's not the end of the world. Mum and Dad didn't pass any exams at school, and they've done all right."

"They didn't?" she sniffed.

"No, they didn't have that sort of exam when they were at school. And they're right, we are old enough to look after each other sometimes without them. They've worked hard to bring us up and they deserve some time to themselves."

I stroked Scamp's head.

"Scamp is getting to be an old boy, there's nothing we can do about that. He's nearly thirteen now, but he's still fit; he can still go for walks and chase a ball, just not so fast. We've all grown up together and only just noticed how big we've all become.

"Here's an idea: Let's forget about work and exams this Saturday, and do something fun, just you, me, and Scamp. Not Maureen, not Brian. . . ."

"Not Ted?" she asked, cheekily.

"No, not Ted," I replied, prodding her arm. "Just us. Then if Mum and Dad want to do something on their own, they can."

"What shall we do?" she clipped her hair back and blew her nose, looking happier already at the thought of a treat.

"We'll think of something. Now, what about that tea?"

~*~

Audrey was up and dressed for school much earlier than usual the next morning, just so she could make sure that Mum and Dad had come home safely.

Over breakfast, they told us about their evening out.

"It was so nice to be out on our own!" Dad winked at Audrey. "We met an old school friend of your mum's and her husband, and they've invited us out on Saturday for bingo and dinner, so you girls will have to amuse yourselves."

147

"We've already made plans," said Audrey, with such a grown-up air that we all laughed, even her.

"I've got my dance class first thing, but after that we've decided to have a mini holiday, as we've worked so hard lately. We've both got some pocket money saved, as we haven't been going out much, so after my class we're going to take Scamp out to the park for a nice playtime, then we're going to go to Woodfield shopping, and have our tea in the department store café; what's it called, Sylvie?"

"Allbright's," I replied, and continued, "Audrey needs some new pencils. She can't keep on working with those two-inch stubs she insists on keeping." My sister poked her tongue out at me. "And I'm going to treat myself to a new fountain pen. The one I had when I passed my Eleven Plus is worn out; the rubber bulb's leaking."

"And then we'll all have plenty to tell each other over breakfast on Sunday morning," Audrey finished.

"I think that's a really good idea, girls." Mum smiled at us. "Sometimes you need a break from everyday things, so you can sit back and appreciate what you've got. I think Daddy and I have been so wrapped up in bringing you two up that we've forgotten to stop and notice what sensible, clever, kind, funny young ladies you've become. We're very proud of both of you, and whether you pass or fail your exams, and whatever you decide to do with your lives, we're always here to help and advise you; but now you're older, you can start making some decisions for yourselves, and help each other without needing us all the time."

"It's funny," Audrey looked thoughtful. "Sometimes you have to do things apart from people, so that it makes it even better when you're together."

"Very true," said Dad, putting on his bicycle clips. "You're getting quite grown up, young Audrey, but not too big for a lift on my crossbar as far as school, hmm?"

Audrey grabbed her satchel, stuffed a last piece of toast in her mouth, and ran for the door.

"Bye! See you teatime!" she yelled.

I looked at Mum and shook my head.

"She's so loud," I said, in mock sorrow.

Chapter Sixteen

Happy the Bride the Sun Shines On

"Oh, you look lovely, Sylvie." Mum smiled as I slowly walked down the stairs, taking care not to trip on my skirt. "You've lost a bit of weight since that dress was fitted, though."

"It's just the worry about the exams and excitement of the wedding. I'll put it back on when we go on holiday — all that sea air, and fish and chips! Let me help you with that." I bent to help her fold up the Zed Bed I had slept on.

"No! Not in your dress! Dad can help me. You just make sure Audrey's ready on time and see if Grandma needs any help."

Audrey banged her way out of the bathroom, wrapped in her dressing gown, with curlers in her hair.

"Are you finished upstairs, Sylvie?"

"Yes, you go and get ready. Call me when you need me to comb your hair out."

"Did you get much sleep on that bed?" she asked, swinging on the newel post.

"It wasn't bad, actually, just a bit creaky."

"Hmm, probably more sleep than I did; Grandma snores worse than you!" She ran upstairs and slammed the door of the box room where she had spent the night.

Grandma had spent the night in our room, to save her having to travel to our house on the morning of the wedding. Now everyone was up and getting ready and Mum's careful plan was about to swing into action.

Gill was staying next door at Maureen's house, and as Audrey, Maureen, and I were all bridesmaids, Aud and I were to go next door and wait for the wedding car and Gill's dad, now known as Uncle Cyril, to arrive.

Mum and Mr and Mrs Fielding were going to walk down to the church with Grandma and meet the rest of the family and Gill's mum there, while Dad called for Uncle Johnny to make sure he didn't look out of the window when the car came for us. The car would then drive us around the block, to give Uncle Johnny and Dad time to walk to the church before we made our grand entrance.

Doors closed above us, and Audrey and Grandma made their way down the stairs, Grandma resplendent in lilac, and Audrey looking like a fairy in her lemon bridesmaid's dress, instead of the clomping great carthorse she usually sounded like coming down the stairs.

I frowned at her in pretend confusion.

"Who is this dainty girl, and what has happened to my sister?"

She pulled a face behind Grandma's back.

"I'm the daintiest thing that ever lived, or how would I have so many dancing medals?"

"True," I acknowledged, "but usually when you're around it sounds like a battle's going on."

"Now then, girls," Mum quickly brushed Audrey's curls and re-tied the bow on the back of her dress. "Off you go next door, gently, Audrey, and help Gill and Maureen. Let Mr and Mrs Fielding know we're ready, please. You both look lovely." She kissed us, and we trooped next door, feeling self-conscious, as curtains twitched all down the road. Everyone was waiting to see the bride.

Gill was sitting on a dining chair, with the train of her dress hooked over the back, while Maureen, with a mouthful of hairpins, attached a veil to her hairdo.

"There. Shake your head a bit. . . . Good; that'll stay on all day."

Gill stood up and turned to kiss Audrey and me. Audrey gasped. Maureen and I, along with Mrs Fielding, had made the dress, so we knew what it looked like, but even so, it looked far better on, with shoes, veil, and bouquet, than it had during fittings.

It was modelled on Princess Elizabeth's wedding dress, with a flared skirt, a wide waistband that curved up to a point in the middle, a v-necked bodice gathered under the bust, and long sleeves. There was a lot less material in it than in the Princess' dress, because of rationing, but it was new. Gill had borrowed her mum's veil, so that covered "old" and "borrowed", and Grandma had given her a tiny enamelled brooch in the shape of a bunch of forget-me-nots, so that was the "blue" part.

"You look beautiful, Gill." I told her. "The others are making their way to the church, and the car should be here in ten minutes. Are you nervous?"

"Not really," she replied. "It doesn't seem real yet; I'm not sure John will recognise me in this getup. I'm more worried that I'll start giggling when I see him, if he pulls one of his faces!"

"He'd better not, in church, or Grandma will tell him off!" Audrey shuddered slightly. She had first-hand experience of being told off in church by Grandma.

"Oh! Girls, I've got something for you." Gill rummaged in her handbag and pulled out three tiny boxes, handing one to each of us. Audrey had hers open before Maureen and I had even thanked Gill.

"Oh. . . . Look! Isn't that lovely!" In each of the boxes was a small silver heart pendant on a thin chain, and on the back of each heart was engraved our initials and the date.

"Thank you, Auntie Gill!" Audrey hugged the bride, and Maureen and I followed, a little more respectfully of her dress.

While we were fastening our necklaces around each other's necks there was a knock at the door.

Gill's hands flew up to her cheeks, which became very pink.

"Oh! This is it! Here we go, girls."

"In another hour, you'll be really my auntie!" cried Audrey, opening the door to Gill's dad.

He stood still, admiring his daughter, as we fell into line behind her. He coughed gruffly.

"You look beautiful, darling. Are you ready?" He offered his arm and Gill took it, smiling, with tears in her eyes.

Maureen hiccupped a sob.

"Mo, if you so much as sniff during the service, I will tread on your foot." I hissed to her, but the others heard, and the emotional moment was broken as we all laughed.

~*~

The car was huge! A big Bentley, with the top folded down, enough room for three in the back, and a little fold-down seat facing us for Audrey to sit on. Uncle Cyril sat in the front next to the driver.

All along the street, doors opened and people came out to watch, except for at Uncle Johnny's house, where Dad was carefully keeping the groom away from the windows, so he wouldn't see his bride too soon.

Maureen and I felt a bit embarrassed as we drove past all our neighbours in such grand style, but Gill looked serenely happy, and Audrey loved every minute; waving and smiling until I had to give her a subtle kick to tell her to stop showing off.

The driver parked behind the church, and stood by the side door, waiting for a signal from Gill's brother Roger that the groom was safely inside, then we slowly glided around the block again to the front of the church, and Uncle Cyril and the driver helped us all out of the car.

Roger met us at the church door with the youngest bridesmaid, Gill's three-year-old niece Vivian, then scuttled inside to tip the nod to the organist to start up The Wedding March.

Vivian was supposed to walk in front of Gill and Uncle Cyril, but panicked when the doors opened and she saw the huge crowd of people, heads turned to look at us, so Audrey took her hand and the two of them followed behind Maureen and me, as we carried Gill's short train.

The only head not turned to look at us was Uncle Johnny's. He stayed facing forward until Gill stood beside him, then as she handed me her bouquet, he turned and grinned at her.

Maureen and I shepherded Audrey and Vivian into the front pew on the bride's side of the church, which felt odd, as the rest of the family was on the groom's side. The vicar made a short speech about why we were gathered there, then invited us all to sit down. Among the rustle of best dresses and the creaking of new shoes, Maureen whispered to me.

"Sylv, look who's playing the organ."

I glanced up and to my left, towards the organ loft, and there, perched on a stool high above the congregation, was Ted. I knew he'd been practising the organ but had had no idea that he was going to play for the service. He winked at me, and I gave him the tiniest wave, my hand half-hidden behind Gill's bouquet.

Uncle Cyril's voice cracked slightly when he answered the question "Who giveth this woman. . . ." and I had to step hard on Maureen's toe.

When the time came for Uncle Johnny to repeat, "I, John Reuben, take thee, Gillian Anne. . . ." I saw Gill's shoulders start to shake, and when she had to make her own vows, the name "Reuben" came out as a squeak, followed by a snort. Reuben was my great-grandfather's name, but Uncle Johnny clearly hadn't told his wife-to-be what his middle name was.

Gill managed to get herself under control, but was on the edge of giggles throughout the rest of the ceremony, and when the vicar led them away into the vestry to sign the register, everyone in the church heard her say, "Reuben!" and give a peal of laughter.

The only person who managed to keep a straight face was Grandma, but when little Vivian turned around in her seat and asked, "Mummy, what is a Roobin?" even she cracked a smile.

While the bride and groom were doing the legal part, Ted played "Eternal Father, Strong to Save." Not exactly the most cheerful hymn, with the line about "those in peril on the sea", but appropriate for a naval family.

By the time the bride and groom emerged for the blessing, the hilarity had calmed down a bit, but they looked so happy and excited that the whole congregation applauded, accompanied by a disapproving sniff from Grandma.

There was no need for the car to take any of the wedding party to the reception, as it was in the church hall next door, so we all walked, in a gaggle of chattering people, covered in confetti. All my cousins were there, and as we hadn't seen each other since Christmas, there was a lot to catch up on before we sat down to the wedding breakfast.

Maureen, Audrey, and I were seated at the top table, with the bride and groom, Grandma, Mum and Dad, and Auntie Agnes and Uncle Cyril. Vivian was with her parents, on her mum's lap, as she was too little to sit in a proper chair.

Maureen and I were given a glass of champagne each with our meal, and a refill for the toasts afterwards, although Uncle Johnny whispered to us that we'd better not let his friend Fred see us, as Fred was a policeman. Maureen looked quite worried until I explained that he was just teasing, and Fred would have other things on his mind beside whether we were legally old enough to drink.

During Uncle Cyril's speech, I had to step on Maureen's foot again, but then when it was Dad's turn to speak, as the best man, and he raised a glass to "the beautiful bridesmaids" I felt my own eyes fill with tears. I blamed the champagne.

Uncle Johnny's speech contained at least three references to "my wife", and he sat down, flushed and smiling to huge applause, then, to everyone's surprise, Gill stood up.

"I know it's not traditional for the bride to speak," she said, smiling sympathetically at Grandma, "but, with the help of Brother Tom and my new nieces, Sylvie and Audrey, I have prepared a little surprise for my husband.

"I'm sure you're all wondering when we'll shut up and have our first dance, and you're probably also wondering what we'll dance to. Well, Roger, if you would kindly oblige. . . ."

Roger made his way between the tables to the side of the little stage behind the top table and took hold of the rope that operated the curtain, waiting for the signal from his sister. Audrey and I knew what was coming, and smiled at each other, but Uncle Johnny looked completely bemused.

"May I present," Gill continued, "The Flying Frigates!"

There was uproarious laughter in the hall from most of the adults, but I didn't think the name was that funny.

Roger pulled the curtain rope and the red velvet swung back to reveal a four-piece band, dressed in Navy blues, and with banners attached to their music stands that carried the letters "FF" in gold on blue. Audrey nodded at me and pointed to our handiwork. The band blasted into "All the Nice Girls Love a Sailor", and everyone cheered.

The men were old shipmates of Uncle Johnny's who Dad had managed to track down.

My Uncle's face was a picture as he took in the grins and nods of his friends, who seamlessly changed the tune to "I'll Be with You in Apple Blossom Time". Uncle Johnny kissed his bride, hugged her and whispered something in her ear, then led her out onto the floor in front of the tables to dance.

As the first dance ended, Gill swished her way back to our table and gently pulled Grandma to her feet, slowly leading her out and handing her to Uncle Johnny, as the band switched to "If You Were the Only Girl in The World" and mother and son slowly danced together. More than one pair of eyes was damp as Grandma made her way back to her seat, then the band whirled into "Lily of Laguna", and all the married couples quickstepped their way between the furniture.

The band took a bow as the men pushed the tables back against the wall and arranged chairs for those who wanted to sit out, then Uncle Johnny declared the dance floor open.

He danced with everyone — all the bridesmaids, including little Vivian, who balanced on his feet; his sisters, sisters-in-law, friends, and neighbours, while Gill glided around the room showing her wedding ring and being congratulated and kissed.

At nine o'clock, the car arrived to take the happy couple home to change, then to the station, to start their honeymoon.

Uncle Cyril and Gill danced a slow waltz to "Scarlet Ribbons", which made everyone cry, then we followed the bride and groom out to the car in the fading light to see them on their way. Dad and Roger had crept out at some point and tied old shoes and tin cans to the back of the car, which made everyone laugh again. Gill stood with her back to all of us, her bouquet held high over her head.

"Ready, girls?" she cried.

I caught Ted grinning at me and clasped my hands behind my back, pulling a face at him.

Gill hurled the bouquet high in the air and backwards, and several pairs of arms reached up. They hadn't counted on my little sister, however, who flung herself forward and grabbed the flowers on the way down. Holding her prize high, she turned and grinned at the assembled crowd, who laughed uproariously.

We waved the happy couple off and most people sauntered back in to carry on dancing.

I sat on the front wall of the hall, watching the car disappearing into the distance, my eyes blurred with tears, holding a freesia bloom that had fallen from the bouquet. I felt silly being sad, because it had been such a happy day, and wiped away my tears.

A waft of pipe smoke floated by, and Dad took a seat on the wall beside me.

"It's a bit of an anti-climax, once they've gone, isn't it?" He put an arm around my shoulders and hugged me. I nodded, not quite trusting my voice.

"Never mind, we can start looking forward to our holiday soon, once you and Audrey have got these exams out of the way, and then you, my chicky, will be a big grown up woman, free of school forever."

"I'll have to start looking for a job once the exams are over," I said, uncertainly.

"Have a rest first and enjoy your holiday. You and Audrey have worked so hard, you deserve a break. Speaking of Audrey, we'd better collect her and your mum, and get home. Agnes and Cyril are going to run Grandma to our house to collect her things, then drop her home, so you girls can have your room back tonight."

Audrey came running towards us, with her slightly battered bouquet.

"Wasn't it a lovely day?" Her eyes were sparkling; I had seen Uncle Johnny give her half a glass of champagne, but I wasn't about to tell tales on her.

"But when I get married, I won't go away until the dancing's finished!" She twirled back into the hall to fetch Mum, as Dad and I shook our heads, laughing.

Chapter Seventeen

Summer Holiday

Audrey's suitcase came bumping down the stairs behind her, like Winnie the Pooh behind Christopher Robin.

She looked anxiously at the hall table.

"No post yet?"

"No," I replied, checking my handbag for the fourth time. "Maybe the letters will come in the afternoon post. There's still an hour before the taxi arrives."

"How can I enjoy my holiday, not knowing whether I've got the scholarship or not?" Audrey wailed. "My whole future depends on this!"

Mum and I exchanged amused sidelong glances at my sister's histrionics, but inside I felt just as anxious about my School Certificate results.

"There must be so many exam results for the postmen to deliver today, they're probably just running a bit late. Like Sylvie said, we've got an hour yet."

~*~

Fifty minutes later, we assembled on the front path with our luggage, waiting to see who would turn up first: the postman or the taxi.

"I've got an idea," I said. "Dad, can I borrow the booking letter from the chalet site for a minute, please? I'll bring it straight back."

He handed me the letter and I slipped down our path and up to Maureen's door.

"Mo, can I ask a favour? I'll need to borrow a pencil and a bit of paper."

I handed the letter back to Dad.

"Problem solved. Maureen's going to keep an eye out for the postman, and once he's been, she'll let herself in and open any letters addressed to Audrey and me, and send us the results in a telegram to the chalet site. I've given her a few bob for the telegram."

"Good thinking, Sylvie," Mum approved. "Then, whatever the results, at least you'll know and be able to get on with enjoying your holiday."

"Not if I fail," Audrey moaned, gloomily.

What I hadn't told them was that Maureen was also waiting for a letter. She had applied for a job in the Co-Op Insurance office in Woodfield, and was waiting to hear whether she'd got the job. Although Dad had said he wanted me to enjoy my holiday, I felt guilty that I hadn't even started looking for a job.

The taxi arrived with the toot of a horn, and the driver helped us load our luggage, some in the boot, some on the roof. We were only going as far as the station by taxi, but it felt like a luxurious start to the holiday.

We were lucky with the train into London, and managed to find four seats together, with our luggage stuffed into the racks above and spread over our laps, but on the coast-bound train, we had less luck. The train was packed with families with luggage, and the best we could manage was two seats together for Mum and Audrey, with me diagonally opposite, and Dad standing. He could have found a seat in the next carriage, but didn't want to leave us to deal with the luggage at the other end. The train was cramped, but nearly everyone was going on holiday, so the atmosphere was friendly and cheerful, and before long we were pulling into our final station, where the light had that strange pearly look that it does at the seaside.

We disembarked with all our baggage and shuffled to the bus stop to catch the special bus for the chalet site.

We had just missed one, so we sat down on the wall nearby to gather ourselves and rest for a while, smelling the good sea air.

"Aud, do you remember when you were really little and Auntie Maude took the two of us to the seaside for the day?"

Mum laughed.

"And you came back with so many shells and pebbles in your pockets that you must have weighed twice as much as when you set out."

"Mummy, when was the last time you and Daddy went to the seaside?" Audrey asked.

"That was just after we got married," Mum replied, smiling sideways at Dad. "It was January, so not the best time to be at the seaside, but we had a lovely time." She smiled nostalgically.

"All aboard!" called the bus driver, as he pulled up to the stop. We clambered on and settled our bags for the short trip to the chalet site.

It was only after we had unloaded ourselves at the site office that I remembered about the results letters and the telegram.

"Dad, don't forget to ask if there's a telegram for me," I reminded him.

"Come in with me, and you can ask for yourself. They might not give it to me, anyway. I don't look much like a Sylvia!"

The lady behind the counter handed Dad the key to chalet number seventeen, and rattled off a list of instructions while he signed the book for all of us — rules about not having pets in the chalet, not smoking, or drinking alcohol, not leaving sand in the bath or on the carpets. . . .

Once she ran out of steam, I asked my question.

"Please, is there a telegram for me? My name's Sylvia Ford."

The lady turned to a bank of pigeonholes behind her and pulled a small envelope from the one marked seventeen. She checked the name and handed it to me.

161

For a moment, I just stared at it, then Dad broke the silence.

"Thank you. Come on Sylvie, let's collect the bags and get to the chalet, then you can open that and give us the news."

I realised that he didn't want the lady in the office knowing our business, and probably wanted to avoid either Audrey or me crying in public if it happened that we hadn't passed.

"Well?" cried Audrey, jumping up and down.

Dad handed her the key.

"You run ahead and find number seventeen. I'll carry your case. Once we're in the chalet, Sylvie will open the telegram."

She sped off without needing any further encouragement, and by the time the rest of us caught up with her she had the kettle on and had claimed the top bunk in the room we were to share. I didn't mind; she was quite a sound sleeper.

We sat nervously on the edges of the brown settees and I slid my thumb under the flap of the envelope. The piece of paper was so small and flimsy, it didn't seem possible that it could be so important.

I read the words quickly to myself, and sat for a few seconds in silence before reading them aloud.

"Aud scholarship. Sylvie matriculation exemption. Mo starts Mon."

Maureen was a woman of few words.

Audrey burst into tears of relief, and Mum rocked her in her arms in a way she hadn't done for years.

Mum's eyes met mine over Audrey's head, full of sympathy.

"Oh, I am sorry, Sylvie. You worked so hard."

"What do you mean?"

"Well, exemption means you didn't pass, doesn't it?"

"Oh! No, no, it doesn't. It means I passed. It means . . . it means that I passed with the highest marks possible." I gulped. "It means that, if I wanted to go to university — which I don't,"

I added quickly, knowing that my parents couldn't possibly afford for me to go, "I could go straight away, without having to go into the sixth form or do any more studying or exams."

Dad moved to sit beside me so he could read the telegram for himself.

"Would you believe it! Two girls of mine winning scholarships, and one clever enough to go to university at sixteen."

He looked across at Mum with misty eyes.

Audrey had calmed down a bit and lifted her head from Mum's shoulder. I handed the telegram over so they could read it.

"What does Maureen mean by "Mo starts Mon" at the end?" Audrey asked.

"She applied for a job with the Co-Op, in the insurance department, doing typing and filing. She starts work on Monday. She didn't tell anyone except her parents and me, in case she didn't get the job."

The thought nagged at my mind again, despite huge relief at my results, that I should be looking for work.

Dad broke into my thoughts.

"Come on then, girls, let's get unpacked and put our glad rags on. I'm taking you all out for dinner tonight. Fish and chips all 'round!"

~*~

It was well past Audrey's normal bedtime by the time we arrived back at the chalet, but we were on holiday, so no-one cared. I let Audrey get herself settled first, as she was so excited I knew that the only way to stop her talking was to walk out of the room and leave her alone to get undressed and in bed.

Dad was sitting on the doorstep smoking his pipe, so I sat beside him, looking up at the black sky, studded with stars, and listening to the soft crash of the waves.

"When we get home, I'll start looking for a job," I said, into the quietness.

"There's no rush, Sylvie. I know you want to contribute, and that's good of you, but we're doing all right. You've got the best School Certificate result possible, so don't rush to take any old job just to earn money. You have to work at something that interests you. I've no education, but I love what I do."

"You're right, Dad. I won't take just anything, but I will start looking." I stood up and kissed the top of his head. "Goodnight."

"Goodnight," he replied, puffing at his pipe. "And . . . Sylvie?"

"Yes, Dad?"

"I'm very proud of you, both of you, and always will be, whatever you choose to do in life."

I felt the back of my nose prickling and rushed inside to hug Mum and kiss her goodnight.

I lay in my bottom bunk, arms folded behind my head, and sighed happily. It seemed just at that moment as though the whole world was at my feet.

~*~

It's amazing how fast a week can go when you're feeling happy and enjoying having no responsibilities.

We shrimped, hunted in rock pools, rowed on the boating lake, went for late evening walks on the beach, built sandcastles, ate ice cream until it came out of our ears, and relaxed more than any of us had done since the start of the war.

Audrey and I put on several pounds each, Dad reckoned just from breathing the sea air, but I think the fish and chips and cakes had something to do with it.

All too soon it was time to leave, and the suitcases were packed again, not as neatly, the chalet checked for any stray forbidden grains of sand; a last long walk along the beach garnered a few more shells for Audrey's collection.

"This has been the best summer holiday ever!" Audrey sighed, as she slumped into her seat on the train.

"It's the only one you've ever had!" I laughed at her, but she was right; it had been such a wonderful, carefree, golden week, and I felt ready for anything, especially searching for a job.

~*~

Maureen waited until we'd been home all of ten minutes before she arrived on the doorstep, and there was a lot of hugging and congratulating to do.

"Have you two looked at your actual results letters?" she asked, pointing to the two envelopes on the sideboard.

We abandoned our suitcases in the middle of the floor and unfolded our letters. Audrey's stated that she had achieved top marks in maths, science and art, and mine that I had gained a Distinction in History, French and English, with Merits in all other subjects.

"And what about your job, Mo? Do you like it?"

"Oh, yes! It's much better than I thought working would be. I'm in a room with lots of other girls about my age or a bit older, and although we work really hard, we can chat a bit, too, and sometimes we have to take letters in to the boss' office to be signed, or to the post room to be sent out, so I'm not just sitting typing all day. And there's another thing. There's a job going that I think might suit you. I got talking to a woman called Cath Perry in the canteen; she's secretary to Mr Wilson, who's the head of the Dairy office, and he needs an administration assistant."

"What's one of those when it's at home?" Dad broke in.

"Cath said it means someone who's really organised and efficient, good with numbers, good at taking instructions and explaining things clearly, and someone who can solve problems and think on their feet. I told her, 'That sounds just like my friend Sylvie,' and she said to write a letter to Mr Wilson, telling him about your scholarship and School Cert., and about being in the Guides and being patrol leader. I can hand the letter in for you on Monday, if you like."

I felt breathless after listening to Maureen's gabbled explanation, and remembered what Dad had said about not rushing into anything.

"Let me think about it, Mo; I've only just got back from holiday."

She made her way towards the door.

"I'll let you all get on with your unpacking, but think about it, Sylv. It would be great for us to be working in the same place; just like being back at junior school, only we get paid!"

~*~

I talked to Mum and Dad about the job over the weekend, and we weighed up all the pros and cons, but in the end, it was Audrey who helped me make my mind up what to do. By Saturday evening, she had grown tired of listening to us talking around and around in circles, and spoke up in an exasperated tone.

"We don't really know what this job is about, do we? And maybe this Mr Wilson won't think that Sylvie is right for the job after all, but the only way she's going to find out is to apply for it. And I know I'm only eleven and I don't know anything about going to work, but surely if you're offered a job and you don't want it you're allowed to say, 'Thanks, but no thanks?' You don't have to take it."

We all looked at my little sister in admiration.

~*~

The next morning, I knocked at Maureen's door as soon as we came home from church. Her mum answered the door and congratulated me on my results.

"Thank you, Mrs Fielding," I replied. "Is Maureen in? I was wondering if I could borrow her typewriter; there's an important letter I need to write."

Part Six
1951

Chapter Eighteen

A Beginning and an End

Scamp looked up at me from his basket and wuffed softly. It was nice having his company early in the morning, while the rest of the household was sleeping.

I started work at eight o'clock, so I was usually out of the house by quarter past seven, and Scamp was always awake to give me a lick and a cuddle before I left, although recently he found it harder and harder to get out of his bed, and his muzzle and ears were almost completely grey.

I gave him a tickle around the ears, told him to be a good boy, and left the house quietly to walk to the bus stop.

~*~

I enjoyed mornings in the Dairy office; they were always busy and bustling. Some of the tanker drivers had already left on their delivery rounds, and had dropped their dockets in my tray before they set out, while others came in whistling and singing, always with a joke or a cheeky comment, to drop the previous day's dockets and pick up new ones.

My morning job was to sort the dockets by area and then by driver number, and place them, in the right order, into the right trays for the accounts office. Once the accountants had written the information they needed in their books, the dockets were given back to Mr Wilson, who would then tally up each driver's total for the day and call them out to me, so I could write them on a big blackboard at the end of the room. At the end of the week, each driver's weekly total was written up in his log book when he came to collect his wages.

~*~

Once Mr Wilson found out that I could speak French, he started calling out the numbers to me in that language, which was quite fun, then another day he decided to use his fingers to signal Roman numerals to me.

~*~

During my first week in the office, I had wondered about a strange rumbling noise that could sometimes be heard in the corridor beside the room where I worked. I asked Miss Perry, or Cath, as I called her when we were having our break, what the noise was.

"Oh, don't worry about that," she said airily. "Next door is the Co-Op Funeral Services office, the mortuary, and the chapel of rest. It's just some poor departed soul being wheeled to the chapel."

I must have looked quite horrified, as she went on, "It's nothing to be scared of, dear. It comes to us all, and, let's face it, you couldn't have quieter neighbours when you need to concentrate on your work!"

I wasn't yet quite comfortable with the idea of dead bodies passing by outside my office door and had so far managed to avoid meeting one of the trolleys when I nipped to the Ladies or went for my break.

~*~

That morning seemed busier than usual. One of the drivers was on sick leave, and the others were called into the office to take on different parts of his round, so there was quite a cacophony of talking, arguing and joking until they all left for their day's work. I knew that the next day's dockets would be muddled, as some of the drivers would forget to mark down that they were covering Sid's round.

Cath made us both a cup of tea once the hubbub had calmed down, and I settled to work on my piles of dockets. I was about a third of the way through when the door opened and Mr Wilson came in, looking very serious.

"Miss Ford, will you come through to my office, please?"

I shot a worried look at Cath and followed him out of the room. What had I done wrong? I'd only been there two weeks; surely, I wasn't going to be sacked so soon?

My boss opened his office door and showed me in. To my surprise, Mum was sitting across the desk from Mr Wilson's big leather chair.

She stood and came towards me as I walked in, seeing my worried face.

"It's all right, Sylvie, Dad and Audrey are fine, but. . . ." she looked at Mr Wilson, apologetically.

"Sit down, both of you, and I'll leave you to it. Would you like a cup of tea, Mrs Ford?"

"Yes, please," Mum replied gratefully, and he left to arrange the tea, closing the door softly behind him. I heard him murmuring to Cath, asking her to make two more cups and telling her something else that I didn't quite catch.

Mum held my hands and spoke gently.

"Sylvie, it's Grandma. She died very peacefully in her sleep last night. Auntie Mabel went to wake her this morning and take her breakfast in, and she was gone. Dad thinks it was a heart attack. She just went to sleep and didn't wake up again."

My eyes filled with tears, but it felt wrong to cry at work.

"Dad. . . ?" I asked.

"Dad's gone up there to help Auntie Mabel and wait for the doctor and the undertaker. I thought it would be best if you came home. I'm not going to take Audrey out of school; it's best that she finds out when she comes home, after everything's organised."

"If there's nothing I can do, maybe it's best that I stay here. I don't want to take advantage and take time off when I've only just started here."

Mum looked at me sympathetically.

"Sylvie, Grandma was with the Co-Op Insurance, which means her funeral will be arranged by the Co-Op."

I still didn't grasp what she meant.

"She'll be coming here, very soon, to the chapel of rest. I don't want you to be here when they bring her in."

I started to cry properly then; it suddenly seemed very real. Mum hugged me.

"It's nothing to be scared of, but it would be better for you not to see her coming in; the coffins the undertakers use aren't fancy ones. It's a bit . . . clinical."

I remembered that Mum had already lost both of her parents. She knew what she was talking about.

"If you want to see her to say goodbye, we can visit her in the chapel when the undertakers have done what they need to do."

I took a long shuddering breath.

"Yes, I think I'd like to do that."

"All right, then. Dad's probably already said his goodbyes, but I'll come with you later this afternoon. It's a very grown-up thing to do Sylvie, and I'm proud of you for wanting to. Now, here comes Mr Wilson with the tea. We'll drink it quickly and then go home. He's already agreed that you can take the rest of the day off."

I thanked Mr Wilson, for the tea and the compassionate leave, and we drank up as quickly as we could, Mum and my boss making small talk, then I collected my handbag and told Cath what had happened.

"Mr Wilson told me," she said, patting my hand. "I'm ever so sorry, dear. I'll look after things here, don't you worry."

Mum and I sat silently on the bus all the way home, each lost in our own thoughts.

~*~

It felt weird to be at home in the middle of the day when I was supposed to be at work. I couldn't settle to anything, not knowing when Dad would be back, and half-wanting Audrey, half-dreading her coming home and having to be told.

Scamp seemed to sense that something was wrong and ambled over to sit by my feet, with his chin resting on my knee, his brown eyes looking up at me.

Dad came home just before Audrey. He looked tired and strained, and sat down on the settee without taking his boots off, which he never did.

"I've been up to the register office and seen the undertaker. The funeral's going to be on Friday at eleven, up at High Trees church. Mabel's in a bit of a state, but Maggie's on her way home to help. They said we can visit the chapel of rest any time this afternoon, but I said my goodbyes this morning. I called in at Johnny's office and he said he'll take you and the girls if you want to go, Amy."

"Sylvie and I will go, but I think Audrey's a bit young, and she's only just started at her new school. I don't want her getting over-upset."

A key rattled at the door and Audrey burst in, ready to chatter about her day until she saw us all sitting so seriously and stopped in her tracks, wide eyed.

"What's happened?"

Dad drew her towards him and sat her on his knee, as though she were five years old again.

"Your Grandma died in her sleep last night, Chicky. She didn't know anything about it; she just went to sleep last night and didn't wake up again."

Audrey flung her arms around Dad and sobbed.

"Oh, Daddy! You haven't got a mummy anymore!"

I hadn't thought of it like that, and it set me off crying again.

Mum blew her nose and stood up.

"I'll go and change into my black skirt, so I'm ready when Johnny comes."

I was already in my new black office skirt and white blouse, so I didn't need to change.

"Mum and I are going with Uncle Johnny to see Grandma in the chapel of rest and say goodbye," I explained to Audrey. "Mum thinks it's best if you stay here."

"Yes, I'll stay and look after Daddy," she said, wiping her nose.

A knock at the door brought a strange-looking, serious Uncle Johnny, in a dark grey suit and black tie.

"Amy," Dad called up the stairs, "Johnny's here."

The three of us squashed onto the front seat of Uncle Johnny's van and drove back to the Co-Op offices. It was only half past four, and everyone was still at work. I hoped we wouldn't meet any of my colleagues as we pulled up, but Geoff, one of the tanker drivers, was just strolling across the yard.

"Hello, Ducks, skiving off?"

I gave him a half smile.

"No, my Grandma died last night. We're just coming to see her and say goodbye."

He whipped his hat off and looked awkward.

"Oh, I'm sorry to hear that. No offence meant, Ma'am, Sir."

"None taken," Uncle Johnny assured him, and Mum gave him a smile.

We didn't have to go down the corridor where they took the trolleys to get to the chapel of rest; there was another door around the corner, with a reception office and a kind lady at the desk.

"We're here to see my mother, Mrs Ford," Uncle Johnny told the lady. "This is my sister-in-law and my niece."

The lady smiled gently.

"My condolences to all of you. If you'd like to follow me, I'll take you to the chapel. Spend as long as you like there, and if you need anything, there's a bell push just beside the door."

She showed us to a small room with deep cream carpet and purple velvet curtains.

There was a little table with a Bible and a cross on it, set beside a tall vase of white lilies, and on the far side of the room were three chairs beside a narrow bed, which was spread with a purple coverlet. Under the coverlet, looking exactly like herself, was Grandma.

Mum gripped my hand tightly as we approached the bed, and I held my breath, trying not to blink, thinking that if I stayed still enough, I would see Grandma breathe, but she was impossibly still.

I let out my breath in a long sigh.

"All right?" asked Mum, squeezing my hand.

"Yes," I whispered. "It's not scary at all, is it? It's Grandma, but she's . . . sort of not there. She looks really peaceful, doesn't she?"

"She looks a lot more peaceful than some of the times I remember!" said Uncle Johnny, with a smile. "I can almost hear her now: 'What are you all crying for? Worse things happen at sea!' She always said that, even after I joined the Navy, which wasn't really helpful!"

I choked back a laugh, and Mum squeezed my hand.

"It's all right to laugh, Sylvie. Grandma wouldn't want us to go around all miserable and serious. If it wasn't for her, your dad and Uncle Johnny and all the aunts and uncles and cousins wouldn't be here. She had a good life, and she brought up a big, close family, who will miss her, but she would be proud of all of you."

We sat for a while longer, then Mum and I kissed Grandma, which felt a bit odd, as she was very cold, and left Uncle Johnny to say goodbye to his mother alone.

~*~

Ted met me from work the next evening. Although he was a year younger than me, he had also left school in July and was now an apprentice electrician, and on Tuesdays he studied at the college in Woodfield, just down the road from where I worked. Maureen's working hours were different from mine, so it was nice to have someone to travel home with once a week.

"How was it today?" he asked as we took our seats on the top deck of the bus.

"Weird, but all right; everyone was very kind. The worst part was lunchtime — I went out for a walk and every old lady looked like Grandma. They didn't really, but you know what I mean."

"I know," he replied. "I felt like that when my grandad died. Every time I saw an old man about the same age as him, I thought, 'Why are you alive and my grandad isn't?' It's not a nice feeling, but it's natural. It gets better — you don't forget them, but it gets easier to remember without feeling sad."

"I was quite scared of Grandma when I was really small," I told him, laughing to myself at memories of running down to the hen house to avoid a telling off.

I felt my eyes welling up and pulled out my hanky, just in case.

"She was very strict, even with the aunts and uncles after they were grown up, and some of them married with children of their own. She never let any of the uncles drink alcohol; they all had to sign the pledge as children, but they all used to slip out to the pub after dinner on Christmas Day. The aunts used to use me and Audrey and all our cousins as a diversion so she wouldn't hear them leave and come back."

Looking down at my lap, I realised that I had pleated my hanky neatly into a fan without thinking, and smoothed it out again over my knee.

"She was a good woman, though, and she brought all her children up to be sensible people. We're a close family."

I smiled, thinking how nice it would be to see all my cousins on Friday, sad as the reason for the get-together was.

"My grandma told me something good after my grandad died," Ted said. "She said that no-one is ever really gone, if there's someone who remembers them, even if that person never met them, and only has memories that other people have passed on to them."

He rang the bell for our stop, luckily, as I hadn't noticed that we were nearly home.

"I like that." I thought over what Ted had just said and nodded. "Yes, I'll tell Dad that. Or you can tell him yourself. Why don't you come in for tea?"

"Not now, Sylvie. This is a time for you and your family to be together, but you know where I am if you need me, just to talk or have a good cry."

He paused, leant forward, and kissed my cheek, then turned and walked quickly away.

Friday was one of those late September days that start cold and grey, but then brighten into low sunshine that highlights the colours of the turning leaves.

I was glad that Grandma had such a nice day for her final journey.

Dad travelled to Grandma's house with Uncle Johnny in the van, and Gill took Mum, Audrey, and me in her car.

The house seemed strange without Grandma's all-seeing presence, and a few times I caught myself looking around for her, as one of my cousins said or did something I knew she would disapprove of.

The atmosphere was calm, although quite a few of my aunts and cousins looked a bit wobbly around the mouth. Everyone moved slowly and talked quietly as the Three Ms, my three unmarried aunts, made tea and poured lemonade in the sunny kitchen.

Uncle Johnny stood for a moment with his hand resting on the back of Grandma's big wing chair, his head bowed, then turned and smiled at us all.

"This is how the house was when I was a kid: full of people. How we ever fitted seven of us kids and our parents in a three-bedroom cottage, I'll never know!"

"A lot of us older ones were in the forces or in service by the time you came along," Uncle Arthur reminded him. "You were the baby, so you had Mum and Dad all to yourself for a few years."

He patted his youngest brother on the shoulder and handed him a cup of tea.

There was a soft sound of tyres on the road outside and Dad pulled back the net curtains to look out.

"She's here." He turned to his suddenly solemn family.

"It's time to go."

Grandma's children filed through the door as the undertakers slowly lifted the coffin from the hearse. Dad and his brothers took a corner each, helped by the undertaker's assistants in the middle. The sisters followed behind, then the in-laws and grandchildren, as we walked the few hundred yards to the church.

Friends and neighbours lined the path from the gate to the church door and took off their hats and bowed their heads as we walked past.

The church was full of flowers, arranged by Grandma's friend on the church committee, and the vicar stood by the door to welcome us as we filed in.

The vicar started the service by talking about Grandma's years of devotion to the church and popularity in the village, then offered a prayer and led us in a hymn.

Dad rose to speak after the hymn, representing all Grandma's children, and telling stories, some amusing, some touching, of their childhood. Then he smiled directly at me and finished, "A wise person I know handed on a piece of knowledge to me the other day that she learned from a friend." He paused and looked around the church.

"She told me, 'No-one is really gone as long as there is someone who remembers them, even if that person never actually met them.' We all have our own memories of my mother, and as long as we keep them alive, and pass them on to our children and grandchildren, she will live on."

The final hymn was "Abide with Me", then we all slowly followed the coffin bearers out to the church yard, where Grandma was lowered to join my grandad, who died before I was born.

The grave was beside a beautiful butterfly bush, with long cone-shaped purple flowers nodding in the gentle breeze.

As we stood silently, listening to the vicar's deep voice reading the committal, the bush filled with butterflies, sipping at the late summer flowers.

On the words "In sure and certain hope of the resurrection to eternal life", Dad stepped forward and scattered a handful of soil onto the coffin and, at his movement, the butterflies took off in a cloud of fluttering colours.

Chapter Nineteen

The Festival of Britain

"The Skylon is suspended fifty feet from the ground, with its topmost point reaching three hundred feet into the sky," Brian read from his pull-out-and-keep guide, "the Dome of Discovery is ninety-three feet tall, with a diameter of three hundred and sixty-five feet. . . ."

"And it costs five shillings to get in!" Maureen interrupted.

"I'm going to spend my time and money in the Pleasure Gardens," she continued. "They've got tea rooms, restaurants, fountains, gardens to stroll in, and fairground rides. We'll have a nice lazy day, eh, Dennis?" Dennis grinned sheepishly. He didn't say a lot, and went along with whatever Maureen suggested.

"Mrs F and I want to see all the new kitchen gadgets," Mrs Fielding said, nodding at my mum. "Not that we can afford any, but it's interesting to see what's around, plus there are all the art exhibitions in the museums."

"I'd like to go in the Dome. I've got two pounds pocket money saved up, so I can pay for Brian, too." Audrey looked at Dad anxiously. We both knew better than to ask for anything that was expensive or unnecessary.

"I'd like to see this Dome, too," said Dad, pausing in filling his pipe as the train rattled and swayed over a set of points.

"What about you, Gerry?"

Mr Fielding nodded.

"Why don't we all split up into groups when we get there," Dad suggested, "then we can do our own thing, and meet up at the Pleasure Gardens this evening for a meal? We might as well push the boat out. It's not every day that something like this comes along."

"Actually, the last time was exactly one hundred years ago." Brian read from his guide. "Prince Albert had the idea for the Great Exhibition in 1861, but it says here that the Festival is more a celebration of Britain than a World's Fair, which the Exhibition was."

Uncle Johnny ruffled Brian's hair.

"Thank you, Professor." He grinned. "Now, back to the subject in hand. Who wants to do what?"

"Gerry and I will take the kids to the Dome," said Dad, waving his pipe at Brian and Audrey. "We can split up when we get in there, so you two can do what you like as long as you don't leave the Dome. Understood?"

The pair nodded and grinned at each other.

"You ladies want to look at all the domestic invention stuff, Maureen wants to spend the day in the Pleasure Gardens, what about the rest of you? Sylvie, are you and Ted going with Maureen and Dennis?"

"Yes, I'd like to see the gardens, and we both want to go on the rides. Apart from that carousel on the pier when we were on holiday, I've never been to a funfair."

"In that case, John and I will go with the older kids, you four to the Dome, and the other two Mrs Fs to the exhibits," said Gill, decisively. I could see why she made such a good Guide leader.

"Shall we meet in the Pleasure Gardens at six for some supper? Brian, have a look in that guide of yours and tell us somewhere to meet that's easy to find."

Brian ran his finger down the page.

"It says there are Foaming Fountains on a lake. That should be easy to find: You'll be able to hear the water."

"Good idea." Gill smiled approvingly.

The train started to slow, and we gathered our belongings. We had one more short train ride, then a walk along the South Bank. Maureen was already complaining about her feet, and we'd hardly walked anywhere, so I wasn't sure that she'd last the day. I'd told her not to wear her new winkle-picker shoes.

As we came nearer to the new Festival Hall, the crowds thickened.

"I'm glad we left it later in the year to come," Mum puffed, squeezing her way between groups of people. "It must have been really crowded when it opened in May. At least it's cooler now, and we've been lucky with the weather this weekend."

We stood and gazed at the new concert and exhibition hall that had been specially built for the Festival.

"It's not exactly an attractive building, is it?" said Ted, frowning.

"It's all about function and design these days." Dad laughed. "Doesn't matter what it looks like, as long as it's got some clever new feature and can fit twice as many people as an old building. It looks like a great big block of concrete to me, but I'm a Victorian, what do I know?"

We turned away to the hall and followed Audrey and Brian towards the Skylon.

We'd all seen pictures of it in the papers, but seeing it in real life was much more of a surprise than we expected. Even Brian was happy to forget his facts and figures and just look at it.

It looked like a giant cigar, pointed at both ends, and appeared to be floating over the Festival grounds, tethered by strong wires. The information board said that it was made of steel lattice, and the wires were, of course, holding it up.

Uncle Johnny pointed up at the pinnacle of the tower. "Apparently, some student or other climbed up there and tied his college scarf to the top, not long after it opened. I pity the poor council bloke who had to get up there and take the scarf down!"

We wandered around the Skylon, taking it in from all sides, then grouped together to make our plans for the rest of the day.

Dad handed Mum and Mrs Fielding a map of the tube and told them how to get to the exhibitions in South Kensington, then showed the Pleasure Gardens group where to go to catch the boat that would take us downriver to Battersea.

"It's now . . . eleven hundred hours; everyone synchronise watches," Uncle Johnny joked. "We'll see you by the lake at six."

~*~

It was pretty cold on the river, even though the day was warm for October, and I was glad that I'd worn my raincoat. Gill had also worn a coat, and the boys and Uncle Johnny had sweaters on under their jackets, but Maureen was in a cotton dress and cardigan, and started shivering as soon as the boat left the pier at Westminster. Dennis took off his jacket and draped it around her shoulders, then sat with his arms folded and teeth clenched the whole way, trying to pretend he wasn't cold.

~*~

The Pleasure Gardens were a riot of sound and colour; people laughing and talking, children running and playing, music from the fairground rides twisting and overlapping in the air as the rides spun and whirled and their riders squealed; from somewhere farther off, the sound of a brass band wafted down on the breeze.

"Let's find a café and get a hot drink," Maureen suggested, hugging herself to get warm.

"Look." Ted pointed to one side. "There's a little tea shop over there with tables in the sunshine overlooking the river. Let's sit there and have something hot, then we can get our bearings and decide what to do first."

Hands wrapped around steaming mugs of cocoa, we leaned back in our chairs and tipped our faces up to the warm October sun.

Ted had picked up a leaflet on the way into the gardens, and studied the printed map as he sipped his cocoa.

"Oh, look, a miniature railway! What about that, Sylvie?"

I leaned across to look at the map.

"That's a good place to start, then we can work our way around through the gardens, and go on some of the rides later. I don't fancy being spun around too much straight on top of a cup of cocoa."

Maureen looked at the map and winced.

"That's a long way to walk. I'd rather sit here for a bit in the sunshine then go on the rides. What do you think, Dennis?"

Dennis shrugged and grinned.

"Whatever you want to do is fine by me," he said, but I had seen his eyes light up when Ted mentioned the miniature railway.

"I'll tell you what," Gill spoke up. "Why don't you boys and Sylvie go and have a ride on the train, and Maureen and I will wait here for you and warm up?"

With a plan agreed, the four of us set off towards the miniature railway in the far corner of the grounds, while Gill dug in her handbag for some sticking plasters for Maureen's blisters.

~*~

The miniature railway was bigger than I'd expected it to be. There were five carriages, with seats for twelve in each, set in pairs of two facing each other, so we managed to find four seats together. The front, back, and middle carriages had a kind of canopy over them, while the other two were open. We chose an open one, and I felt guiltily glad that Maureen had stayed behind, knowing that she would have wanted to be in a covered carriage to keep her perm tidy.

The engine driver was a bit of a character; he was dressed in striped trousers, a white jacket, and a peaked cap, and had a big, twirly handlebar moustache.

He checked that everyone was in and comfortably seated, then blew the whistle and released the brake. The engine chuffed away, leaving the carriages behind! Everyone shouted and called, and the driver looked back, pretending to be confused, but he was overacting so badly that I knew it was all a gimmick. He reversed the engine up and coupled it to the carriages, and we were off.

The train rattled along the short track, passing by the backs of some of the other attractions, accompanied by squeals and laughter from the smaller children. Dennis leaned back and relaxed as though he was on his daily journey to work. I half expected him to pull out a newspaper and start reading it. Ted and Uncle Johnny leaned out of the carriage to watch the points change and see how many wheels each bogey had, and technical things like that, while I sat back and watched the reactions on the children's faces.

The train pulled into a platform at the other end of the line, where there was a little snack bar. You certainly wouldn't starve on your day out; there were food stalls at every turn.

We waited while the engine shunted back and turned around, then climbed on board for the journey back.

~*~

Uncle Johnny and Dennis left us at the Fountain Lake, which was where we were to meet up later, and headed back to collect Gill and Maureen.

Ted and I wandered slowly through the gardens, stopping at the Dance Pavilion, where a band was playing foxtrots and quicksteps, and embarrassed husbands were being dragged onto the floor for a quick twirl around.

"Shall we?" I asked Ted, grabbing his hand.

"I can't dance!"

"Oh, come on, just for a few minutes; it'll be fun!"

He was right. He really couldn't dance.

We shuffled awkwardly around the floor for a few bars, then gave up and wandered over to the grotto.

We strolled around the grotto in silence for a while, not really looking at anything. I didn't want to make a fuss about Ted's awful dancing, but I had to say something to break the atmosphere.

"You're such a good musician, how come you don't have any sense of rhythm at all?" I asked, incredulously.

He scuffed the floor with his toe and looked embarrassed.

"I don't know. I can hear the rhythm in the music; my feet just don't seem to want to follow."

He changed the subject.

"Shall we go and find something for lunch? Then how about a turn on the boating lake to let our food go down before we go on the rides?"

"Smashing idea!"

~*~

As we stood in the queue for the Chair-o-plane ride, a familiar voice cut through the noise from behind me.

"Sylvie! Sylvie!"

I looked around, and right at the back of the queue were Audrey and Brian, with Dennis and Maureen just in front of them. Audrey was waving frantically, and Brian had the biggest grin on his face that I'd even seen. He looked as though he was having the time of his life.

Dad and Mr Fielding stood beside the ticket booth, smoking their pipes and talking, and as we inched forward in the queue, Mum and Mrs Fielding appeared and joined them.

As the ride began to load, Ted and I let some of the other people go ahead of us, so we could be in the next plane to Maureen and Dennis.

"Two more seats for the Chair-o-plane, roll up!" called the ride attendant.

"Wait for us!"

Uncle Johnny and Gill ran towards us, hand in hand, and joined the queue, the attendant roping off the entrance to the ride behind them.

We swapped a few quick stories of our day as the queue moved forward, then had to separate as we stepped, two by two, into our miniature aeroplanes, and the attendant strapped us in.

The ride slowly started to move and, as it spun, the arms holding the planes lifted upwards and outwards, and we rose higher and higher, faster and faster.

Ted looked back over his shoulder and waved at the others, but I was too scared at first to do anything except hold on to the side of the seat.

The ground seemed a long way below us, and we were spinning so fast that I couldn't focus to see where my parents were down below. I started to relax as the speed levelled out, and managed a glance over my shoulder. Audrey and Brian both had their arms in the air; Audrey's hair was all over her face and she was screaming and laughing. Maureen was also screaming, holding on to Dennis' arm with her eyes closed tight. Uncle Johnny and Gill were waving at people on the ground.

"All right?" Ted asked, and I nodded. My face ached from smiling so much, it was such a wonderful feeling of freedom to be flying high above the ground.

All too soon, the ride slowed, and we glided down towards the ground, trying to tidy ourselves before we stepped out of the seats.

"Come on, everyone! Let's go on the Big Dipper!" Audrey cried as we gathered together with Mum and Dad and the Fieldings.

"Not for me!" Mrs Fielding said, quickly, and Maureen shook her head.

Dennis hesitated, always reluctant to do anything that Maureen didn't want to do, but I could see that he really wanted to go on the Big Dipper.

Mum looked at Dad with a question in her eyes.

"I'm too old for that sort of thing!" He laughed. "I'll stay here. Why don't you go on with Sylvie, then Dennis can ride with Ted?"

Uncle Johnny and Gill decided to come, too, so we joined another queue and managed to get ourselves seated all together in one carriage, Audrey and Brian at the front, with Mum and me bringing up the rear.

The carriage slowly cranked up the steep slope, which seemed to go on for ever.

Mum grabbed my hand and held it tight; I wasn't sure whether she thought I was scared, or whether she needed encouragement.

As the train of carriages reached the top of the slope, Mum gripped even tighter.

"Oh dear, Sylvie, I'm not sure that this was such a good ideeeeeeeeeeeeee. . . ." She screamed as the carriages plunged over the crest and flew down the other side.

We just about caught our breath as the momentum pushed us up another slope, then we were swooping down again.

In front of us, the two boys had their hands in the air, showing off, but the rest of us gripped the bars across our laps. Audrey was screaming and laughing, but Brian was suspiciously quiet.

The carriages looped around the track again, then just when I started to feel that I couldn't stand it anymore, we slowed and jolted to a stop, breathless and laughing.

I pulled Mum to her feet and we staggered out of the carriage and down the steps to congregate with the others.

"Where's Brian?" I asked Audrey.

"I think he had too much ginger beer and candy floss," she replied, looking anxiously towards the ticket booth.

A very pale Brian emerged from behind the booth, wiping his mouth on his hanky. We all watched in concerned silence as he walked towards us, looking slightly green.

He wadded up his soiled hanky, stuffed it in his jacket pocket and grinned at us.

"That was wizard! Let's go on it again after supper!"

Chapter Twenty

Future Plans

We perched on the seat at the bus stop opposite the town hall and waited for the Mayor to come out and throw the switch to officially start Advent.

Ted usually finished work at one o'clock on Saturdays, but this first day of December he stayed late, as his firm had been given the job of wiring up the Woodfield Christmas lights, and he had been personally entrusted with the fairy lights on the tree in the town centre.

"Have you spoken to Maureen recently?" he asked, as we waited, tapping our feet to keep them warm.

"No, now you mention it, I haven't. She hasn't eaten lunch in the canteen all week; she said she was too busy and was just eating a sandwich at her desk. I haven't seen her much at home, either. I wondered if she was avoiding me."

"I met Dennis after work yesterday," he told me, keeping a watchful eye on the town hall door. "You'll like this — apparently he and Maureen are unofficially engaged."

"What?!" I turned to him in surprise. "That's ridiculous. They're only sixteen."

"That's why it's unofficial," he explained. "They haven't told anyone except me, because they know their parents will say exactly the same, but they've decided they're going to get officially engaged on Maureen's eighteenth birthday."

"That's two years away," I scoffed. "Anything could happen before then. Why do they want to be grown up so quickly? I know I'm at work and everything, but I'm still technically a child, and most of the time I feel like one. Some of the girls at work tease me about still being in the Guides, but I don't want to grow up too soon."

I felt cross at the thought that my friend was moving away from me, with feelings and ideas that I wasn't ready for yet, and upset that she hadn't told me her secret, but realised that she was probably scared to tell me in case I let anything slip to her parents or mine by mistake. Plus, I had a nosy, blabbermouth sister.

Ted cleared his throat.

"I know they're too young and everything, but I was thinking: If we carry on seeing each other, then one day . . . I mean, not now or anything, but, well, we get on all right, don't we? We're good friends, we like the same things, our families like each other. . . ."

I looked at him in dismay. I liked him a lot, and if I was honest, I could quite happily imagine us being married, five or ten years on, but I wasn't ready to even think about it yet.

A spatter of applause across the road dragged my attention back to the present.

"Oh, look, here comes the Mayor."

Saved by the bell.

With the wind blowing from behind us, we couldn't really hear what the Mayor said. Something about "great pleasure", "meaning of Advent", and "merry Christmas", but we were cosy in our bus shelter and didn't want to step out into the cold.

The Mayor reached out a hand to the switch and I could sense Ted holding his breath.

Another mumble, and the lights came on. There were stars hanging from the street lights, lanterns outside the shops, and, with a sigh of relief from Ted, twinkling lights all over the Christmas tree in the square.

"Job done." Ted grinned. "Come on, let's get home. It's too cold to hang about."

We chatted on the bus about everything and anything, except Maureen and Dennis.

"Are you coming for Sunday dinner tomorrow?" I asked, pulling on my gloves as the bus stopped at the top of my road.

"Yes, please. Must dash — band practice tonight!" And off he ran.

~*~

I tried to put thoughts of Maureen and Dennis out of my mind as I opened the door. The house was warm, with a smell of something tasty coming from the kitchen.

Audrey was sitting by the fire with a pad on her lap, sketching something, with Scamp curled at her feet.

"Come through and pour yourself a cup of tea, Sylvie," Mum called from the kitchen. "Dad might be a bit late — he's still up at the aunts' — so I've made a bacon roly-poly; it'll just simmer till he gets back."

"What's happening at the aunts'?" I asked, searching for my favourite cup.

"Your dad and Uncle Arthur had to see the solicitor and sign some papers this morning to do with Grandma's house. She left it equally to the Three Ms, so Dad and Arthur had to sign and witness papers, as they're her executors. You know how your Uncle Arthur rambles; he's probably explaining all the legal jargon to the girls in detail, and all they want to know is that they've got somewhere to live!"

"What are we going to do about Christmas?" I asked, lifting the lid of the pan to peep at the roly-poly, wrapped in its cloth, bubbling away. "It won't be the same without Grandma."

"I thought we'd have Christmas dinner here this year. It'll be a bit of a squeeze, but we can fit everyone in if Gill lends us some dining chairs and crockery. There would be too many memories for your aunts to cope with, if they had everyone there so soon after losing Grandma."

"Good idea." I smiled at her, secretly pleased that we

wouldn't have to trudge up that long hill in the cold to Grandma's house this year.

"Uncle Johnny can pick the aunts up in Gill's car on Christmas morning while Gill helps us get the dinner ready."

I carried my tea through to the sitting room and sat beside Audrey. She turned her sketch pad to show me.

"What do you think?"

It was a sketch of a dance dress, pale green, with a sweetheart neckline, a bodice gathered under the bust, and an impossibly full skirt.

"It's lovely, Aud, but I don't know how we'd afford that much material. You definitely need a new dress for the Nationals, though, and we've only got three weeks, so we'd better go shopping next weekend."

Audrey and Brian had qualified for the National Ballroom Championship, which was to be held in London the weekend before Christmas, and Audrey's sudden growth spurt had turned her old dance dress into a ballerina length with three-quarter sleeves.

I weighed up some thoughts in my mind.

I had been saving from my wages, as Captain had decided to arrange a trip to the Guide Chalet in Switzerland in the spring, but with over three and a half months to go, maybe I could give Audrey that money for a dress and still save enough to go to Switzerland at the beginning of April. I decided not to say anything for a while and have a good think about it.

~*~

Scamp wuffed softly as he heard Dad's feet on the front path, and Mum filled the kettle to make fresh tea.

The cold air blew in with Dad, and Audrey shivered as he hugged her, the cold from his coat seeping into her.

"Did the lights come on first time, Sylvie?" he asked.

"Yes. It all looked lovely, but we didn't stay long, as it was so cold. How did you and Uncle Arthur get on? Is everything done now?"

We took our places at the table as Dad told us about his day and Mum sliced the roly-poly.

"Yes, all taken care of, although your Uncle Arthur makes things very long-winded. The girls own the house now, jointly between the three of them, so provided they don't drive each other mad that's them settled. And there's a surprise for you girls as well. Grandma had been saving her pennies for all her grandchildren, even before you were born, and she has left you fifty pounds each."

"Fifty pounds?" Audrey gasped.

I was silent in amazement. That was nearly a quarter of my yearly wages.

I could see Audrey's eyes shining at the thought of the beautiful dresses she could buy for fifty pounds, and I think Mum had the same thought.

"Here's an idea, girls: Why don't you take ten pounds of it each and spend it on something you need or want now, then save the rest of it?"

I nodded.

"Captain is arranging a trip to Switzerland, to the Guide chalet at Adelboden, at the beginning of April. I've been saving from my wages in hopes that I could go, but ten pounds would be more than enough to pay for it and give me some spending money, so I can use what I've already saved to get a passport. I'd also like to take an evening class in shorthand and typing; it would be useful at work now, and later on I might be able to get a better-paid job with more responsibility."

That sounds like a sensible plan, Sylvie," Dad commented. "You know, Mum and I could have helped you pay for the Switzerland trip; we want you girls to have some fun when you get the chance."

I reached across the table and squeezed his hand.

"What about you, Audrey? I suppose you're going to blow the lot on a sequin and diamond dance dress?" Dad nudged her.

She looked at him sideways with a little smile.

"Actually, I've got a big plan." She waited until she had all our attention.

"I'm going to use some of my ten pounds to buy material for a dress for the Nationals, and new dancing shoes, then I'm going to save everything that's left." We looked at her in surprise, waiting for what was coming next.

"When I leave school, I want to go to college and study dress design. I want to open my own shop one day, selling clothes I've designed myself."

We all gaped at her.

"I thought you were going to do something in maths or physics?" I asked.

"Well, in a way it is." She picked up her paper serviette and folded it.

"Look; this is just a triangle, isn't it?" She folded it again.

"Now it's a cone. If you cut the top off the cone it's the skirt for a dress. If I'm going to design dresses, I need to know how to make solid shapes from flat material. That's maths. And knowing how different types of material drape and fold is sort of physics." She flapped the serviette as though the dress was moving in a dance.

"Well, you two have really thought things through, haven't you!" Mum smiled at us.

"Since the war, things are different," she went on. "My generation either worked for a while and then got married, or went into service, like your aunts, but the war opened up so many real jobs to women that there's no rush for girls to get married and settle down these days."

I thought of Maureen and her unofficial engagement and felt glad that our parents approved of what Audrey and I wanted to do.

~*~

The following Saturday morning, Audrey and I were on the doorstep at Ashcroft's before Mrs Ashcroft had a chance to turn the sign to "open". Audrey was fizzing with excitement at the thought of buying material, finally off ration, for a brand-new dress that she'd designed herself.

She explained to the shopkeeper what she wanted, words tumbling out, and Mrs Ashcroft nodded patiently, waiting for a pause to give her suggestion.

"I've got a lovely eau de nil duchess satin, just in, that would suit you perfectly," she said, looking at Audrey's dark blonde hair and green-grey eyes.

"Your drawing looks lovely — I've got a pattern with a bodice very similar to that, but you'd need to add more material through the skirt, and maybe change the sleeves a bit." She led us across the shop to a rack of patterns and pulled one out.

"I can let you have this half price, as it's the last one and the packet's a bit shop soiled."

Audrey studied the drawing on the pattern envelope.

"Yes, I think we can alter that to make the dress I want, don't you, Sylvie?"

"Provided you do the maths, yes!"

"Now, let's have a look at that satin," Mrs Ashcroft grunted, heaving a bolt of fabric from under the counter.

The light green satin flowed across the worktop, and I could tell from just feeling it that it would be a dream to wear. Not so easy to sew, maybe, but we had three weeks of evenings and two weekends to finish it.

"It says we need three yards of fifty-inch wide material, no nap, but I want to add some godets into the skirt, so . . . may I borrow a pencil and paper, please, Mrs Ashcroft?"

She scribbled some figures and muttered to herself.

"I think another yard will give me enough fullness. I can get three godets with twenty-five-inch hems across the width, and the fourth one can have a seam down the back. Four yards, please!"

"It's quite expensive, girls. It's four shillings and sixpence a yard." Mrs Ashcroft looked worried.

"That's all right," Audrey assured her. "My Grandma has left me some money, so I can afford to splash out a bit, and it's for a special dancing competition — I'm in the national final for my age group."

"Well, congratulations! I hope you win. Now, let's see about some lining. . . ."

~*~

Audrey unfolded the paper pattern carefully on the kitchen table and studied the shapes.

"I think if we re-shape the neck like this. . . ." she drew a curve on the paper, "then make the sleeve wider here and add a band, and then I'll make the pattern for the godets out of newspaper."

Mum watched as she taped sheets of paper together and cut confidently, then disappeared upstairs and came back holding an old sheet.

"Here, you can make up the bodice in this to make sure it fits before you cut into the material."

Audrey looked up from her cutting.

"That's called a toile," she said knowledgeably. "It's French; I read about it in a book about dressmaking in the school library."

By Sunday afternoon the cotton bodice was stitched and fitted, and Audrey had adapted the pattern from the alterations we made to the toile.

Mum cleared the table and helped me lay out the satin. We folded it carefully, right sides together, and placed and pinned the pattern pieces. I checked and double-checked that all the pieces we needed fitted onto the material, then took a deep breath and started to cut.

~*~

The dress was finished with a whole week to spare.

Audrey had the idea of adding tiny weights, taken from the hem of a net curtain, into the hem, so it would drape and flow beautifully.

As soon as the last thread was cut, she snatched the dress out of my hands and ran to try it on.

It took her so long to come back downstairs that, in the end, I went to find her. She was standing by the long mirror in Mum and Dad's room with tears in her eyes.

"Audrey! What's the matter? Don't you like it?"

She whirled around and hugged me.

"I love it! I just can't believe that I designed this myself. I know we used a pattern and everything, but it all worked: the neckline shape, the extra fullness in the skirt, the wider sleeves. . . ."

She twirled and watched the skirt billow out.

"The judges won't be able to keep their eyes off you." I smiled at her. "Come on, come down and show Mum and Dad."

~*~

The dance hall foyer was full of people milling about, unsure where they should go. The National Championships covered all age groups, so there were children of nine or ten in miniature tail suits and ballgowns, right up to an elegant elderly couple, who were quietly practising steps that they must have danced together for sixty years or more.

Ted found an usher and asked where Audrey and Brian needed to go.

"Through this door here, follow the corridor round to the right, then the second door on the left is the room for the thirteen-to-seventeen-years age group."

We weren't allowed to go with them, so we gave our tickets to the ushers at the big gilded doors to the main hall and were shown to our seats in the second row. The front row was reserved for the six judges, who had a long table in front of them, with a lamp set up between each pair of chairs.

The hall slowly filled up, and the chatter subsided as the judges filed into their seats.

A tall man, who was apparently a famous ballroom dancer and former national champion, introduced the judges in turn, to polite applause, then called to the floor the first couple in the twelve-and-under category.

The lights dimmed, leaving just small pools of light over the judges' table, then the first pair of dancers walked onto the dance floor, followed by a spotlight.

Each couple was to perform a waltz and one other dance of their choice, then there would be an elimination round for each age group, where all six couples would dance at once, and if the judges decided they were out of the dance, their number would be called to tell them to step off the floor. In each age group, there were medals available for first, second, and third.

The elimination round for the twelve-and-under category was quite comical, as there was a big difference in height between some of the couples. A tall, gangly girl and her short, stocky partner placed third, a tiny pair of nine-year-olds came a shy second, and the gold medal went to a very professional-looking couple who smiled broadly while dancing, but looked as though they couldn't stand the sight of each other once off the dance floor.

Audrey and Brian were third to dance in their age group, after a dumpy couple who bounced around the floor like a pair of rubber balls, and a pair who danced beautifully until the boy caught his heel in the girl's dress and dragged them both tumbling to the floor.

Audrey and Brian's waltz was smooth and flowing, and their quickstep to "Let's Face the Music and Dance" was light and lively.

Mum, Dad, Ted, and I looked at each other and nodded. It was looking good for our two.

The next couple danced very correctly, but with absolutely no expression or emotion, followed by a duo who threw themselves into the rhythm, but whose footwork was less than accurate.

The final pair took to the floor and bowed. I swayed towards Mum and whispered, "This is the couple that Audrey said won last year. It's their last year in the under-eighteens class, so they want to win again."

The music started and the dancers began their performance. Audrey and Brian hadn't put a foot wrong in their dances, but this couple had something special that I could only put down to experience. They flowed seamlessly, each knowing exactly what the other person was going to do.

Ted glanced at me anxiously and I shrugged. Audrey and Brian were the youngest in the category, and in fact had only just scraped in, as Brian was still a week away from being thirteen. They would have plenty of time to try again, but I knew how ambitious Audrey was with her dancing.

The champions ended their second routine, and the compere called all the other couples back onto the floor for the elimination round.

The pair who had fallen had lost their confidence and were the first to go out. The enthusiastic partnership went next, after a few stumbles, followed by the bouncy couple. Three couples left — our pair, the impeccably correct duo, and the champions.

The judges watched carefully, and the dance seemed to go on forever. The precise but dull couple were eliminated, leaving the oldest and youngest pairs in the group dancing against each other.

The judges conferred again, heads together, then held up a number. Audrey and Brian were out.

The winning couple swirled into their bows as the music ended, and all the competitors were allowed to join their families in the audience to watch the senior class and wait for the medal ceremony at the end of the competition.

I expected Audrey to be disappointed, but she was so excited she could hardly sit still.

"Silver medal in our first ever national competition!" She gripped my hands and bounced in her seat.

"What about you, Brian, are you pleased?" Ted asked him.

"Yes, we did well," he looked at his watch, "but I hope they hurry up with the last group and the medals, or I'll miss the football results."

The competition had over-run for time slightly, because the judges took so long to decide on a winner of the adult class, but in the end, it was the elderly couple who joined the other gold medallists on the top step of the little podium, with the silver and bronze medallists, including Audrey and Brian, ranked either side of them.

The compere quietened the audience with downward motions of his hands and made one final announcement.

"There is one more award to present. All you ladies look so glamourous and elegant in your beautiful dresses, and we have a very special guest here today to award this trophy to the best-dressed lady. Please welcome Miss Marguerite Hepworth."

I saw Audrey clasp her hands together to try to control her excitement. Miss Hepworth was one of the best-known dress designers in London, and was rumoured to have designed clothes for Princess Margaret.

Audrey had told me that she had been asked to write a description of her dress, but we had assumed it was just so the compere could describe it properly when he commentated on the dances.

Marguerite Hepworth took centre stage and the compere handed her the trophy.

"I must congratulate all of you ladies on your beautiful dresses, but to me, there is one that stands out, for simplicity of line, elegance of cut, and clever design that enhanced her movements as she danced. I am told that it was designed by the thirteen-year-old dancer herself and made up by her elder sister."

Audrey's face was pink in anticipation; were any of the other dancers thirteen-year-olds with elder sisters?

"The award goes to . . . Audrey Ford."

Mum, Dad, Ted and I leapt from our seats and clapped until our hands stung, as Audrey stepped down from the podium, swept a beautiful curtsey, and accepted the trophy.

~*~

Dad carried the dress carefully in its full-length bag as we strolled back to the station. Audrey was now bundled up in her coat, with her hair stuffed under a woolly hat, looking nothing like the elegant young lady who had come away with a medal and a trophy.

The medal was around her neck, hidden under her coat, but she clutched the trophy in her gloved hand and kept lifting it to look at it.

"You know, winning a silver medal at dancing is lovely, but this trophy is more important. This is the first award I've won as a designer, and it means that I've chosen the right career, don't you think?"

"The first of many," I corrected her, hugging her proudly.

Part Seven
1952

Chapter Twenty-One

The New Elizabethans

"Good morning, Co-Op Dairy . . . Oh, hello, Steve, what's up? Wireless? No, why? What? When? Oh, no, and that poor girl so far away in Africa. . . ."

I put down my pen and openly earwigged Cath's conversation. Her boyfriend usually rang her up during her lunch break, and it was only quarter past eleven. It sounded serious. The phone in Mr Wilson's office rang and made me jump guiltily, so I put my head down and pretended to be working, ears flapping.

I could hear muttered conversation from Mr Wilson's office, then his door opened quietly.

Cath ended her call and put the phone down, looking at our boss with a weird expression.

"Girls, I. . . ." He cleared his throat. "Girls, I'm sorry to have to tell you that His Majesty the King died in his sleep last night. Head Office just rang up to tell me, and to instruct me to close the office for the rest of the day as a mark of respect. You may go home. God save the Queen."

Cath and I rose uncertainly to our feet and murmured, "God save the Queen."

I felt a lump in my throat and tears prickling at the back of my nose, and a strange sense of fear. Our King was gone, and our new Queen was so young: only twenty-five, just seven years older than me. Not only had she just lost her father, when she was thousands of miles away from home, but now she had to take charge of the country.

Cath and I tidied our desks, gathered our coats and bags, and switched off the lights. Cath was weeping softly into a hanky, but I felt too stunned to cry.

Out in the street, the news had started to spread. People were standing in small, hushed groups, talking quietly or just standing in silence. The morning fog had started to lift, and the weak February sun was trying to break through. The wireless hire shop across the road was crowded to the door as people listened to the slow and sombre music that had replaced the day's scheduled programmes, waiting for any more announcements.

I said goodbye to Cath and walked to the bus stop, the heels of my shoes sounding loud in the muffled street. The flag over the town hall slowly lowered to half-mast as I watched, and the town hall staff stood in silence outside, heads bowed, then quietly walked away.

"I thought I might find you here. Want a lift?"

I hadn't noticed the van pull up at the bus stop, but I was glad to see Uncle Johnny, and not to have to catch a bus home with everyone in such a strange, quiet mood.

I slid into the passenger seat of the van and tucked my bag down by my feet.

"We heard the announcement on the wireless at work and my boss closed up straight away." Uncle Johnny spoke over his shoulder as he pulled away from the bus stop. "I thought you'd probably be sent home, too, and might struggle to get on a bus, with everyone shutting up shop."

"Thanks, Uncle Johnny. I'm glad you came past; I was feeling a bit lost and upset, and just wanting to get home. Poor Princess Elizabeth. Her Majesty, I mean."

"It's going to be strange singing 'Queen' instead of 'King'. When your dad was born, Queen Victoria was still alive, but he was only two and a bit when she died, so none of us remember what it's like to have a queen who actually reigns, not a queen consort."

Mum, Dad, and Audrey were all at home by the time we arrived, and Gill was with them, not wanting to wait on her own for Uncle Johnny to come home. They stayed for a while, talking about the sad news, then left to go to visit Gill's parents.

"Sylvie, I'll pop 'round later to let you know if Guides is still on for this evening. Ma might want to hold a short meeting out of respect, and I expect we'll parade at church on Sunday."

Mum had already found a strip of leftover blackout material and was attaching pieces of elastic to make black armbands for us all.

"Our new Queen is the same age as Auntie Gill," Audrey commented. "Brian said she'll leave everything up to the Prime Minister, because girls can't run a country, but I think he's wrong. Auntie Gill would make a good queen; she's good at making decisions and telling people what to do, and if I was a queen I wouldn't let a lot of old men tell me how to run my country."

"I feel sorry for the old Queen — Queen Mary, I mean," said Mum. "She's already lost her husband and two of her sons, another son's estranged from her, and now this. I suppose the Duke of Windsor will come home for the funeral, but let's hope he leaves that woman behind. It all worked out for the best, really. We got the best king we could have had, and now a new young Queen who's been brought up to do her duty, but if he hadn't been forced to be King that poor man might have lived longer."

I glanced across at Dad. He was only three years younger than the King, and suddenly I saw him as just a man in his fifties, no longer young, and mortal. I had always seen him as my dad, who knew everything and could mend anything that broke, and would always be there, but now, thinking of that other family of mother, father, and two daughters, I realised that he wouldn't always be there, and one day I would have to take on responsibilities — maybe not as important as those the young Queen was about to shoulder — but adulthood suddenly seemed one step closer.

~*~

We gathered in the church hall in silence, some adjusting unfamiliar black armbands over uniform shirts, others looking sheepish because they hadn't found time to make one. Mum and I had made a few extra bands, which I handed out.

Captain strode in and we all came to attention and saluted.

"Good evening, Guides. This will just be a short meeting, but I felt that we should come together to show our respects to his late Majesty, and, as we will be parading at church on Sunday, to practice flag drill. This will be an important service, and I don't want any mistakes."

She looked sternly at me, and I blushed, remembering how I had clanged the company flag against the hanging light as we entered the church at the last church parade.

Lieutenant brought the flags from their place against the wall, and handed the company flag to me and the Union flag to Jasmine, tucking the ends of the staffs into the holsters of our flag belts, as we formed up in our patrols.

"We will slow march into the Horseshoe this evening," Captain announced, "as the organist will be playing a slow voluntary before the service on Sunday. By the left, slow march."

Our feet sounding loud on the wooden boards, Jasmine and I led off; she, on the right-hand side of the room, marched two steps forward, then about-turned to the right, and I mirrored her on the other side, the rest of the company dividing in two to follow us.

We slowly competed a full circle, the two halves of the parade overlapping and crossing, and continued until Jasmine and I were back in our starting positions, with the rest of the company forming into a horseshoe shape behind us.

Jasmine looked at me, counting, as the feet behind us marched on the spot, then she nodded, we raised our flags a few inches, and, with three more crashing steps, the parade came to a halt.

Captain and Lieutenant stepped forward and saluted. Jasmine and I returned the salute, and, without looking down at our hands, passed the flags to them, trying not to fumble. We saluted again, then the company turned to face inwards towards the centre of the horseshoe.

"Well done, Guides," Captain praised us, as she set the flag to one side. "We will now hold a minute's silence in memory of the late King."

She blew her whistle and we clasped our hands and bowed our heads. Someone sniffed, overcome with the emotion of the day, but otherwise there was complete silence.

Captain blew her whistle again, and we raised our heads.

"We will now sing the full National Anthem, followed by Taps."

A few people sang "King" by mistake, but by the third verse everyone had got the hang of it.

The words of Taps; "all is well, safely rest. . . ." made me think of the young Queen, making her way home by aeroplane, to take her throne, and I hoped she was resting.

Chapter Twenty-Two

Edelweiss for Elizabeth

"So how do you say, 'good morning' in Swiss?" Maureen asked.

"There's no such language as Swiss," I replied, checking that my rucksack was still in the overhead rack, as I had already done six times since the train left London.

"They speak French or German in Switzerland." I told her. Maggie sniffed.

"Well, they needn't think I'm speaking to them in German after what they did to us during the war."

I could see Gill looking cross, and I was about to speak, when Maureen piped up.

"Don't be daft, Mags. The Swiss were neutral; they didn't do anything to us. And Hitler wasn't even German, he was Austrian, so don't go on about Germans. The Swiss can't help what language they speak. It's like someone from Scotland having a Scottish accent — they can't help that, either," she finished, somewhat illogically, but forcefully.

Maureen, Jasmine, Maggie, June, and I were sharing a six-berth sleeper compartment with Gill once we arrived on the other side of the Channel, so we had taken a compartment on the London train together, while Captain was in the next compartment with the others who would share her sleeper down through France. Jasmine wasn't technically in the Guides anymore, as she had decided not to move up to Rangers, but she had already booked the trip, so she was with us in her slightly outgrown Guide uniform.

It was just starting to get dark when Captain opened the door to our compartment. We weren't sure whether we should stand up and salute or not, so there was a bit of bobbing up and down before Captain opened her mouth to tell us what she had come to say.

"Guides, we will soon be arriving at the ferry port. You will need to have your passports ready, and you may be asked how much money you are carrying. Please remember that the travel restriction is ten pounds per person." Maureen glanced at me and winked. I knew she didn't have anywhere near the full allowance, but, thanks to Grandma, I did, although I wasn't about to mention it.

"You are not only representing your Company, but the whole Guiding institution. You are in uniform, so how you behave will reflect on Girl Guides worldwide. I trust you to be on your best behaviour whilst travelling, and when we reach the chalet in Adelboden." She paused.

"I also have some important news," she continued. "Just before we left, I received a letter from our Chief Guide, Lady Baden Powell. She has asked every Guide Company in the country to put together four to six pages towards making a book, which will be presented to Her Majesty the Queen on her coronation, reflecting the lives and thoughts of Girl Guides across Britain. I would like you all to contribute something, be it a poem, drawing, or piece of observational or reflective writing, so get your thinking caps on.

"Now, please gather up your luggage ready to go through customs. Lieutenant, please check the compartment before you leave to make sure nothing is left behind."

We passed quickly through the customs point and boarded the ferry. It was now almost completely dark, and only the red and green lights on the buoys out at sea could be seen.

None of the other Guides had been on a ferry before, and this one was much bigger than the small boat I had taken on my trip to the Isle of Wight. We stood on deck for a while, but the evening air was cold, as it was only just April, so we soon headed down the stairs, which Captain said were called the companionway, to find something to eat.

There was a buffet restaurant selling soup and sandwiches cheaply, so Maureen, Jasmine, and I chose a table and took turns to go to the counter for food.

As we left Dover, the sea was quite smooth, but the further we steamed into the Channel, the rougher it became. Maureen gave up on her egg sandwich halfway through, and by the time she had finished her soup she looked quite pale, but Jasmine and I tucked into our cheese and tomato rolls and celery soup with gusto, washing it all down with coffee.

We wrapped up warmly and went back up on deck after supper to see France appear, leaving Maureen curled up in an armchair in the passenger lounge.

The lights of Calais slowly became larger and larger, and soon an announcement was made for all passengers to re-join their groups and prepare to disembark. We were in France!

Even the air smelled different. Jasmine said it was a mixture of coffee, garlic, and those funny little brown cigarettes that everyone seemed to smoke.

We queued to go through customs again, and Maggie's face was a picture when the official spoke to her in French and she couldn't reply. I translated his question to her and her reply to him, and we were allowed to pass.

Maureen sailed through, smiling and saying, "Bonne nuit!" to everyone. Little did they know when they grinned back at her that she had just used up a third of her French.

~*~

The station was busy and bustling, even at ten o'clock at night. We were all starting to flag a little, even Captain, and once again I put my French to use, asking which way we should go for our train.

The compartments were small, but ingeniously fitted out. There was a long seat on each side, with a high, firm back, and then, above it, what looked like the back of another seat attached to the wall. We settled our bags and tried to peer into the darkness at France, then there was a hurried announcement, which I couldn't entirely catch, and the train jolted forwards.

An attendant rapped at our door, and eventually made us understand that he was there to make up our beds for us. We huddled out into the corridor to give him space and watched as he stood on the lower seat and raised the top beds, which were lying against the wall, fastening them into place with arms that swung out from underneath. He did the same with the backs of the seats that we had been sitting on, then the seats themselves became the lowest beds. He pulled sheets and pillows out from under the lower beds, then showed us a bell to press if we needed anything and wished us a good night.

Maureen was still feeling queasy, so she took one of the lowest bunks opposite Gill, while Maggie quickly claimed one of the topmost ones, and instructed June to get into the opposite bed.

Jasmine and I shrugged at each other and heaved ourselves up the narrow ladders into the middle bunks.

The rocking of the train was surprisingly soothing, and I must have fallen asleep almost straight away, but I was rudely awakened by a cold foot stepping clumsily on the edge of my bed and almost kicking me in the nose.

"Maggie!" I hissed. "What on earth are you doing?"

"I need to go to the toilet!" she whispered back. "Come with me, Sylvie. I don't want to go down that corridor on my own in the dark."

I sighed and slid out of bed, trying not to step on Maureen, and escorted Maggie along the narrow, jolting passage to the tiny compartment.

I leaned against the wall, dozing and watching Northern France flash past outside, thinking of all the British soldiers and airmen who were lying buried out there in the dark, having made it safe for us to make this journey.

Maggie came out of the lavatory looking a little pale.

"It's open at the bottom!" she whispered in horror. "You can see the track going by underneath while you're sitting there!"

I decided not to use the drinking fountain outside our compartment during the night.

We stumbled back to our beds as the train rocked its way through the darkness, and I fell back into a deep sleep.

In the early hours, something jolted me awake. The train had stopped. There were voices shouting outside, and a hissing of steam. Gill stirred and woke, and, seeing me half sitting up, whispered across the compartment.

"It's all right, Sylvie, they're just uncoupling the sleeper carriages from the rest of the train. We'll be attached to another engine now to carry on down through France and into Basel. Do you want to see Paris?"

I nodded, and we crept out of bed and tiptoed to the window. Outside were porters and railwaymen, bustling about their work in a cloud of steam. A sign on the platform read "Gare du Nord", which I knew meant North Station.

"Look over there, Sylvie. Do you see that dome, all lit up?" whispered Gill.

"Oh, yes! How beautiful! What is it?"

"That's Sacre Coeur. It's a cathedral. That's Paris you're looking at."

We watched in silence as the engine finished shunting, and our carriages, now coupled to a different engine, moved off. The Paris skyline faded into the darkness and we crawled back into our bunks to sleep through France.

~*~

I think I must have been half aware of the train stopping and sounds of people boarding, but it was a knock on our compartment door that woke me at around six o'clock.

The man at the door raised his uniform cap, and asked to see our passports, speaking German at first, but repeating himself in French when he realised that I didn't understand. I woke the others and we rummaged in our bags for our documents, Maggie grumbling under her breath about a man coming in when we were sleeping; but we were all fully dressed, so I couldn't see what she was beefing about.

As we had been awoken so early, we took turns to stagger along the corridor to the lavatory and quickly wash our faces, then Gill and I took a walk to the buffet car, where hot, sweet rolls had just been loaded on. We bought a selection of rolls and pastries and a jug of coffee, and stumbled unsteadily back to the others, passing Captain and one of her compartment mates on the same errand.

We munched our breakfast while watching the morning light unfold over Switzerland, gasping at how beautiful the countryside was. Jasmine consulted her map, and informed us that we had crossed the border at Basel and were heading towards Berne, where we were to change to a coach for the rest of the journey.

As the train climbed higher, the houses were set further apart, in small mountain villages that looked exactly like the drawings in my old copy of "Heidi", which now belonged to Audrey. The houses were mostly made of wood, with shallow pointed roofs, decorated around the eaves with what looked like wooden lace.

There was still snow on the tops of the mountains and among some of the valley villages, but here and there we saw a few herds of mountain goats, and heard the clang of their clunky, square bells as they grazed on the spring grass.

We took turns to sit closest to the window and enjoy the view, calling the others to look when we saw something unusual or exciting.

The train pulled into the Berne station just after one o'clock. After a short debate between Captain and Lieutenant whether we should find somewhere to eat or carry on to the Guide chalet, we climbed aboard a waiting bus, stowed our bags as best we could, and set out on the last stage of our journey.

Captain had prepared a list of phrases in French and German which she thought we might need, and had typed them out neatly so we could carry them in our uniform pockets. Maureen and I pulled out our lists and tested each other on them, giggling and unsure of the pronunciation of some of the words.

"Of course it's good to be able to say what we want, but the problem comes when someone replies," Maureen commented, frowning. "None of what that man said on the train is on these cards."

"It might be," I replied thoughtfully, "but he said it so fast I couldn't spell it in my mind, if you understand what I mean."

Maureen nodded and applied herself studiously to her card, but I knew she would just get by with "Bonjour" or "Guten Tag" and a smile for the whole trip.

Just when I thought that the whole bus must be able to hear my stomach rumbling, the driver called out "Adelboden! Alles fur Adelboden!"

We quickly gathered our luggage and climbed down from the bus into the cold mountain air.

"Breathe in, girls!" Captain urged us, throwing back her shoulders and inhaling deeply. "The air is so clean and healthy here, and we'll be getting plenty of exercise over the next few days, so let the mountain atmosphere blow the cobwebs away."

Consulting a typed page of directions, she led us down a steep road, and suddenly there was the Guide chalet in front of us.

I had expected a slightly larger version of the chalet we had stayed in at the seaside, but this was a huge building!

Set down in the valley, the bottom of the building was made of stone, nestled snugly between the slopes, but higher up it was panelled in wood, like the houses we had seen on the way up, only much bigger.

The sloping roof had the same lacy wooden trim around the eaves, and each window was framed by a pair of wooden shutters.

"It's like a posh hotel!" Maureen gasped.

"There'll be Guides from other companies staying here, too," Captain explained, "some from England, but some from other countries in Europe."

The main entrance was at the top of a long flight of stone steps. We huddled behind Captain, feeling suddenly shy, but the lady behind the reception desk was warm and friendly, and spoke good English as she checked our names against her list and looked at our passports. We had been allocated to two dormitory bedrooms which each slept six, so we decided to stay in our travel groups.

"There will be luncheon in the dining room in thirty minutes," the receptionist advised us. "Please to help yourself to the buffet."

~*~

The dining room was large and echoing, and filled with girls in various kinds of Guide uniforms, chatting in several languages and serving themselves from a long table at one end of the room.

"For the rest of our stay, we'll be taking a packed lunch with us, but today there's a welcome lunch buffet laid on, as everyone arrives," Captain explained.

To us, who had become used to rationing and having to think carefully about meals, the table spread before us was the height of luxury. There were fragrant rolls, pats of golden yellow butter, pots of jams and honey, slices of cheese and ham, and jugs of coffee, hot chocolate, and milk.

I buttered a roll and filled it with cheese and ham, then took another flaky, crescent-shaped roll and spread it with butter and jam. I poured a mug of milky coffee, and took a seat between Maureen and a slim girl with dark hair who was dressed in a different kind of uniform.

I smiled at her and tried a few words in French, and she replied that her name was Madeleine and she was from Lille in France. She pointed to some other girls further down the table who were dressed like her and explained that they were from her company.

After a couple of mouthfuls of food and a large swig of coffee, Maureen boldly leaned across me and said, carefully, "Bonjour, je m'appelle Maureen."

Madeleine smiled at her and replied slowly, realising that Maureen's French wasn't as good as mine.

Maureen returned the smile enthusiastically, nodded, and tucked into her food without saying another word.

~*~

The lunch was a long, drawn-out affair, as more companies arrived over the next hour, and gradually the groups started to mingle, some more confident than others. Quite a few of the girls from France, Germany, and Holland spoke good English, and several spoke two or more languages.

The captains and lieutenants gathered together and compared journeys and plans for their stay, the Dutch captain translating, all of them carefully watching their charges as they moved around the hall.

With nods and smiles, the captains parted, then all blew their whistles and held one hand up in the "to me" signal.

Each company gathered around its leader to listen to instructions.

"All the captains have decided that after supper this evening we'll have a sing song, here in the dining room, so all the Guides from different countries can learn each other's songs. The rest of the afternoon until supper is free for you to explore the chalet, make friends, and go for a walk if you wish, but please do not go beyond the village. The local captain tells me that there's a souvenir shop in the village, which you may like to visit. We meet back here at six for supper. Company, dismiss!"

We saluted smartly, then wandered away to discuss what to do. Madeleine strolled over to us with a friend in tow, and offered to show us around the village, as she had been to the chalet before. Her friend, Marie-Louise, spoke good English, so she paired up with Maureen, while Madeleine, Jasmine, and I fumbled our way through conversation in French.

The souvenir shop was full of fun things, mostly hand made locally, from tiny bells like those the goats wore to expensive cuckoo clocks. Maureen bought a bell and a tiny carved wooden goat, and the French girls bought little celluloid dolls in Swiss costume.

Jasmine and I found a rack of beautifully carved walking sticks with sharp points on the bottom. They were carved with the word "Adelboden" and a picture of a flower.

The shopkeeper came over to us, and explained in halting English that the sticks were called Alpenstock, and were very useful for walking on mountains. He showed us a little basket of curved metal badges, some engraved and some enamelled, showing scenes from the local area, and explained that they were for attaching to the sticks to show which places had been visited.

Jasmine and I decided to buy a stick each, and we chose two badges to start our collection; one with an engraved picture of the chalet, and one showing the Jungfrau mountain.

I asked the shopkeeper the name of the flower carved on the stick.

"We call Edelweiss," he said. "He blooms in summer, next month, but you may see a bloom on low hills where no snow there is."

We hiked back up to the chalet, Jasmine and I striding out with our sticks, and paused on a wooden bridge across a small stream, so that Maureen could take a photograph of us with her new Brownie 127.

She put her purse and her shopping down at her feet and snapped two shots, just in case one didn't come out.

As she bent to pick up her belongings, she slipped slightly, and, as if in slow motion, we watched in dismay as her foot tapped her purse and sent it spinning over the edge of the bridge and into the water.

"Oh, no!" she cried, running to the other side of the bridge. "My money!"

The stream was shallow but fast, and the purse was whirled away down the hillside to where the water grew deeper. We chased down the hill after it, but it was too late. It was gone.

Maureen's eyes filled with tears. I knew how hard she had saved for this trip, and I put my arm around her and hugged her.

"You can have half of what I've got left," I told her. "Look at it as a gift from my Grandma."

She sniffed and thanked me.

"I'll pay you back when we get home."

I hugged her again.

"Come on, let's go to our room for a while, then you can wash your face and get ready for supper."

She dried her eyes.

"I'm starving! It must be this mountain air. I hope the supper is as good as the lunch,"

"We mustn't eat too much, though," Jasmine teased her. "You can't sing properly on a full stomach!"

~*~

The breakfast was strange, and not like anything we had ever had before: oats and wheat flakes, with dried fruit and nuts, eaten with yoghurt. It was different, but very tasty, and washed down with fresh milk and coffee.

Lieutenant gathered the ten of us together once we had eaten. Captain was staying behind with the other leaders to plan activities for the evening, and the chalet staff had arranged for local guides to take small parties of us to Interlaken by bus to see a glacier.

"Girls, I'm going to telephone my husband to let him know that we've arrived safely. I'll be back in five minutes; any messages?"

Gill had arranged a clever system with Uncle Johnny. She had agreed to ring him up at his office each morning, and if any of us had messages for home we could pass them on, and Uncle Johnny would write them on the Guides noticeboard in the church hall. Likewise, if our parents had any messages for us, they could pin them on the board and my uncle would pass them on the next morning.

No-one had any messages, so Gill hurried off to telephone from the booth in the reception area.

She came back with a serious expression on her face, but didn't seem to have any news to pass on.

We piled onto the bus, along with our Swiss guide, and drove away.

~*~

When I first saw the glacier, I thought it was just a fast-running river, but after staring and blinking a few times I realised that it was solid ice. Our guide explained that the ice was in fact moving, but so slowly that it was almost impossible to see.

The sun shone on the dazzling sheet of white as we climbed beside it. I was glad that I had bought the Alpenstock, and patted the newly nailed-on badge that I had just bought in the gift shop at the bottom of the glacier.

We reached a plateau in the sunshine, and our guide announced that we would have an hour to explore and rest before making our way back down to the bus. Chattering, we started to move away in twos and threes.

"Sylvie? Can I have a quick word, please?" Gill called.

I looked at Maureen and shrugged. I hadn't done anything wrong as far as I was aware.

Gill led me away from the others and we perched on a large rock in the sunshine.

"Sylvie, I've got something to tell you," Gill began. I looked at her anxiously, my heart sinking, thinking of our new Queen, far away from home, hearing bad news.

"The family are all right, don't worry," Gill reassured me, quickly. "It's Scamp. John said that Audrey came down to breakfast this morning and found him in his basket. He died in his sleep. He was a good age, Sylvie."

My eyes filled with tears. Scamp had arrived when I was just two, and I couldn't really remember him not being there. It must have been worse for poor Audrey; she had always had Scamp in her life.

I lifted my head and turned my face into the sun, to stop the tears running down my face. I looked around me at the bright green grass, waving softly in the spring sunshine, the blue sky, the white mountain tops, and the sparkling ice.

"I hope Heaven for dogs looks like this," I said, shakily.

Gill patted my arm.

"I'm sure it does, and Scamp is running happily now. I'll leave you alone for a bit. Do you want me to let the others know what's happened?"

I nodded, blowing my nose.

"Yes, please."

I stood up and walked away from the rock, not wanting to watch the others looking at me sympathetically when Gill told them, and sat down on the grass in a patch of sunshine.

I felt suddenly completely alone, and wanted my family very much. My hands felt for the solid earth, to reassure myself that the rest of the world was as it had always been.

Thinking fond thoughts of my little dog, my fingers wandered among the grass and found a small delicate bloom. Distracted, I looked down and saw a tiny white flower, just like the one carved on my stick. Edelweiss!

I picked three small sprigs from the plant and tucked them in my shirt pocket for safety. I knew they wouldn't last long, but if I could get them back to the chalet I could press them between paper, then when I got home I could place them on Scamp's grave in the garden.

Feeling better at having found a way to remember him, I gathered myself together and walked slowly back to join the others.

~*~

The games and songs after supper took my mind off my loss for a while, and I sang and laughed with the others, but once I was in bed and the lights went out, I could feel tears welling up again.

I tried to remember Scamp as a happy puppy, bouncing around and making us laugh with his wet kisses and flailing tail. I remembered how he always tried to cheer us up when we were sad, and smiled to myself in the darkness. I resolved to enjoy the rest of my trip and remember all the fun times with my dog.

I rolled on to my side and tried to sleep, but my thoughts ran on, to our new Queen and how bravely she had coped with the loss of her father. Standing strong, just like those little white flowers that were now tucked safely inside my passport between pieces of paper.

I remembered that I still hadn't thought of anything to contribute to the Coronation book, and turned onto my back, arms behind my head, thinking. An idea came to me, and I fumbled for my notebook and pencil in the pocket of my uniform shirt, hung over the chair beside the bed, then quietly reached for my bag and found my torch.

I dived under the covers, switched on the torch and began to write.

"This flower I give to you, Your Majesty, as a symbol of your new reign. Though it is fine and delicate, it is strong. It grows in high mountains, among the rocks and ice, standing proud, with its face turned to the sun.

"It is beautiful and fragile, but it is hardy, breaking through the cold soil to herald the joy of the coming spring, as the start of your reign brings us joy and hope."

Scamp wouldn't mind sharing his flowers with the Queen.

Chapter Twenty-Three

Something New

"Oh, Sylvie, what have I done?" Gill wailed. "I've got a bump where it should be smooth, and a smooth bit where it should be bumpy." She held her knitting out to me in despair.

"Don't panic. You just knitted when you should have purled. I can fix that." I took the needles from her, dropped the stitches back a few rows, and picked them up again the right way around.

Uncle Johnny and Ted were at a football match with Audrey and Brian, and Mum and Dad had gone to the pictures, so Gill and I had decided to have a cosy afternoon in front of the fire while I taught her to knit. She was making a cardigan for her friend's new baby, but the baby would probably be at school before she finished the garment.

"I wish I'd learned to knit when I was a child," she sighed, "but I was too busy climbing trees with my brother. Still, they do say you're never too old to learn."

I counted the stitches across the raglan sleeve of the jumper I was making for Audrey before answering.

"It's really strange." I frowned, thinking how to explain what I wanted to say. Gill's words had struck a chord and gave me a small clue as to why I had been feeling so discontented lately. "Once you're at work, time seems to stand still and go fast at the same time. When you're at school, there's always something to look forward to — a holiday, or going up a year, and something new to learn, but once you start work it's just all the same. It's nearly Christmas already, and I've been working for over a year now; the time has flown past, but in doing the same thing every day."

"Is your job boring?" Gill asked, pausing to read her pattern.

"No, not at all, but it still feels weird not to be learning anything; to come home and just have an evening doing nothing if I want to."

"You did that shorthand and typing course," she reminded me. "That was learning something new."

"Yes," I mused. "Maybe I should take another course or learn a new skill."

"I've got an idea!" Gill put her knitting down so she could talk without losing her place. "I know this is your last year in the Rangers, but how about taking a badge? You haven't taken the Child Nurse badge, and I'm sure my friend Barbara would let you look after her two children for a day. Pass me my handbook, there, on the sideboard. Let's have a look at what you have to do to earn the badge."

We put our heads together over the book and studied the requirements. I would have to be able to bath and dress a baby, change a nappy, and make up a feed, as well as cooking a healthy meal for an older child, explain the dangers for small children in the home and what measures should be taken to avoid them, and teach a child something new.

"You can do that, Sylvie," Gill encouraged me. "You can already cook and, having a younger sister, you shouldn't have any trouble with the three-year-old. You just need to learn how to look after a baby. Barbara can show you what to do, then, provided you can do it again by yourself with Barbara supervising, you'll pass easily."

I considered the idea. It would be good to learn something new, and playing with children was fun. I was just a bit nervous about having to look after a tiny infant, as I had never had much to do with babies.

"I suppose it'll be useful when I have children of my own one day," I said, although I couldn't imagine being a mother for a long while yet.

"You never know what'll come in useful!" Gill grinned at me, with a twinkle in her eye. "I'll speak to Barbara next time I see her and arrange it. Now, what does this mean here; 'yarn forward'?"

~*~

The following Saturday, Gill dropped me at her friend Barbara's house. She stayed for a cup of tea, and the two friends chatted while I talked to the little girl, whose name was Marina, and gingerly held baby David, who was just three months old.

By the time Gill left to go Christmas shopping with Uncle Johnny, Marina was begging me to play Snakes and Ladders with her, and David was fast asleep in my arms.

Barbara carried the empty cups through to the kitchen, and I followed her and watched while she made up baby David's feed, noting carefully how to warm the bottle and how much water to add to the milk, then I sat in the old wooden armchair in the kitchen and Barbara showed me how to feed him slowly, so he wouldn't get wind. Marina watched solemnly the whole time.

Barbara's husband, Graham, appeared at the kitchen door while I was feeding the baby, and we were introduced.

"Barb, have you got a bit of old rag I can have?" he asked. "I've just oiled the gate hinges and I don't want you getting oil on yourself when you go out."

Barbara left to find a cloth, and I felt a sudden panic at being left alone in the room with the two children, but David continued to suck at the bottle, and Marina kept up a running commentary, telling me all about the time David had been sick on her daddy's shirt.

The baby's mother re-appeared just as he was about to drain the bottle, and quickly took it away.

"Don't let him suck an empty bottle, Sylvie, or he'll get really windy!"

She showed me how to sit him up and rub his back gently, to help the milk go down.

"Now let's go and put him in his cot, then you and Marina can have a game of Snakes and Ladders before lunch."

I followed her upstairs, holding the precious bundle carefully, and laid him in his cot. I raised the side of the cot and locked it in place, making sure that there was nothing near him that he could get fingers or toes caught in, and nothing that might cover his face.

Marina fetched the Snakes and Ladders box and laid the board out. I decided to pretend not to know how to play the game, so she could tell me the rules, which made her feel very clever and superior.

Apart from the dice flying off the table a few times and having to be rescued from under the settee, the game went quickly, and even though Marina lost, she didn't whine or cry, and when Barbara told her to put the game away and get ready for her meal she only pouted a tiny bit.

"Sylvie's going to help me make your lunch, Marina," Barbara told her, taking her hand and leading her to the kitchen. "Can you put the place mats on the table, and set the knives and forks out for us?"

The little girl nodded and went about her job solemnly, pausing at each place to consider which side to place the knife and the fork.

Lunch was beans on toast, so I had no problem with that part, and Marina told me that I cooked it just as well as her mummy did. Graham said my lunch was better than Barbara usually made, but he winked at his wife, so I knew he was teasing.

After lunch, Marina sat quietly on the settee, nodding over her thumb, while I read her a story, then it was time for her nap.

"Sylvie come and tuck me in?" she asked, so I led her quietly upstairs, so as not to wake David, and pulled the covers around her shoulders, promising to come and see her next week.

I heard voices as I tiptoed back downstairs. Barbara was at the door talking to Gill, and Uncle Johnny was in the car, leaning out of the window to join in the conversation.

"There she is." Gill smiled as I walked into the hallway. "Barbara's been telling me how well you've done; she said Marina's your friend for life, now."

I grinned. "It's been fun playing with her; she's a sweet little girl."

"We'll be here the same time next Saturday, Babs," Gill said, as I put my coat on. "I'll be doing my serious Lieutenant bit, though." She laughed.

"I'm sure Sylvie will pass with flying colours." Barbara smiled, waving us down the path.

~*~

I thought I had better wear my uniform to actually take the badge, as it was an official Rangers meeting of a sort, but decided not to wear my lanyard, in case the baby tried to chew it, or got it caught around his neck. I put it in my pocket, anyway: being prepared, like a good Guide.

To my surprise, it was Captain who called for me.

"Good morning, Sylvie. Gill's not well this morning; John popped 'round and said he's called the doctor out, as she's been very sick, so she asked me to stand in."

I felt nervous. I was fairly sure Gill would pass me on this badge, but Captain, even when she was being just my Auntie Agnes, was quite strict and intimidating, and I knew she wouldn't cut me any slack just because I was family. I was also worried about Gill.

"Is it the flu?" I asked. "I hope she's all right. She and Uncle Johnny are supposed to be coming to us for Sunday dinner tomorrow."

"I think she'll be fine by then," Auntie Agnes reassured me. "John just wanted the doctor to come to make sure."

She looked me up and down.

"You're not wearing your lanyard, Sylvie!" Captain commented as we climbed into her car.

"No, Captain. I thought it safest not to, around small children, in case they pull on it or play with it."

She nodded.

"Sensible girl. While I drive, you might as well tell me all the other safety ideas you've learned, then we can mark that part of the test as complete."

~*~

Marina came running to the door to meet us, followed by Barbara with a sleepy David in her arms.

Marina pulled up short when she saw me in my uniform, so I quickly took my hat off and bent down to greet her.

"Sylvie all smart!" she said. Then, noticing Captain behind me, she yelled, "Auntie Aggie!" and lifted her arms to be picked up.

It was going to be hard to remember to say "Captain" and not "Auntie Aggie" during my test.

"David's just woken up," said Barbara, stroking her son's sparse hair, "so I thought you could bath and change him first."

I gulped a bit. Nothing like plunging in at the deep end. Or the not-deep-enough-to-be-dangerous end, but I remembered watching Mum bath Audrey when she was tiny.

I always wanted to be the one to test the water with my elbow, as it seemed such a funny thing to do.

At thirteen, Audrey would die of embarrassment if I saw her in the bath, but now she was a real friend and companion. Strange how huge changes happen so slowly that you don't notice them.

I changed my shoes, rolled up my sleeves, and pulled my

apron from my bag, then dug to the bottom of the bag for a small package.

"Marina, here's something for you to look at while I'm busy with David. Once he's bathed and changed, I've got a fun art project for us to do together."

I handed her the package and she pulled off the paper.

"Big girl book!" she exclaimed, opening the little picture book and pretending to read the one-line sentences on each page.

Barbara had set the baby bath and towels in front of the fire, with David's little clothes warming on the fire guard.

I filled the bucket at the sink and added hot water from the geyser little by little, testing the water with my elbow, then carried the heavy bucket through to the sitting room and filled the bath, testing again.

I carefully undressed the giggling baby and lowered him gently into the water, supporting him on my left arm while I quickly washed him, then lifted him out and wrapped him in a fluffy towel, drying him all over, especially between his little fingers and toes.

Captain watched me like a hawk, but that was the worst bit over — I had been dreading dropping him.

I quickly folded the muslin liner and placed it on the nappy, creamed the baby's bottom, then folded the nappy and pinned it securely.

He babbled and squirmed as I wiggled his feet and hands into his little romper suit, but finally he was dressed, and still smiling. Barbara held him while I made up his bottle, watched carefully by Captain, then I took him on my lap and sang nursery rhymes to him while he drank. His eyes started to close before he reached the bottom of the bottle.

I placed him in his carry cot beside the settee and pulled out another package from my bag.

"Come on, Marina, come and sit here so David can see what we're doing if he wakes up. We're going to make a picture!"

I pulled out of the package a piece of card and a paper bag full of felt and fabric flowers that I had already cut out, plus some wax crayons and a small bottle of glue with a rubber tip.

I took a small square of coloured paper and folded it in half.

"This is going to be our vase," I told Marina, drawing an outline of half a vase on the paper, "then we're going to fill it with flowers. If I let you use these special scissors, do you think you can cut this out, really carefully?"

I looked at Barbara as I spoke, showing her the blunt ended children's scissors that I had borrowed from Audrey's old toybox, and she nodded.

Marina took the scissors and carefully cut around the shape, then I showed her how to unfold it and glue it to the card.

"Now, can you draw some straight lines for the flower stems? Then we can do the fun part!"

With her tongue out to help her concentrate, the little girl took a fat green crayon and drew some wiggly stems, then I emptied out the bag of flowers and let her place them and glue them on the picture.

"That's lovely, Marina!" Barbara praised her.

"Now all you have to do is sign your picture, like a proper artist," I told her. "Can you write your name, just there, at the bottom?"

She nodded and wrote "MARNIA" in straggly capitals. Close enough.

Captain sat back in her chair and laughed.

"I was so engrossed in watching you two that I forgot to make any notes! That was such a clever idea, Sylvie! Well done."

Graham joined us for lunch, which was scrambled eggs and tomatoes on toast. Timing the eggs so they were cooked but not rubbery at the same time that the toast was ready was tricky, but everyone seemed satisfied with the meal, and Captain marked another tick on her pad.

"Well, this is nice." Barbara relaxed in her chair as I washed up the lunch things and Captain dried. "You can come every Saturday morning if you like, Sylvie, and give me some time off. I think you've done very well."

She rose and opened the bread bin, taking out the dry end of a loaf.

"Why don't you take Marina out onto the green to feed the ducks while Captain and I have a chat?"

I knew that they wanted me out of earshot so that Barbara could be honest about how she thought I had done, so I helped Marina into her coat and shoes and led her across the narrow lane to the green. We were still in view of the house, but I felt very responsible, and held tight to Marina's hand so she didn't throw herself into the water with the crusts.

~*~

Barbara came to the door and called us in. She had made a pot of tea and passed the biscuit tin around.

Captain sipped her tea and smiled at me.

"I think we can safely say that you've passed. Sylvie, you did very well. I'll present you with your badge at meeting on Thursday."

"Oh, thank you, Captain. I really enjoyed today. I feel much more confident around small children, now."

"That's a good thing." Captain smiled, glancing at Barbara, who grinned back.

~*~

"Mmm, that dinner smells good!" Uncle Johnny hung his coat on the peg and helped Gill out of hers. Gill smiled but looked a little pale.

"How are you feeling?" Mum asked her, as she moved the paper off the settee to let Gill sit down.

"All right, just a little bit wobbly," Gill replied.

"Dinner will be about ten minutes. I'm just waiting for the greens. Would you like a glass of water?"

"Yes please, Amy, that would be lovely."

Audrey came running down the stairs to kiss our uncle and aunt, and she and Uncle Johnny were still discussing the previous day's football results as we took our seats at the table.

"I hear you passed your Child Nurse badge with flying colours, Sylvie," Gill remarked as she passed the gravy boat across the table to me. She hesitated and looked at Uncle Johnny, who gave her the tiniest of nods, followed by an encouraging smile.

"That's going to come in really useful because. . . ." she paused and looked around the table, her cheeks flushed, "I'm going to have a baby."

"Oh, congratulations!" Mum pushed her chair back and hurried round the table to kiss her sister-in-law. "So that's why you've been so ill; I did wonder."

"Yes." Gill grinned. "Hopefully that will stop soon, but it's worth it."

"When will the baby arrive?" Audrey asked.

"Early summer," Gill replied, "sometime around the beginning of June."

"Oh, good! Then I can look after it during the summer holidays. Oh! And I won't be the youngest of the cousins anymore!"

Chapter Twenty-Four

Long Live Elizabeth

We scurried to and fro in the rain, carrying chairs, cushions and crockery down our path and up Maureen's, trying to keep everything dry.

"It's a good thing that gold coach has got a roof," Maureen yelled above the downpour as she passed me with Mum's big teapot.

I almost collided with Gill at the gate, or rather with her stomach, which arrived everywhere a good three seconds before she did.

Uncle Johnny escorted her into the house and Mrs Fielding pulled up the big armchair for her and found a footstool.

"Thanks, Mrs F," she puffed, kicking off her shoes. She winced as she sat down.

"Are you all right, Gill?"

"Yes. I've been having a few phantom contractions, but I'm not due for another week yet." She smiled faintly.

Uncle Johnny had run back next door, and carried in a small card table, which he set up at Gill's elbow.

Maureen and I arranged chairs as close as we could to the television cabinet, with cushions on the floor for Audrey, Brian, Ted, Dennis, and anyone else who wanted to get closer to the twelve-inch screen.

"Ten o'clock," Mr Fielding said. "Where is everyone else?"

Mum and Dad bustled though the door with a cake tin and some more plates.

"Audrey's gone to call for Brian. She'll be here in a minute. It doesn't start until quarter past. Ted and Dennis are just coming up the path," said Dad, holding the door for them.

Mr Fielding closed the curtains and adjusted the green-shaded lamp on top of the television, then proudly turned the knob to on.

"It needs time to warm up," he said, peering anxiously at the screen. "Should I unplug the telephone? We don't want any interruptions."

"Who's going to ring us up in the middle of the Coronation?" Mrs Fielding laughed, as Audrey and Brian burst in, shaking themselves like wet dogs. "We're the only people we know who've had the phone put in! Sit down and stop fussing, Gerry."

The picture on the screen flickered and rolled, then settled down to a view of Buckingham Palace. The commentator's voice was serious and respectful, talking about what an important day it was in the life of our nation.

"It's not raining so much there," Mum observed. "Those poor soldiers in their wool uniforms will be soaked. Still, at least it's not too hot. You'd never believe it was June, looking at that weather."

"Ooh, look, here comes a carriage!" Audrey squealed. "It's the Queen!"

"No, it's not," Brian corrected her. "If you listened to what the man says instead of talking over it, you'd know. It's the Queen Mother and Princess Margaret."

The crowds in the street cheered everything, even the serious old men in military uniforms who looked as though they would rather be out shooting something than dressed up in their medals.

A fanfare announced the departure of the State Coach from the palace, and the crowd roared again.

"There she is!" Maureen clapped her hands "Our Queen! Doesn't she look lovely!"

"Oh, I forgot to put the kettle on!" Mrs Fielding jumped to her feet. "I've just got time before they get to the Abbey. I don't want to miss seeing her dress."

Mum slipped out to help her, and I took the opportunity to sink onto a cushion next to Ted while people were moving about.

Cups of tea and a packet of biscuits were passed around, and everyone started to settle down.

We all gasped as the Queen stepped out of the coach, and her six attendants, all dressed in white, stepped forward to hold her heavy train and follow her into Westminster Abbey. The commentator's voice described her dress, which was embroidered with emblems from each of the countries of the United Kingdom, and her ermine fur cape and red velvet train.

"It's a pity we can't see it in colour," Gill commented.

"They're filming it in colour, to be shown in the cinemas," Uncle Johnny told her. "Maybe we can go next weekend, if Pickle hasn't made an appearance."

He kept referring to the baby as "Pickle" because Gill had blamed her early morning sickness on pickled gherkins.

"I don't think I could fit into the seat!" Gill laughed, catching her breath with a gasp.

Uncle Johnny took her hand.

"Are you sure you don't want to go to the hospital?"

"Positive. It's not frequent enough to be anything, and even if it was, I want to see that crown put on her head before I go anywhere."

The procession had reached the altar, and the Queen was seated in a grand chair while the Archbishop of Canterbury read out vows to her, to which she answered, "I will".

After one particularly long list of promises, the Queen replied, "All this I promise to do," and Audrey giggled.

"I bet she couldn't remember all those things she just agreed to do, if you asked her!"

Brian had lost interest, now there were no horses or soldiers to look at, and his attention had wandered. He re-focussed his eyes on Audrey as she spoke, then turned back to the screen, squared his shoulders, and concentrated, as the Queen was dressed in a cloth of gold coat, with a belt tied around her waist, and led to the Coronation chair.

"Oh, doesn't she look young," Mum whispered, "like a little girl in her dressing gown, bless her."

"Why do they keep giving her things, then taking them away from her again?" Brian frowned.

"Shh, it's symbolic." Audrey nudged him.

We all fell silent as the Archbishop lifted the crown and slowly walked towards the Queen. He lifted the crown high, for everyone to see, then lowered it ceremoniously and placed it on her head.

"God save the Queen!" called the congregation in the Abbey, three times.

"God save the Queen," we repeated, sincerely, moved at the sight of the young girl, seated alone on her throne, surrounded by so much history and tradition.

The newly crowned Queen processed back down the nave with Prince Philip, followed by all the clergy in their robes, and we all leaned back and sighed.

Gill's sigh sounded louder than anyone else's, and slightly shaky, and Mum looked anxiously at her.

Outside the Abbey, the various ranks of soldiers, sailors, and airmen from all the nations of the Commonwealth were marching past. Brian and Dennis perked up and paid attention, but Ted turned to me with a wry smile; he was expecting his call up papers for National Service at any time, and was half excited, half dreading the thought.

"If I was year older, I could be marching with them," he said thoughtfully.

Mrs Fielding got up.

"Any more tea?" Heads were shaken all 'round.

"I'll go and start on the sandwiches. Call me when the Queen comes out of the Abbey. No, sit still, Amy. Maureen will help me."

I slid into Maureen's empty seat next to Gill and grasped her hand.

"Are you really all right?" I asked anxiously.

"I'm fine," she said, smiling, but the smile didn't quite make it to her eyes, and she gripped my hand so hard I thought she might break my fingers.

"Uncle Johnny. . . ." I started, but he had noticed and was already on his feet.

"I'll bring the car 'round; I think it's time we got you to the hospital."

"My bag. . . ." Gill puffed.

"I'll get it. I know where it is." I ran down the path, up the next door one, and straight up the stairs to my aunt and uncle's bedroom. Gill had told me about her hospital bag, packed and ready under the bed, so I found it easily and ran back out to the road.

Mum and Dad were helping Gill into the front passenger seat, and I threw the bag into the back seat.

"Will you let my parents know, Tom?" Gill panted.

"Brian's on his way 'round there now to tell them. Don't worry," said Dad. "You'll be fine. Johnny, you've got Gerry's phone number?"

"Yes." Uncle Johnny put the car into gear. "I'll ring you up as soon as there's any news. Now get back indoors, all of you; you're getting wet and missing the Coronation!"

~*~

We trooped back in and settled down to our ham and tomato sandwiches while we watched the long procession leading the Queen back to the palace. I couldn't concentrate; the telephone on the sideboard seemed to have grown to twice its size, just because we were all waiting for it to ring with news, so I was quite glad to help Mrs Fielding carry plates and serve the Victoria sponge cake that Maureen had iced with a crown and the date.

Ted and Dennis watched the marching soldiers of all nations with keen eyes, commenting on how poor their marching was compared to that of the British soldiers, and Brian hung on their every word.

Dad and Mr Fielding lit their pipes once the food was cleared away and sat back to wait for the flypast, which was due to happen at two o'clock.

The television showed the crowds gathered outside Buckingham Palace, despite the cool, damp weather, all shouting, "We want the Queen! We want the Queen!"

Their wish was eventually granted, as the Queen, the Duke of Edinburgh, the Queen Mother, and Princess Margaret, with little Prince Charles and Princess Anne, all strolled out onto the balcony to wave and smile at the crowds.

"Those crowns must really make their heads ache after a while," Mrs Fielding observed.

The royal party kept looking up to the sky, waiting for the aeroplanes to come over, while the commentator talked on and on about the history of the palace.

"He's filling time," Mr Fielding said. "Maybe the flypast is late because of the weather." But right on cue, exactly at two o'clock, the formation passed over the palace, tiny dots on the television screen.

Prince Philip was seen pointing at the planes and telling little Prince Charles to look up and wave.

"Those kids will sleep well tonight!" Mum laughed. "He was so good in the Abbey, not fidgeting too much."

The live broadcast ended, and a lady in a studio announced that the Queen would be on air to make a speech at eight o'clock. Mr Fielding switched the set off and opened the curtains. We all blinked at each other, owlishly, surprised that it was still light outside; it seemed much more than six or seven hours since the broadcast began, but the clock showed otherwise.

"Just think, that little boy will be our King one day," said Audrey.

"Everyone has to start somewhere," Brian commented profoundly.

Our laughter was interrupted by the shrilling of a bell, and we all turned to look at the telephone, suddenly quiet.

Mrs Fielding approached the instrument as though it was a hand grenade, and gingerly lifted the receiver.

"Handley eight four three?"

"Yes, hello, John, I'll put Tom on for you."

Dad put down his pipe and took the receiver, his eyes flickering around the room, watching our anxious faces.

"Johnny, how are things?" he asked. "Already? Everything all right? Oh, I'm so glad! Just let me tell everyone here. . . ." He moved the receiver slightly away from his mouth and announced, "It's a girl! Eight pounds, five ounces; mother and daughter doing fine. Father's a bit shaky!" He laughed, and we all cheered. Dad made a waving motion to quieten us, so he could hear what his brother was saying. "Sylvie? Yes, I'll put her on."

He beckoned me to the telephone and I gingerly took hold of the handset.

"Uncle Johnny? It's me, Sylvie. How is Gill?"

My uncle's voice sounded tinny and strange down the line.

"She's fine. Very tired, but very happy."

"Have you decided what to call the baby?" I asked.

"That's why I wanted to talk to you," he replied. "Her first name is Elizabeth; she couldn't really be called anything else, being born on Coronation day, but as you're her oldest cousin, we'd really like it if you would be her Godmother, and we'd like to give her Sylvia as her middle name, if that's all right with you?"

My eyes filled with tears, and I had to steady myself for a few seconds before I could reply.

"I would like that very much, Uncle Johnny. May I tell everyone?" He assented, and I cleared my throat and looked around the room.

"Her name is Elizabeth Sylvia Ford."

"Long live Elizabeth!" Audrey shouted, loudly enough that our uncle could hear her.

Everyone rose to their feet and echoed her salute to the newest member of the family, raising their cups and glasses.

"Long live Elizabeth!"

About the Author

Andrea Gilbey lives in leafy Hertfordshire with her cat. She works full time in the fashion industry and enjoys drawing, painting, graphic art and photography to relax and unwind.

Andrea has published five illustrated children's books for pre-schoolers and upwards, and with Southern Indiana Writers colleague Ginny Fleming, worked on the Written in Our Hearts Cookbook in aid of the Davy Jones Equine Memorial Foundation.

Andrea's illustrations are inspired by friends, family and the world about her. She has written a non-fiction social history book, and a children's novel.